SEDUCED BY MY EX'S DIVORCE ATTORNEY

PIPER RAYNE

Cover design: RBA Designs

Line Editor: Gray Ink Editing

Proofreader: Shawna Gavas, Behind The Writer

Join our newsletter and receive Jailbait, a 11k prequel to Real Deal for FREE

About Seduced by my Ex's Divorce Attorney

The perfect man for her is the one she hates most. #gofigure

Dating is hard.
    Dating in your thirties is even harder.
    Dating in Chicago is harder still.

I haven't given up on finding my happily-ever-after, but in the age of swiping right and Netflix and chill, I'm wondering if everything is as temporary as my marriage turned out to be.

Truth is, there is one guy I can't get my mind off of.

Roarke Baldwin has salt and pepper hair I've dreamed of running my hands through and I'm pretty sure that if I checked he really does have a six pack of abs underneath his suit. And I've always wondered what that stubble on his face would feel like between my thighs.

The problem? He's the one man I hate more than my ex-husband…

His divorce attorney.

SEDUCED
BY MY EX'S DIVORCE ATTORNEY

What are the worst four words to hear in the English language besides 'we need to talk?'

'We overbooked. You're out.'

Especially six weeks before you're hosting a gala to pop the cork on the new charitable foundation you started.

Normally, the buzz of the alcohol would've lifted my spirits, or at least let me have an ounce of optimism in this shitty situation. There has to be a venue in one of the largest cities in America that has availability on short notice. Weddings get canceled all the time. Not that I'm wishing a broken heart on anyone so I can steal their venue spot, but if I'm being cynical—and I'm speaking from experience here—it's a lot better to never say I do, than to say it then have half your worldly possessions stolen from you in divorce court.

Let's all be honest, love fogs up a sane mind more than a bottle of tequila on a Mexican beach. One minute you're all 'woohoo,' licking salt and sucking back limes under a makeshift tiki hut poolside. The next you're hunched over the trunk of a palm tree with your stomach rejecting the good times you promised.

Love's bred from the same false high. Except the regret doesn't always come on the same night. Sometimes it creeps up on you like a long night of drinking expensive champagne. You think you're having a sweet time, drinking conservatively and keeping away from the hard stuff. Then you pass out on the way home to wake up wondering what the hell you did and where the damn Advil is.

My experience with marriage was the latter.

I'd known Todd my entire life. Grown up with him from our first week at Montessori school together. He chased me around the playground and gave me a locket in the first grade. He asked me to the carnival in third grade. I wouldn't call what we had kismet. Half the time he annoyed me, but he was kind and considerate. A good guy. Before walking down the aisle, I convinced myself that passion and spontaneity were overrated.

The fact that I predicted his proposal down to the month he bent down on one knee in a public setting proved I was constantly one step ahead of him. If it weren't for his cheating dick, maybe I would've still believed that marriage wasn't boring and redundant.

"Another round ladies." Lincoln, our usual waiter at the speakeasy I'm a member of, Torrio's Table, delivers another round of Vespers for my co-workers and me.

"I know he's young but damn." Chelsea's gaze follows his ass as he walks away.

I admire too, because Lincoln *is* easy on the eyes. Not even a nun could argue that.

"I'm sure Dean would love to hear that."

Chelsea sweetly smiles over at Victoria. "You can act like you're not looking, mama saint, but you're not fooling anyone. Not to mention, me looking doesn't mean he holds a candle to my man."

Both my employees recently found new men in their lives. They're both willing to give love another try, believing that fate's GPS somehow steered them wrong the first time with their failed marriages. Well, in Chelsea's case she just sort of looped back to her ex-husband.

Are they happy?

Definitely.

Will it work out?

I don't know.

I hope it does.

But I've been where they are. Sex until dawn and breakfast in bed. Scary how fast things pivot to masturbation and grabbing a banana while waiting for your Starbucks.

I hope they both have happily ever afters, but right now, I need them to get out of la-la land and find me a venue.

"I have no idea what to do. It's July. Invitations have been printed which means I have to get them reprinted, but I don't even have an address. Girls, we need to brainstorm." I twirl the glass by the stem between my finger and thumb.

"We'll figure something out." Victoria's sweet gaze lands on me.

The door opens into the secluded room and my worst nightmare saunters in with that cocky ass grin on his face. "As if I need anything else bad tonight."

Chelsea spots the guy she thinks has been soaking my panties for the last few months, turning back my way, smirking.

"Ignore him." Victoria squeezes my forearm. She's the sane one out of the two of them.

Roarke Baldwin swaggers across the room and nods and waves to some other patrons like he's running for fucking Congress. I'm still waiting for an answer from management on how he got his membership to Torrio's. Before my divorce, he was never here.

His gaze remains on me the entire time he passes our table.

I let a breath leave my lungs once he clears my vision without stopping. Until I feel movement in the booth behind me across my back, alerting me that he can hear our conversation. Chelsea's eyes stay on the back of his head, confirming my thoughts.

"I'm sure we'll figure something out." I fluff off the topic of the venue because I don't want the man behind me knowing I'm at a disadvantage.

"We'll find a venue. Don't worry," Chelsea blurts out and I'm really hoping it's the hormones in her body that are making her ignore the fact that I tried to squash this topic. "What kind of a place double books and doesn't know it until six weeks out?"

I drag my finger across my throat.

"I agree, I felt like cutting their throats when they called. I'm happy you feel the same way because I thought it was my pregnancy hormones kicking in. The other night, I got so mad at Dean because he didn't wipe off Grover's paws when he came in from outside," Chelsea continues rambling.

"Chels." Victoria widens her eyes and bops her head in the direction behind me.

"Oh," she mouths and slinks back into her booth. "Sorry," she mouths again, biting her lip.

My eyes close and the booth behind me shifts.

Please be getting a drink. Lincoln's swamped and he's on

the opposite side of the room, so it makes total sense if Roarke was headed to the bar.

Chelsea's gaze follows him and I don't need a tracker on the man to know where he's at, watching Chelsea does just fine. Even Victoria's watching him. I can tell he's at the bar. *Thank God.*

A few seconds later their eyes widen and their faces lose color. Their unspoken reaction makes my internal radar blip and bleep, signaling that he's drawing closer. The scent of his musky cologne wraps around our booth as tightly as the viper he's proven to be.

Once we're in his clutches, he eyes the empty spot next to Chelsea.

For reasons unknown to me, she slides over closer to Victoria.

He folds himself into the booth, glass clasped in his hand, his gaze focused solely on me. "Ms. Crowley, I couldn't help but overhear you're in need of a venue?" His perfectly styled salt and pepper hair is the first sign that he's dangerous. It suggests he's older and more experienced than I am. He's had years at the practice of fucking with people's lives—both professionally and personally I'd bet. Lord knows his profession relies on his ability to twist words and plant seeds of doubt.

A solid piece of ice clanks against his glass, splashing the dark amber liquid inside when he sets it down on the table.

"I'm not interested." I sip my drink, purposely pressing my lips around the edge of the glass hoping to drive him as batshit crazy as he drives me.

"What if I can get you a venue?"

His arrogance never ceases to amaze me. Like I'm some damsel in distress and he's going to gallop into my town on his white horse to save the day. No thanks.

The girls' gazes dart over to me like they're watching the latest drama and someone just announced a surprise pregnancy. Maybe they'd like some popcorn to keep their jaws from hanging.

"I'm sure your price is more than we can afford." I tamper down my emotional side—the irrational one that demands I reach across the table and wrap my hand around his throat until his face turns red.

"Oh, Ms. Crowley, you have it all wrong. You know as well as I do the art of negotiation is simple. I give you something you want and you give me something I want."

I twirl my glass on the table, the liquid splashing from side to side.

Don't ask.

Throw your drink in his face.

Unfortunately, I've been trained to not show anyone they're getting a rise out of me.

'Calm your temper,' my dad's voice rings out in my head. *'Do not show them what you're feeling. Under any circumstances.'*

I plaster a half-cocked smile on my face. "And what is it you want Mr. Baldwin?"

I lock eyes with him, and maybe my father trained him, too, because there's not one flicker of doubt to be found.

"You."

My stomach stirs with a million butterflies. Some die and fall to the pits of my belly while others soar with the thought of him telling me exactly how and where he wants me.

Chapter Two

"**O**h, Mr. Baldwin—"

"Call me, Roarke." His arrogance shines through his eyes over the rim of his glass. His Adam's apple bobs, prompting sweat to puddle between my breasts.

"I don't think so." I sip from my own drink, needing the coolness to chill my skin back to the icy hatred I need to deal with this vulture.

"Why?"

Chelsea makes a squeaking sound and Victoria reaches over and squeezes her knee.

"Why what?" I ask in a voice devoid of emotion.

"Why won't you call me Roarke?" The ice in his glass clinks again as he sets it down and my eyes clock his expensive watch. His crisp white buttoned shirt sleeves peek out of his dark charcoal suit. He even has a crimson pocket square in his front pocket which separates him from every other suit in here.

Which is fitting since he walks around like he's the fucking King of England.

"Roarke would make it sound like I liked you. I do not."

His hand covers his heart and his gaze darts over to my friends. "Is she always this straightforward?"

The girls who I hired for their sharp tongues and intelligence look like a pair of starry-eyed lovesick teenagers right now.

Roarke doesn't wait for them to answer because like most things with him, I'm certain he doesn't care what anyone else's opinion is about anything.

"Your words, Ms. Crowley, they hurt. I've done nothing to warrant your hatred."

I tilt my head and draw in a slow, deep breath trying my best to rein my temper in.

One….two…three.

Yeah, that didn't work.

"You took from me. You stole a lot from me. Things he didn't deserve." I school my face to hide how angry I am.

"Now, now. My client paid me to do a service for him. I did that service."

I huff but quickly quiet myself and straighten my back. "Your client didn't work for that money. He didn't work for that vacation home. He didn't sweat for anything. His surgeon salary was untouched for most of our marriage."

Why am I rehashing my divorce like we're in mediation again?

I put my hand up in the air before he can deliver his rebuttal. "You know what? Never mind. The divorce is over and I'm rid of that name now. It is what it is, but I will assure you, Mr. Baldwin, I do not need your help now, nor do I need your assistance in the future. Thank you for your kind offer, but we're fine."

The fucking bastard smiles like I just jerked him off

until his cum dripped down my fingers like a melted ice cream cone.

"All right then. I'll leave you ladies to figure out a solution yourselves." He slides out of the booth with the finesse of a man who's never suffered from clumsiness.

"Goodnight, Mr. Baldwin."

"Han… Ms. Crowley." His knuckles rap on the wood of the tabletop, his eyes still taking me in.

Saliva puddles in my mouth but I refuse to swallow. I'll never let him witness my physical attraction to him.

"Is there something else, Mr. Baldwin?" My eyes train on his, the ache between my thighs growing.

"Should things change, you know where to find me." He winks and Chelsea's eyes follow him for a moment. Since the booth behind me doesn't shift, I assume he's moved on to make the people on the other side of the room miserable with his presence.

Usually, I'd resort to curse words and another drink or two after reliving my divorce with the man who facilitated it, but the ladies need to trust that their boss can handle an egotistical male who's trying to be the white knight galloping in to save the day.

"Holy shit," Chelsea says, her hands clutching her stomach like she's about to vomit. "I thought Dean and I were intense. You two."

"Chels." My tone holds a warning.

"Good for you, Hannah. He can go suck it." Victoria downs the rest of her Vesper.

I smile politely at Victoria. Chelsea's still awestruck, her eyes having a hard time not veering over to Roarke.

"He's just so…" Chelsea never learning her lesson continues to ramble. "Commanding." Her eyes sweep over ours. "Like he'd do nasty stuff to you, but you'd enjoy every minute and then end up begging for more."

I don't disagree with Chelsea. Roarke Baldwin screams 'strap me to a bed and show me how a real man does it.' Not that I would say that. Ever.

No, I'd fall to my knees and show him exactly how a woman can transform *him* into making her breakfast the next morning. But if I let one toe dip in that water, I'm sure he'll swallow me up like a hungry crocodile. That's why the electric fence is between us, so it can zap me every time my damn lady parts want to take a dip.

"Chels. Dean?" Victoria reminds her of her fiancé.

Chelsea waves her hand in the air and rolls her eyes. "Please, Dean knows he's the only one for me. I'll tell him all about Roarke Baldwin when I get home and he'll probably be extra alpha tonight to prove he's the real man." She looks absolutely giddy thinking about it. A flush appears on her cheeks as though she's imagining what he'll do to her. "I give Hannah credit though. I would've crumbled and I'm a hard case to break."

"Chelsea, all Dean had to do was get you alone in his office," Victoria says.

Her cheeks redden even more.

Sometimes I wonder what if? What if I wouldn't have settled with Todd? What would fate have brought my way if I'd stayed single?

Roarke Baldwin?

My subconscious needs a real talking to.

"Chelsea, I don't care what you have to do. I'll pay whatever the cost. Find me a venue," I say, shifting the conversation back to business.

She nods, knowing we're shifting into go time.

I hired her because I saw her capability of turning no's into yes's so I feel assured that she won't fail me now. There's no way I can go to Roarke Baldwin and let the man have one up on me. At least not without losing my dignity.

Chapter Three

When I arrive at the office the following morning, Chelsea's in her office carrying on and on to Victoria.

Usually, I'd be happy to listen, but I need her on her A-game this morning. I don't need to hear about the mind-blowing sex performance of Dean last night.

Dropping my bags on the chair in front of Victoria's desk, I make my way down the short hallway to join them.

"Look at me. I can't stop." I hear Chelsea chuckle.

"You're glowing," Victoria says.

"You can't what? Stop smiling. Enough with the—" My heels stop on the carpet and my arms land on the sides of the doorway.

Chelsea's red and bloodshot eyes greet me. Oh no. Please say no.

"What's wrong?" I ask.

Victoria smiles softly at me indicating it's not the conclusion I'm drawing.

"Chelsea is experiencing first trimester pregnancy,

that's all. When your hormones are zooming all over your body like little space cadets."

"Can't I shoot them down like Centipede?" Chelsea grabs a tissue and blows her nose.

Man, I thought PMS days were bad around here.

"First of all, Centipede is a bug. Maybe you're talking about the Space Invaders game?" Victoria always has the mom wisdom around here.

Chelsea completely disregards Victoria's response. "Dean thinks there's something wrong. He says I shouldn't be crying so much."

"How much are you crying?" I ask, sitting and crossing my legs in the chair in front of her desk.

As always, Victoria hovers by the door in case someone calls.

"Well, I cried at a commercial the night before last and again as I was scrolling through Facebook. I never noticed how much sad stuff is on there. I mean a man surprising his son after coming home from the war? Come on. Who doesn't cry at that?" She raises her hands in the air and shakes them as though asking for a prayer to be answered.

"That's normal. I get teary-eyed with that kinda stuff, too." Victoria attempts to be the consoling friend.

A hopeful look crosses Chelsea's face for a second. "I cried thinking about Grover. Thinking how I barely know him and how he'll never grow as close to me as he is Dean. That he's going to die one day and I never knew him as a puppy."

I glance at Victoria who returns my look of bewilderment.

"See? Look at you two exchanging looks like I'm a lunatic. Maybe Dean is right. What if this is some sign that my hormones are crashing?"

"It's not." Victoria walks over and props herself on the

edge of the desk, placing her hand on Chelsea's shoulder. "This is all normal. With Jade, I cried because Pete brought me a banana milkshake instead of a strawberry one."

"I'd be mad, too. These cravings are no joke. Dean went out last night at ten pm to get me Chick-Fil-A."

"Were they open?" Victoria asks like she's done a late night run before only to be disappointed.

"No. He got there right as they were locking the doors. The damn teenage manager couldn't be bribed. And guess what?"

"You cried?" I ask.

Chelsea nods, tears welling in her eyes all over again.

Ding, ding, I got the answer right.

"You two are not making pregnancy sound appealing." I stand smoothing out my skirt.

"Wait until you meet him or her. All these crazy emotions are all worth it. I promise." Victoria kisses Chelsea's forehead like the mom she is. "Tell Dean not to overreact. He's in for a long ride."

Chelsea laughs, her tears drying and I don't want to be a jackass of a boss, but I really need her to secure us a new venue for the gala. Preferably today. I was up all night figuring out who owed me a favor. Since half of my contacts disappeared the minute I signed my divorce papers, the list has shrunk considerably.

"Oh, Hannah, I'm waiting for callbacks from a few venues. Don't worry, I won't cry to them on the phone."

"Great, keep me posted." I walk out of the office wondering how the next six or seven months of her pregnancy will pan out.

Victoria follows. "I put the messages on your desk this morning. Reed said he'll call in some favors too and see if he can work anything out for us, but he's in court most of today."

"Thank him for me, but he already has a lot on his plate."

"He's happy to help." She sits down at her desk, her hands instantly positioned on her keyboard.

I'm thankful every day that Jagger called me to tell me about how his assistant was relocating.

The white and gold decor in my office cheers me up slightly as I head to my own desk. The non-traditional office flair reminds me I'm in charge now and I don't have to conform to anyone else's wishes.

When I leased these offices for the RISE Foundation, I decided that no way was I going with boring old black, grey and brown. I wanted something vibrant, new…something to make me excited about life again. Someone offered their advice that the feminine palette diminishes my power when someone visits my office. That it says I'm soft and they'll get what they want from me.

Okay not someone—my father. But RISE is mine and I'm the one who has to stare at these walls and sit at this desk day in and day out. I'm damn well going to be happy.

Picking up the messages from the corner of my desk, I sort through them, all from people I contacted about donating to the silent auction. It doesn't disappoint me at all that none of them are from Roarke Baldwin because I definitely don't want him to contact me.

Nope. Not one bit.

FOUR O'CLOCK ROLLS AROUND and since Chelsea has yet to bring me a contract for a venue, I'm assuming her fairy godmother wand is broken.

A knock sounds as I hang up from a phone call with Lennon Banks, the woman who wants to open up a branch of RISE in San Francisco, but how can I arrange that when I don't even know how things in Chicago will go? We've managed to get after-school programs at five schools off the ground—including Victoria's daughter Jade's school. But I'm not satisfied with that. We need more. Our goal is to lead girls to find their voices and never refuse to use them.

"Come in," I say as I move some papers to the side of my desk.

Chelsea's head is down as she opens the door. She normally lights up a room with her contagious smile and her sharp wit, so I'm crossing my fingers that it's the pregnancy that's responsible for her mood and not the fact she couldn't find a space to hold our gala.

She plops down in the chair across from me. "I'm sorry, Hannah. I failed."

I press the intercom button. "Victoria, can you come in here please?"

A second later, Victoria walks in and sits down next to Chelsea, her own frown already in place. Chelsea must have already shared her news.

"I've literally called everywhere, Hannah. Well, everywhere but the Days Inn or the Budget Motel. If you want I will though." Chelsea looks at me, hopeful.

I place my elbows on my desk, my fingers running over both temples. Think, Hannah, think. You know people.

"I'm sure you tried everything," I say, trying to reassure her.

Chelsea nods, holding up her hand and counting the hotels off one by one. "The Ritz, the Westin, the Hilton, Four Seasons, The Drake, The Swissôtel. I've called them all. I guess September has taken over as the new wedding month because that's all I kept hearing from the event coordinators."

"We could head to Lake Geneva. Make a weekend out of it?" Victoria chimes in and the idea is great, but to get all those people out of the city with a little over a month's notice? No way.

"I wish. Too far. Anything in the burbs?"

"I've called the entire Oakbrook area. Schaumburg's booked too."

"What about north of the city?" I ask.

"I'm sorry, Hannah, nothing. I'm on every waitlist going, but anything that did come up would be last minute."

Victoria bites her lip.

Chelsea looks like someone told her Santa Claus wasn't real.

"Both of you. Go home." I wave them off.

"What's the game plan?" Victoria asks, sitting on the edge of her seat.

"I don't know yet. You two go home and I'll work something out."

Chelsea, my usual go-getter, stands, not putting up a fight to leave. I'm sure she wants the serenity of her bed and her fiancé, Dean. "I'll try again tomorrow," she mumbles, leaving my office. "I'm so sorry, Hannah."

"Make sure you get her in a cab or call Dean," I say to Victoria.

She nods. "I'll do that and come back?"

I shake my head. "No. Go home and relax. It will work out. It always does."

With a sigh, I lean back in my chair. I just hope I don't have to sell my soul to the devil, aka Roarke Baldwin.

Ten minutes later, the two of them are gone and I let my panic take over. Alone in my office, I spring to my feet and pace. Heading back to the break room, I glance at another care package from the newest bakery that opened up a block down. My hands itch for the sugar, but I pull open the fridge and grab a diet soda instead.

Walking back to my office, I kick off my heels and continue to pace for a while. Eventually I gaze out the window. The sun is shining in the sky. I love summer and the endless stream of sunny nights.

Roarke pops into my head again. If Chelsea can't find anything, how the hell would Roarke even be able to help me? I'm tempted to call his bluff. He probably can't even deliver on his promise and what does he want with me anyway?

We never did address what he meant by that. Instead we went right into his absurd obsession with me calling him Roarke. He probably thinks that if I did agree to his stupid agreement that I'd be willing to sacrifice myself.

Me naked on his bed isn't as despicable as I wish it was. It's quite enticing if I'm honest. But I would *never* admit to it.

"Jesus, Han, get a grip," I mumble to myself.

My inner angel pops onto my right shoulder. *Roarke Baldwin is a bad, bad man.*

My imaginary devil pops onto my left shoulder. *And you're a bad girl. How will he punish you?*

"Shut up you fucking devil!" I yell.

The office door of RISE opens.

I stop all movement with the very real fear that I've conjured him up in real life. The villain always shows up when his prey is weak.

Am I weak? Maybe a little. After all, there's a war going on between my head and my pussy and my wet panties suggests which one's winning.

"Ms. Crowley, I'm sorry, usually you girls are gone by

now." Misty, the cleaning lady peeks her head inside my office.

Thank Goodness.

"I was just leaving." I slip into my heels, shut down my computer and grab my bag. "Have a great night, Misty." I smile.

"Be careful out there. The sun is going down."

I glance out the window by Victoria's desk, the sun has started to make its descent now. "I will thanks."

"Darkness is when the devil comes out to play." She empties Victoria's trashcan into her big garbage bag.

"Sometimes the devil appears in daylight too. Dressed in a custom tailored suit and wingtips."

She raises her eyebrows. "Man problems, Ms. Crowley?"

My hand lands on the doorknob to the office. "Not in the slightest. Goodnight."

"Night, Miss."

I leave the confines of my office, riding down the elevator alone and it isn't until I step out onto the streets of Chicago that I realize my devil isn't like a thief emerging from a dark alley. He sits perched up in his penthouse or corner office under the guise of one of the most successful men in Chicago. He's the devil in the gray suit and if I don't tread carefully, I'm likely to forget it.

Chapter Four

I tap my pen on the desk as I wait on the line for the Director of Hospitality to return to the phone. I appreciate that she's in the office as early as I am and able to take my call, but she's taken ten minutes already to check her calendar. I'm not asking for space three years down the line. The event is six weeks away.

"Ms. Crowley." Her voice shakes when it sounds over the line.

Probably new.

"Yes."

Tip. Tap. My pen bounces like a teeter-totter against my white desk.

"I'm sorry. I thought we had a cancellation, but the bride called this morning to say the wedding is still a go. Lover's quarrel I guess." Her voice sounds sweet now, like she's happy they didn't cancel.

Too bad I can't say the same.

"Thank you. If anything changes can you put me down as the first call you make?" I ask, leaving my voice dripping with the sweetness of honey. "Please note I'll pay fifty percent more."

I've had hard lessons on what gets me what I want and honey and money are always more effective when used in tandem.

"That's very nice of you, but our prices are our prices."

We say goodbye and hang up and my gaze veers out the window. The feeling of impending doom over rescheduling the linens, the entertainment, the caterer —everything—seeps into my pores like cold rain on my skin. My office phone rings and since it's after hours and I'm alone I answer.

"RISE Foundation."

"Hannah?" The spunky voice of my childhood best friend, Gwen Turner, greets me.

"Gwen?"

"Who else?" she laughs. "Sorry for the early morning wake-up."

"You called the office. It's fine."

"I did?" She pauses for a second. "Oh shit, I'm off my rocker. Sleep deprived and overfucked, drinking every night…lots of fun."

A rustling sound comes over the line.

"What's up? You sound distracted."

She giggles again. "I am. Sorry, but my manager just mentioned booking me another date once I get stateside again. I told him I'm booked the weekend of September fifteenth, right?"

I let out a breath. If Gwen can't speak, then there's no reason to have the gala. She's my biggest celebrity coming and the biggest draw for people to part with their wallets.

"It is. Is there a conflict?" I ask.

"NO!" she screeches. "I told him to piss off. Told him I couldn't disappoint my girl."

"Thanks." The increased pressure to find a place threatens to flatten me like a pancake.

"He even tried to dangle the dollar amount I'd be missing out on. The guy doesn't understand the value of friendship, ya know?"

Guilt piles on top of guilt. Not that Gwen is by any means poor. She's rich. Not as rich as me, but she's earned hers. I inherited mine. There's a difference. A huge difference.

"Oh, Gwen I don't want you to miss—"

"Stop it, Montana. You're worth it. This foundation you're forming is worth missing out on a few thousand. My manager can suck it."

She uses her annoying nickname for me, Montana. Not the state, the character, Hannah Montana. It's the most unoriginal thing she's ever done.

"Suck your tit you mean." A male voice joins our telephone party.

Gwen giggles.

"That's not your manager, is it?" I ask.

She giggles harder and I'm afraid he probably is sucking her tit.

"Maybe, maybe not." She teases like she did when she was sleeping with her professor during her short stint in college.

"Gwen, what is with you and authority figures?"

She can't even use the excuse of daddy issues. Her dad is the most involved and loving man who lets her soar on her own, never interferes, but guides her to make smart decisions so she doesn't end up with something like a celebrity sex tape.

"Oh Montana, slip out of that stuffy business dress and go get laid. Todd sure as hell never fucked you right—it's about time you find a man who will."

An image of Roarke Baldwin flickers in my head accompanied with the tantalizing thought of what's under his suit. He always seems so controlled—his hair perfectly styled, his panty soaking five o'clock shadow trimmed to perfection. What would he be like in bed? A beast? A machine? Could I unglue him as much as I'm sure he'd unglue me?

I shake my head—literally—to clear my thoughts.

"You live in a fairyland."

"Join me sometime. I promise you'll never want to leave." More giggles and rustling echo through the line.

Like the pop of a champagne bottle, I wave the white flag on this conversation.

"Okay, Gwen, time for me to hang up so you can go have your orgasm. Thanks for using me to torture your manager while you delay his rocket ship from exploding."

"Your humor is back, Montana. I miss you."

"Is this foundation really worth losing close to a mil?" the deep voice asks.

I grip the receiver in my hand until my knuckles are white.

"Stop counting money and give me what I really need." After a long moan from Gwen that seems to send a current from Paris to Chicago, I realize—I really do need to get laid. It's been a while.

Hanging up, a gnawing feeling eats away at my stomach. If I have to somehow cancel this gala, I'm now screwing Gwen, too.

For the hundredth time since Torrio's Table the other night, Roarke Baldwin's offer resurfaces to the forefront of my mind.

"What exactly did he mean when he said he wants me?"

"He means he wants you tied up, or maybe he has a

red room of pain at his place." Victoria comes into my office and sits in the chair across from my desk.

"My life is not a movie."

She smiles sweetly, shrugging her shoulders. "Why are you here so early?"

I shrug, tapping my pen back and forth.

"Reed called a few people and everyone's booked. The same thing as Chelsea said, weddings."

I chew the inside of my lip for a second. "Please thank him for me."

"I will. So what are we going to do?" she asks, moving to the edge of her chair.

Victoria is a fix-it person. The word defeat isn't in her vocabulary which is what makes her such a great employee and friend.

"I'm going to have to go deal with the devil," I say with about as much excitement as I feel, which is to say none.

Her smile wipes off her face. "No. There has to be another way."

I shake my head, my pen dropping to the desk. "I'm not sure there is. Plus, it could be as harmless as him wanting me on his arm for some big event. I'll do it for all those girls we could help."

"I hate this. I think we should just reschedule the event. We could do a winter wonderland. Rent some heaters for an outside patio…all the décor inside could be white, silver and blue. It'd be beautiful."

She paints a breathtaking picture and I might have been on board before Gwen's call. But speaking with her reminded me of all the speakers who have committed, booked out time from their busy schedules to come. I'm not going to screw them over when they agreed to help me out of the goodness of their hearts. Chelsea's cousin and her friends are flying in from training in New Zealand to give away a silent auction package of a weekend in Park City with them as tour guides.

"Stop looking like I just told you Reed has a secret wife. I'm not going to sell my body, Victoria." I google Roarke Baldwin, bastard-at-law and scribble his phone number down, sliding the note to Victoria. "Here. Call over and say I need to have a word with the snake."

"I don't like this. I'm just saying," she says before rising from her chair.

There's no sense responding because there's nothing else to say.

Through the frosted glass, I watch her movements. She picks up the phone and I hear the murmur of her voice as she talks, but she hangs up before sending a call through to me.

He's probably in court screwing someone else over.

My throat contracts when she rises from her desk. I can't remember the last time I was nervous and it only makes my resentment for Mr. Baldwin grow.

She enters my office and places a colored sticky note on my desk. "He told his assistant you're to use his cell phone only. The office phone is for clients and you're not a client."

I crinkle the piece of paper, balling it in my fist.

"What a son of a bitch!" I throw the coral piece of paper across the room.

"I don't like this. I think we should reschedule the gala."

I slide my chair out, press my palms on the edge of my desk and push up, heading over to retrieve the note I just flung. "No. Mr. Baldwin wants to play, I can fucking play. The most arrogant predators always underestimate their prey. Roarke Baldwin is the biggest pompous ass I've ever met, and I guarantee he underestimates every woman he comes into contact with, including me."

"You're kind of scary right now," Victoria says, backing away from the desk. "Can I leave the door open a sliver so I can eavesdrop?" She grins.

I laugh and shoo her out of the office with my hand. Chelsea must arrive because a moment later I spot two shadows with their ears pressed against my door.

Chapter Five

I press the numbers on my phone with shaky fingers, bringing the receiver up to my ear and release a deep breath.

He picks up after one ring. "I thought we were friends? Having your assistant call my assistant. Tsk. Tsk, Ms. Crowley."

Aggravation fuses together every cell in my body until I become an impenetrable wall.

"First, we are not friends. Second, I would prefer to talk to you via our office phones."

There's a brief second of silence where he's probably realizing I called him through my office line.

"Ahh… so now you have my number and I don't have yours? That seems terribly unfair."

"I didn't realize you cared about fairness?" I lean back in my chair and cross my legs.

"You don't know that much about me. It's not like you know me *intimately*." He lowers his voice on the last word and drags it out.

I roll my eyes, happy we're not face-to-face so he can't see the flush in my cheeks.

"You may have witnessed how I own the courtroom, but you know nothing about my private life. For instance, you don't know if I like thrillers or comedies. Whether I prefer sorbet to ice cream or if I wear boxers or briefs."

"I don't need to know those things," I say with frustration, shutting my eyes to rid the vision from my head of him in tight black boxer briefs—since that's my preference.

"You want to know though." A sexual innuendo pours out of his mouth and hits its mark between my thighs.

"There you go making assumptions about my wants." I pick up my pen, shuffling through paperwork. Anything to distract me from this ache.

"I not only know what you want, I know what you need, Ms. Crowley."

I smack my hand down on my desk. "Okay Rico Suave, let's talk about this venue you have access to and keep the discussion of undergarments for another time."

A beeping sound interrupts us.

"Hold all my calls please, Kristen." Then nothing for a moment. "Sorry about that but you know how busy I am."

"Yes, I'm sure destroying people's lives takes a lot of time. So let's stop the sexual innuendos and get down to business."

"Let's meet tonight. You frequent Torrio's. I frequent Torrio's. Let's do something crazy and have a drink together."

"I don't need a drink at Torrio's, Mr. Baldwin, I *need* a venue to house my gala. Now tell me your terms and I want the details of this venue you insist you can secure. I refuse to meet you until you supply me with that information." I uncross my legs and tap my foot on the floor under me.

"So demanding. I like it." I can hear him shuffling papers in the background. "I'll have my assistant message your assistant with all the details of the venue. I'm sure it will be to your liking. Then we'll meet tonight at Torrio's. Seven sharp. Consider it our own personal happy hour."

"I'm not committing to anything until I see the venue."

"Then I'll see you at seven." The phone clicks and I stare at the receiver in my hand.

"Prick," I murmur.

A knock sounds on my door.

"Just come in."

The two women practically fall through the door.

"Nice to know there's no such thing as privacy in this office," I say, tossing my pen down on my desk.

"We only heard bits and pieces." Victoria walks in with a muffin in her hand.

"Give us some credit. At least we didn't hide in my office and try to connect to the line."

Chelsea seems much happier today as she sits down in the chair. No red eyes or blotchy skin, her smile wide and bright.

"You're happy today," I remark.

Her smile grows wider.

"Oh let me guess, Dean made use of those uncontrollable hormones last night," I say with a chuckle.

She shrugs, her eyes flitting up behind her eyelids.

"Good for you."

"Wait until you're five months along. That smile might as well be sewn on your lips." Victoria waggles her eyebrows and places the muffin on my desk.

"Tell the bakery to stop sending samples. My God, do they want my ass to be the size of Lake Michigan?" I push it away, my attitude having a lot to do with the bastard I just hung up with.

"I'll tell them." Victoria's abrupt removal of the muffin says I'm being a bitch. I reach out for the delicious looking treat. "It's fine really. Sorry. That man just makes me crazy."

"Let me take it back. I think they think since we're an office of women we want to give all the items a go."

Chelsea throws her hands in the air. "Don't go telling them to stop. Hello!" She points to her stomach. "I can eat whatever I want for the next seven months with zero guilt."

Victoria hands the muffin to Chelsea who happily takes a big bite, crumbs falling to her lap.

"So, we're all going to Torrio's tonight?" Chelsea asks with a mouthful of muffin.

"No. I am. Mr. Baldwin's assistant will be sending you the information on the venue, Vic. Let me know as soon as you get it."

"You're going to have a drink with him?" Chelsea asks, her gaze meeting Victoria's. "Under those dim lights that promise roaming hands and sneaking kisses?"

"No Chelsea. I'm going to Torrio's, where more business transactions happen than hook-ups. Where our usual waiter, Lincoln, will serve me and Mr. Baldwin. We'll negotiate an agreement I find reasonable and then I will leave. Alone."

Chelsea stands, dropping the muffin wrapper into my trashcan.

"Sure. Okay. Sounds like you've got it all figured out." She waves her hand in the air. "Catch you on the flip side when you're all hot and bothered and sexually unfulfilled wishing your dildo was the real thing."

I sit at my desk with my mouth ajar.

"It's the hormones. They make you crazy." Victoria sticks up for her friend.

I'm not upset though. What she just did is the reason I

hired her. She calls people out on their bullshit and right now I know I'm full of shit. Tonight I'm going to wear a pants suit just to protect myself. I'll never admit that what she just said is my worst fear and could be my fate come dawn.

"Let me know when you receive the information on the venue."

"Sure thing." Victoria steps out of the office glancing down the hall, probably to make sure Chelsea is at her desk and not ready to mouth back to me with some more unwelcome truths.

Chapter Six

"Thank you, Sam."

I step into the speakeasy whose membership has been in my family for generations. If only they didn't let assholes like Roarke in here, it'd be the perfect, serene wind down place for me to come after the office.

"My pleasure, Ms. Crowley."

I nod and head into the bar filled with seventy percent males. I'd love it if they attracted more professional women here. It's ridiculous how much of a boy's club it still is.

My gaze sweeps over the room, looking for the king of the good ol' boys, and I find him immediately. He can't be missed. While other men have loosened their ties and abandoned their jackets, Roarke looks like he just started his day in a three-piece suit that fits to perfection, not a piece of his salt and pepper hair out of place. Other men's postures are relaxed in the booths or chairs with their arms loose and legs open, laughing and smiling with the others, but Roarke sits in the booth facing the door with a straight back and his eyes on me.

I don't get a wave, but his gaze locks with mine. No condescending smile plays on his lips, but I don't get a welcoming smile either. I feel like I was transported back into that courtroom when he'd give me a fleeting look before whispering to Todd.

This has to be the lowest thing I've ever done. Negotiating myself in exchange for a venue. What the hell is wrong with me?

I step down the two stairs and break the distance between us. Smiling at a few familiar faces, I delay my impending doom.

He slides out of the booth, standing at the edge of the table, waiting to greet me. Such a noble prince. Not.

"Nice to see you, Ms. Crowley."

"I can't say the same, Mr. Baldwin." I slide down into my usual booth with the girls, except I'm on Chelsea's side this time.

Thankfully, Lincoln is as attentive as he always is. "Vesper?" he asks, putting a napkin down in front of me.

"Not tonight. How about scotch on the rocks."

He nods and heads back to the bar.

"Scotch?" Roarke questions, his eyebrows shooting up to his hairline.

"Yes. I know you probably think I'm a margarita or a daiquiri girl. Sorry to disappoint you."

He chuckles lightly to himself, bringing the glass to his lips. "You never disappoint."

I roll my eyes.

"Let's just cut the bullshit, shall we?" I place my entwined hands on the table.

He sets his drink down, trying like a champ to hold back his smile.

"Bullshit?" he asks.

My anxiety ticks up a level with his one-word questions to everything I say. Is this the lawyer in him?

"Yes, you're using the leverage of a venue to reap something from me. I'm not for sale, Mr. Baldwin. I'm here because the venue will work and if you can deliver like you say you can, I'm more than willing to negotiate terms." I lean forward so he won't miss a word of the next part. "But let me be clear, I will not be naked and strapped to your bedpost."

Lincoln's hand rattles as he sets my drink down, resulting in it tipping and spilling all over the table.

"I'm so sorry." Lincoln grabs the napkin, but the three by three square isn't enough to sop up the mess so he races off to the bar.

"Look what you've done. You got Lincoln all excited about the possibilities." Roarke takes his own napkin and stops the rush of liquid before it soaks my lap.

Lincoln runs back with a rag. "I'm so sorry, Ms. Crowley. That's never happened to me before."

"It's okay, Lincoln," I say.

"I'll go get you another drink."

"Thanks for saving my pants," I begrudgingly say to the man across from me.

"I'd hate to give you an excuse to cut this meeting short."

Before I can respond, Lincoln delivers a fresh drink from the bar. "Here you are, Ms. Crowley. Again, I'm sorry."

He's newer and efficient, although I'm sure they hired him as eye candy for the few women who belong. Too young for me, but the tattoos that peek out of his white linen shirt intrigue me nonetheless.

"Hannah, please and it's fine." I smile up at him.

Roarke's eyes widen. "He can call you Hannah?"

"Yes." I nod.

Lincoln glances to Roarke. "Another, sir?"

Roarke shakes his head in a dismissive gesture and Lincoln heads to the next table.

"Back to what you were saying about bedposts and ties… Let's get one thing straight. I would never ask that of you because when I finally have you, Ms. Crowley…" He says my name with maple syrup coated sarcasm. "I won't need to tie you down to keep you there. You'll want it."

I roll my eyes, letting the scotch burn my throat as I take a healthy sip of my drink.

"You're pretty presumptuous. And if you want me as you say, you went about winning me over the wrong way. I'm not some young girl who's going to fall on my knees for you."

"Dare I say there'll come a time when you will drop to your knees in front of me." When I spear him with a disgusted look, he chuckles. "Why do you think you intrigue me?"

"You know everything about me. You know how much money sits in my bank accounts. How many properties I have. I'm simply an opportunity to you Mr. Baldwin. If you want me, it's strictly because of what I can offer you financially and socially."

He rests his weight on his arms, leaning over the table toward me. The scent of his expensive cologne permeates my senses and I have to will myself not to show him any weakness by leaning back in my seat.

"There you go again, making assumptions." His finger slides out and runs over the top of my hand. "I'm not Todd. I don't want a cent from you. When I told you it was you I wanted, that was it. Nothing else. But I would never force that on you either. The choice is yours."

I push back the burning arousal from his confession. If

he's telling the truth, it sets him apart. No one has ever just wanted me. Including a lot of my friends. There was always some club or designer they wanted me to pull strings for. I have no doubt Roarke is playing me. You're not raised with the Crowley last name and end up just skipping along the yellow brick road not thinking your next enemy couldn't be someone you call a friend.

"Enough of this back and forth," I snip. "What are you proposing?"

He leans back and I move my hands to my lap. His gaze follows and then floats up to my face after pausing briefly at my breasts.

His own hand disappears beneath the table and reappears with a manila folder.

Lawyers.

"What, are you going to make me sign a contract?"

"Look how well you already know me." He grins.

"Seriously?" My gaze flies to the papers he pulls from the folder. "I can guarantee you my word is enough."

"In my line of work, someone's word is never enough. People forget. There are misunderstandings, miscommunications. This way our agreement is in black and white with no room for misinterpretation."

I lean forward, my hands reaching for the contract but he retracts it. I slink back into the booth. "Let me guess if I don't fulfill my end there's a monetary fine for me to pay."

"Tsk. Tsk. Ms. Crowley, stop making assumptions." He reaches into his jacket, pulling out a pair of black-rimmed reading glasses, he positions them on his face and reaches in his pocket again for a pen.

I hate to admit it, but the few times I saw him wearing those glasses in court or during discovery, I couldn't help noticing how much it upped his hotness factor. A pair of glasses should not make a man even sexier.

"Maybe we should have had this meeting at your office with it all being so by the book." I give him a caustic smile across the table.

"I debated that," he says flipping through the papers and not looking up at me. "But the desire to bend you over my desk would've been too strong." He looks up from the papers and winks.

A sudden bolt of lightning electrifies me from head to toe and every hair on my body stands on end. *Bastard.*

"That's never going to happen," I say.

"Still making assumptions I see." He sets the pen down, taking off his glasses and letting his gaze fall over me. "I rarely fail to get what I want."

"Cut the Fifty Shades bullshit." I seize the contract, the pen tumbling down off the papers and landing on the table. "My lawyers will have a look at this."

"Your lawyers aren't going to see this contract. I assure you, it's favorable for both sides." He sits back, giving me time to read it over.

"What are you going to sit here the entire time?" I ask.

"I'd like nothing better than to spend the night with you. I'd prefer other alternatives, but I'll take what you're offering." I stare at him for longer than I should. He has me at a disadvantage—his true intentions are foggy to me now.

"Then get comfortable."

He raises his hand, and Lincoln rushes over. "Another please," he shakes his glass.

"Ms. Crowley?" Lincoln asks.

"Hannah," I remind him. "And no, I'm good."

Roarke's jaw ticks while Lincoln walks away.

"You'll find there's nothing out of the ordinary. No sexual favors. No exchange of money. It's a straight deal. I secure you the venue and you grant me five favors."

I flip through the contract, my gaze running down the pages and see that he's telling the truth—there's no sex mentioned, nothing about nakedness, and no dollar figure.

"What kind of favors do you have in mind?" I ask.

His smile reappears. The same one he had in court the day when he secured my ex-husband far more than he deserved.

"That's where trust comes into play."

Is he kidding?

I place the contract down and slide to the end of the booth. "No deal."

His large hand lands on mine, stopping me from leaving. "Listen." There's a desperation in his tone that keeps me in place.

"I will not sign up to be your prey. Some plaything you call on a whim demanding I do something embarrassing or demeaning."

His hand tightens over mine, but I yank myself free.

"Fine." He snatches up the contract, and clicks his pen, then scribbles something down, initials it, and hands it back to me.

I read over the added verbiage that states that no favor will be embarrassing or demeaning, his illegible initials scrawled next to it.

"You've left me no choice. I could ask you out on a date, but you'd deny me. Five favors that all entail you seeing a side of me outside of the man you think I am. That's all this is. We both know if we ripped up that contract and I asked you to go out with me you'd never give me a fair chance even if I could manage to convince you."

"Why?"

He sips his drink. "Why?" he asks back, raising a brow.

Back to his damn one word questions.

"Yes, why are you going to this much work to prove to me you're not who I think you are? You don't even know me."

"I know more than I should at this stage of our relationship."

His eyes dip to his drink and I'm reminded of the fact he probably hired a private investigator on me, same as my lawyer did with Todd. He probably knows my habits. Knows about my dog Lucy. Hell, he probably knows what tampon brand I use.

"To answer your question, I'm attracted to you and I think we could be good together."

I study his face for a moment, waiting for the punchline, but he seems sincere, which throws me. "A divorce attorney who believes in true love and marriage?"

"More assumptions. I said nothing about marriage, nor would I ever—to anyone. I'm just giving you the chance to know the real me so that perhaps I have a chance with you."

I stare across the table at him, testing to see if he'll crack. He doesn't even flinch.

If I wasn't attracted to Roarke Baldwin, this would be an easy decision, but despite my better judgment, I am. The chance to maybe sleep with him and get him out of my system could be a win-win for us both.

"We have one thing in common." He tilts his head in askance. "I will never get married again."

"Then your decision should be simple." He nudges the contract in front of me.

I read it over, every sentence, every word. He's right, there's nothing that will secure him anything other than five favors, and the papers clearly state that none of them will be monetary or sexual in nature.

I hold my hand out for the pen without looking at him.

I'm strong and the worst that can happen is that I sleep with Roarke Baldwin. That's not so bad. I could live with myself after—I think.

I sign the contract, pushing down the feeling that I've just done something there's no coming back from, and slide it back in his direction.

"See, that wasn't too hard." He folds the contract up in thirds and shoves it into his front pocket. "I'll make sure you get a copy tomorrow."

I down a big gulp of my drink. "And the venue?"

He pulls out a card from his vest pocket and slides it to me. "Call this number tomorrow. They already have you booked. They just need some specifics."

"Have a great evening, Mr. Baldwin." I slide out of the booth unable to sit across from the silver fox any longer without my willpower crumbling and begging him to forget the five favors, just take me home.

"Leaving so soon?" he asks with a cocky grin, like he can read my mind.

"Yes. Goodnight." I turn and take one step away from the table.

"You don't even want to know the first favor?"

I stop immediately and turn to face him again, securing my clutch under my arm. "Is favor number one that you're going to keep me here against my will?"

He chuckles. "No." He slides out and stands, his hand running down the length of my arm and I suppress a full body shiver. "Favor number one is that I can call you Hannah and you call me Roarke. There's no more Ms. Crowley and Mr. Baldwin."

"Fine. Goodnight Roarke." His name falls off my tongue way too easy, and I can't help but wonder what it would sound like if I was screaming it while he drove into me.

I am in such deep shit with this man.

He leans in, his light scruff scratching my cheek before his soft lips land where my cheekbone meets my hairline. "Sweet dreams, Hannah."

Chapter Seven

"Five favors?" Victoria cringes across from me.

Chelsea's eyes light up.

Two completely different reactions from two very different women.

I always enjoyed our morning recaps at the office but now that it's me in the hot seat, not so much. They were waiting this morning to find out exactly what Mr. Bald— Roarke wanted.

"Kinky. I like his style," Chelsea says, the traitor.

Victoria flips through the contract that was waiting in her email this morning. "You're right, there's nothing sexual."

"Seems like a waste." Chelsea shrugs.

"I take it Dean's still tapped in? No more tears." I raise a brow.

"Only from coming so many times." She smiles and I sip my coffee ignoring the grating jealousy.

I haven't had sex in way too long and even then, it wasn't with a man who could do much for me. Having your two friends living their lives with a post-coital glow isn't easy. Maybe that's why I signed that contract last night. Subconsciously maybe I thought Roarke would solve that problem for me.

"It's a little romantic, no?" Victoria hands the contract to Chelsea who flips through it even though I'm sure she's only really searching for the juicy parts.

"A contract is never romantic." I lean back in my office chair.

Chelsea tosses it on my desk. "I kind of agree. But he's gone to great lengths to win you over."

"My bet is that he's still only really interested in sex," I say.

Victoria's lips dip.

Chelsea's lips tip up even more. "Perfect. It's a win-win. You're not looking for a long-term relationship or marriage, right?"

"Yes. But doesn't this make it seem like he's going to win me over by the time this contract is fulfilled and then what? I sleep with him and we both walk away?"

I won't tell them about how restless I was last night. Lucy kept getting up and moving because of my tossing and turning. Eventually she went to her dog bed on the floor. I can't help but think I'm being paid for sex in some twisted way.

"Please. You don't have to sleep with him if you don't want to. Five favors and he already used one up. That's four left. You totally have this." Chelsea acts like my little cheerleader.

"I agree. You do as he says with one arm out. Don't let him get too close. You were cornered and the fact he's using his connections over you says what kind of guy he is. So, just do what he asks you to and be done with it. Whatever you do, don't fall for him." Victoria's inner mama bear roars loud.

"Girls, you know I can handle myself. We're good. No worries."

"Shame really because I bet he knows his way around a woman's body. Foxes know how to hunt." Chelsea stands, taking her box of donut holes with her.

"You're really taking this whole I eat what I want to heart." I point to the powdered sugar covering her breasts.

"Shit," she mumbles and sweeps the white sugar off of her, but it smears.

"Live it up but remember it's hard to work it off your ass off after the baby's out. Trust me on that." Victoria leaves the office.

Chelsea looks at me. "I have no complaints. I'll just have Tad whip me back into shape." She smiles through another mouthful of donut and then heads down the hall.

I swivel in my chair to face the skyline of Chicago through the window. Out of the millions of people who live and work in Chicago, how does my path keep crossing Roarke Baldwin's.

My phone vibrates on my desk and I swivel back around to pick it up.

My dad.

I accept the call and put it on speaker.

"Hi, Dad."

"Hi, pumpkin. How are things at the foundation?"

"Good."

"Did you contact that guy for the gala? He said he'd love to speak there."

"I told you it's about female empowerment so I'm having only successful women give the speeches."

"Don't you think that's kind of reverse discrimination?"

The highway noise in the background tells me he's talking on his Bluetooth while driving. Probably on his way to the golf course.

"No, I don't."

He chuckles to himself. "I've always loved your bull-headedness. Who trained you so well?"

"You did."

"That's right. I taught you how to act like a man."

I roll my eyes. My dad loves me, but there's no doubt he missed the opportunity to raise a son.

"I'd rather think of it as you taught me to be a strong female."

He chuckles again like what I said is funny. I toed that line with my dad for years when I was younger—trying to get him to see that his ideas were sexist and his beliefs were from fifty years ago. Some battles just aren't worth fighting and I don't want to spend my adulthood in conflict with my dad.

"I told your mother that we had nothing to worry about."

"Thanks, Dad." I pick the pen up off my desk and start flicking it side to side in my hand.

"I mean so what about Todd, right? We're lucky to have that bastard out of our life."

I drop the pen. Whoa, back the bus up. I thought we were talking about me being successful and able to stand on my own? That my mother who has never earned one dollar herself doubted my abilities?

"What are you talking about?" I ask.

"Todd," he says louder. Like I'm his golf buddy who turned down his hearing aid. "The announcement of his engagement."

I spring up and out of my chair. "He's engaged?"

"Oh, you didn't know. I assumed you heard before we did. It was all the buzz at the club last night during dinner. Supposedly she's a nurse at the hospital. Seems a little sleazy to me, sleeping with someone who works underneath you, but his parents were raving about her."

The pit of my stomach shouldn't feel as though I just ate a hearty helping of street meat. I shouldn't give one shit about Todd or his upcoming nuptials.

"He took her to Tahiti or somewhere tropical and had the ring put in some shell and wrote something in the sand. You know me, I zoned out after a little while, but your mother, she was worried about how you'd handle the news."

I'm sure she was wondering why I wasn't worth that much planning on Todd's part. I got proposed to at the club during a Friday night fish fry. *Asshole.* Now he takes his soon-to-be wife away on my dime for some elaborate proposal?

I clench my fists but don't respond, unable to find the right words.

"Don't let it bother you. He's a jackass and an idiot for not knowing what he had. His parents are a bunch of dimwits. You know I've always thought that."

I giggle at my dad. He might've been hard on me and yeah, he's a bit of a chauvinist, but when it comes to me, he has my back every damn time.

"It doesn't bother me," I insist. "It just bothers me that he's doing it with my money. What good is a prenup if you still have to give away half your shit?"

"Now Hannah, you couldn't have predicted Grandpa's death to happen a year into your marriage. Nor the fact he was old school and thought once married you stayed married. The old fool thought he was being nice by putting Todd in his will along with you."

"Exactly that. Any true gentleman wouldn't have taken the money, especially when he's the reason the marriage fell apart. He's a surgeon. It's not like he's barely scraping by."

"You afforded him a lifestyle he never would've had even with being a surgeon. You gotta let that go, move on with your life. I'm sure there's another guy out there who's been waiting to snatch you up."

"Snatch me up? Dad," I sigh.

"Oh, Hannah, you need to stop worrying so much. So what if Todd got more than he ever should have? He hired a great lawyer. Too bad it was before we could put him on retainer."

"He wasn't that great," I grumble.

"That's because you were on the opposite end. If he would've been yours, you'd have been kissing his feet."

"I don't think so." I pace back and forth in front of the window.

"At least if you get married again and it doesn't work out, we know who to call." He chuckles.

I roll my eyes again, happy my dad can't see me. If he could, he'd tell me that's no way to behave toward my father.

"No worries there. It was hard enough for me to become a Crowley again after the divorce. I'm not giving up the name a second time."

That's the truth. Who knew how hard government offices made it to change back to your maiden name? When I had gotten married, the attendants would smile and ask me when the wedding was, how he proposed, where we honeymooned. When you tell them you're divorced their lips turn down and they don't ask any other questions.

Of course then again, what are they going to ask? How many years did it last? Whose fault was it?

"Oh pumpkin, you had one failed marriage. Look at

Uncle Harrison, it took him five tries before he found the right one. We just have to protect ourselves better. Next time we know to tighten up the prenup. Simple. Don't go off and punish every other man because Todd was an ass who was looking for his chunk of gold. I told you I never liked those people from the moment they moved in."

"Thanks for the pep talk, Dad." I smile to myself.

"I'm at the course now. I don't want you to close your-self off from other opportunities. Your guy is out there somewhere." He switches the phone off Bluetooth and onto speaker.

"Gregory!" one of his buddies says in the background.

"Great day for golf," my dad says.

"Okay, talk to you later, Dad."

"Yep, talk to you soon. Come by for dinner on Sunday. Your mom is worried about you."

"I'll try," I say, knowing I probably won't.

"Try harder. Bye, sweetie."

The line dies and I lean my shoulder on the glass window.

Todd's engaged.

As much as I was happy to sign the divorce papers, I can't help but wonder, what makes her so special? More special than me.

My phone buzzes from where it still sits on the desk so I step over and see the number I programmed in yesterday on the screen with a notification. I pick up the phone and open it to read the message.

Roarke: *Ready for favor number 2?*
Me: *How did you get my cell phone number?*
Roarke: *Feel lucky that I haven't used it until now.*
Me: *Yay me. What's the favor?*

Roarke: *I have to go out of town this weekend. Family emergency. I need someone to housesit.*
Me: *Housesit?*
Roarke: *Yes.*
Me: *Are you asking me to water your plants and feed your fish?*

He can't be serious. He's going to use a favor for me to babysit his empty house?

Roarke: *No. I'm asking you to spend the weekend at my place while I'm out of town. I have a kitten and he's just getting comfortable. Are you allergic?*

Shit, say yes, Hannah. Say you'll go into anaphylactic shock.

I start to type out the lie and then delete it then start to type it out again, but for some reason unknown to me I can't hit send on the lie.

Roarke: *I'll take your silence as a no.*
Me: *I think this is a little over the boundaries.*
Roarke: *It's not sexual or embarrassing. Do you find me asking you to housesit demeaning in some way?*

Bastard.

Me: *Aren't you afraid I'll snoop?*
Roarke: *Quite the opposite. I'm hoping you do.*
Me: *Who are you?*
Roarke: *I believe I've overheard your employees referring to me as the silver fox, but you can just call me Roarke.*
Roarke: *;)*
Me: *I have a dog and I have no idea if she gets along with cats.*
Roarke: *Puppy?*

Me: *Yes.*
Roarke: *Boy or girl?*
Me: *I take it from all your questions that you don't still keep tabs on me?*
Roarke: *You think I had you followed? Is that what you're worried about?*

I don't answer because I want to say yes, I do. This round robin game we keep going through is growing tired.

Roarke: *Back to the puppy and kitten debacle. Bring your dog. If they don't get along, I'll give you a number to call for someone else to come over. Deal?*
Me: *I suppose so.*

I'm not going to stick up my nose to such a simple favor. Especially one where I don't even have to be around him to fulfill.

Roarke: *Perfect. I'll have a key dropped off today and I'll text you the address. Please keep it confidential. As you're aware, many people don't like me and I'd rather they not know where I live. There will be a note on my kitchen counter with directions.*

So professional like he's going to use me as his servant instead of his sex slave.

That thought shouldn't disappoint me as much as it does.

Chapter Eight

The taxi drops me off in front of the address Roarke sent me.

"Come on, Lucy." I tug on her leash, but her butt slides along the concrete.

She is not the protective German Shepard I thought I was buying.

I tug a few more times and she finally stands and prances across the concrete until a man spins through the revolving door at the building's entrance. Her paws halt.

"Come on." I tug a little bit, but she sits down again, all four paws trying her hardest to grip the cement sidewalk. "Please Lucy," I beg.

Nothing.

"I don't want to go in there either, but we're doing it for the girls. It's two days and then we'll be back home." The dog sitter sounded like a good idea, but I figure if I do bring Lucy and she chases the cat around it's an easy out for me. Voila, favor number two complete.

Then again, what if I can't fulfill this favor and he says it doesn't count?

I shake my head. What are we, in high school? He can't bully me.

"Lucy." I kneel down, my overnight bag falling from my shoulder and smacking the sidewalk. I pet her head, staring into her eyes. "Once we're through those revolving doors, it's just like home."

Her head tips down. Yeah, she's not going for my pep talk.

"Miss?" A man to my side opens up the door beside the revolving ones.

I stand, and Lucy gets to all fours again.

"Please feel free to use this door." The man is dressed in his uniform that suggests he's either the doorman or security.

"Thank you very much."

Lucy actually follows behind me this time. She does love people.

"Who are you here to see?" he asks, rounding his desk in front of the elevators.

"I'm housesitting for Roarke Baldwin."

"Ah…yes…he mentioned that when he left this morning. He said you'd have a key." He punches something on the keyboard. "Hannah Crowley?"

I hold up said key. "That's me."

"He also said you'd need a dog walker four times a day?"

"Um…" Lucy tugs on the leash and I pull her back so I can finish my conversation.

"The building supplies it."

"Would it be billed to Mr. Baldwin?" I ask.

"Well, yes, but he's already paid for it."

Great, tack on another favor.

"I insist on paying the fee myself." I approach the desk,

Lucy finding a little girl coming off the elevator much more interesting than the desk.

I extend the leash as long as I can get it to reach the doorman, who I now see is Will, according to his name tag.

"I am sorry, but that's not possible, Ms. Crowley."

"Not possible? Surely you can send the invoice to me and not Mr. Baldwin?"

He points to the computer screen. "It clearly says here that if Ms. Crowley tries to pay for the service, then I am to politely refuse."

All I see is a mask of red. I don't know what kind of game he's playing, but I'm about to lose my temper. I do my best to hold it in since it's not Will's fault.

"Fine, I'll reimburse Mr. Baldwin directly then. Anything else in those notes of his?" I air-quote notes because him leaving instructions that pertain to me is utterly ridiculous.

"Seems to be about it. He'll be home on Sunday."

I nod. "Yes, I'll be leaving first thing Sunday morning."

Will smiles, teeth yellow from what I can smell is probably years of smoking.

"Then let's get you upstairs." He rounds the desk again, patting Lucy on her head.

Lucy stands and wags her tail confused when he doesn't stop to let her lick his face.

"I'm sure I can manage to get upstairs on my own," I say.

"I'll just keep the doors open for you and press the floor."

I smile, and Lucy and I step into the elevator, my shoulder killing me from carrying her bed, food, along with my overnight bag. I should've said bring the cat to me, but since he mentioned something about it just getting acquainted it's probably better for it to stay in the environment it knows. Plus, I'll admit to being curious to see Roarke's condo.

"Thank you, Will." I grab some cash from the front pocket of my purse and hand it over.

He shakes his head.

"I've already been tipped for the entire weekend. So have the other doormen. Please enjoy your stay, Ms. Crowley."

The elevator doors shut, and I put the money back in my purse.

"He's such a jackass," I murmur. Lucy's head turns in my direction with curiosity. "Two days, little one, and then we're down to three favors left."

The elevator doors open on the eighty-fifth floor.

"What? He didn't have the extra mil for the top floor?" I mumble to myself, tightening the leash on Lucy as we walk down the hallway.

I keep walking and there are no doors anywhere, no signs to where I need to go, and I feel like I'm walking in a circle until I land in front of a door with the number he texted me. He could've given me more specific directions. There's no way he owns this entire floor. Then again, the man screws rich people over for a living. I know from what I had to shell out to my own lawyer that they don't need to clip coupons.

I insert the key, Lucy sniffing the door like she's a drug dog and can't wait to make her master proud. The door lock clicks and Lucy jumps, pushing it open the rest of the way, running into the condo.

Having her leash wrapped tight around my wrist, I lunge forward. My purse lands with a thud and the contents spill out across the expensive marble floors. My overnight bag drops but luckily my computer is cushioned between my clothes.

"LUCY!" I yell, but she's running from room to room, sniffing out the cat, I assume.

I think I'll be using that number soon. I smile to myself as I get up off the floor.

A tiny silver fur ball runs past me and hides under the couch and Lucy resorts to sniffing around the perimeter of the piece of furniture, allowing me to soak in his condo for a minute. It's decorated in hues of grey, blue, and white with dark floors and huge windows that give a different view from each room.

Bastard might not have the entire floor, but he's got half.

I set off to explore some more, finding that his place has three bedrooms, each with their own bath and an office that looks like it's rarely used. A huge living room is in the center of the space and sits open to a kitchen and a long dining table that runs the length of one of the large windows.

Everything is clean and orderly like I assumed it would be. There's no beer cans or giant televisions that overpower a room, no clothes hanging out of a hamper or dried toothpaste in the sink. A perfectionist lives here. Though I already suspected that about him.

Lucy continues to circle the couch, sniffing for her prey.

I notice a piece of paper on the kitchen counter and so I head over to find a list of instructions in his sloppy man's handwriting. I half expected it to be typed up by his assistant.

Hannah,

Thank you. As you probably already know by now, I hired a dog walker. He'll come four times a day and they have access to my apartment so you don't need to be here to meet them. Also, as you probably know by now, all tips to doormen for the weekend are already paid. Please don't try to overtip them—they will refuse you.

I MAKE a childish whatever face and roll my eyes to myself.

"Kitty" gets fed twice a day. Soft food is in fridge. Hard food in cabinet. Water obviously.

I have no plants to water and the cleaning service was there right before you.

One last thing, I'm trying to keep Kitty out of my guest bedrooms, so you can sleep in my bed. Before you sigh, all sheets have been freshly washed.

I'd love for you to stick around on Sunday for dinner, but not enough to use it as a favor. The decision is yours.

Enjoy your weekend,

R

"SERIOUSLY?" The note slips from my hand down to the counter along with a written list of take-out places nearby.

ARF!

"Jesus, Lucy, leave the cat alone." I turn around to find the small little kitten peeking its head out from under the couch. Lucy looks like she's trying to get her huge-ass head under the couch, too, to join him.

Until this moment it didn't dawn on me that it's a little unexpected that a man like Roarke has a tiny, cute and fluffy kitten. A Doberman or a Pitbull wouldn't have surprised me. But this cute little thing? I'll admit it's not what I would have expected from Roarke.

Lucy licks Kitty—which by the way is a stupid-ass name. I sit down on the couch, the kitten crawling out from the opposite end, then pouncing from the coffee table to my lap.

"Whoa." My hand pets the soft grey fur and he begins to purr.

Lucy jumps up onto the couch, wanting to give her own welcome.

"You are a cutie. Kitty doesn't really fit you. I think I'm going to call you… Nickel." He purrs some more and pushes his head into my hand.

Lucy weasels her nose under my arm and flings it up in the worst emotion ever—Jealousy.

My phone rings from my purse so I place Nickel down on the couch and run over to answer.

I should've known to let it go to voicemail.

"Yes?" I answer.

"Is everything to your liking?" Roarke's deep voice sends a shiver up my spine.

"Your condo? It's okay." I walk to the window that overlooks Lake Michigan, watching all the boats coming and going from Navy Pier.

He chuckles. "Sorry it's not as costly as yours."

We both know our condos probably cost roughly the same, and I'm not too big of a person to admit that his views are better.

"Well, what can I say? I could barely afford much after my divorce."

"Touché."

"Oh and I renamed Kitty."

"You did?" He sounds amused. "What did you name him, may I ask?"

"Nickel. Since he's a silver grey color."

"Platinum sounds better."

"Maybe if *he* was a *she*. I get where you're going with the whole platinum being better than nickel, but we are talking cats here Mr.— Roarke."

"You caught yourself. Good job, Hannah." The way he says my name makes it feel like a million flickers of energy ignite in my stomach at the same time.

"Well, everything is good on this front. Favor number two seems like a cinch."

He chuckles again. "I'm glad you're settled. Please help yourself to whatever in the fridge. I had my assistant stock up on some items for you."

"Were you ever in the hospitality field?"

He laughs again. "I told you already, you know nothing about me. I'm just a nice guy."

"Not in the courtroom," I tease.

Oh my God. Are we flirting?

"I can't argue that point. But it's my job and my clients hire the best and that's what I give them. I know you were on the other side—"

"We don't need to go over all that. Thanks for calling. Nickel and Lucy are getting along fine." I turn to view the couch and find Nickel now snuggled into Lucy's neck. "Better than fine."

"Good. I didn't really want to hire some stranger to come in. I'm glad it's working out."

A female voice calls his name in the background and I stiffen.

"If you need anything, I left my assistant's phone number on the back of the paper, or any of the doormen can help."

He gets called again by the same woman.

"Thank you again, Hannah."

"You're welcome," I say, pushing back my irritation at

hearing a woman's voice. What business is it of mine what he's up to this weekend?

We hang up and I tap my cell phone against my chest as I watch the boats sailing along the glimmering lake. That might've been the first conversation where I didn't want to rip his head off.

I'm not sure if that's a good sign, or a bad one.

Chapter Nine

The weekend goes by without incident and I don't hear from Roarke again. On Sunday morning, something wakes me up and I realize that there's noise coming from the kitchen.

I bolt upright, seeing Lucy and Nickel fast asleep in Lucy's dog bed. Seriously? Worst guard dog, ever.

Sliding out of the million thread count bedsheets that smell way too much like Roarke, I tiptoe to the door and peek down the hall.

A suitcase is next to the hallway table with keys and sunglasses strewn on top. Soft music pipes out of the area with a few sounds of someone cooking.

"He did not hire me a cook, did he?"

I turn and look back at the alarm clock.

Nine o'clock.

I have no idea how I slept so late, but I suspect binge-watching Netflix most of the night didn't help. Once the dog walker came for Lucy, I changed into my pajamas and vegged out for the first time in I don't know how long. I usually have to go to some charity event or dinner at the club with my parents. If I liked Roarke even a little, I'd thank him for giving me a Saturday night to myself.

"Lucy," I softly scold for not alerting me to someone being inside.

Not that I think they're doing anything other than making me breakfast.

Lucy picks up her head, looks at me and then plops it back down.

I continue on the balls of my bare feet as I descend down the hall to better assess the situation.

My gaze flickers to the sunglasses I've seen Roarke wear before. And the suitcase totally looks like something of his—expensive and all manly with silver and black. My shoulders lose all their tension.

Then I stiffen again.

Since when has Roarke Baldwin ever made me feel safe?

I hide behind the wall where the hallway meets the open living space, watching him move around his kitchen with his back to me. His hair isn't as gelled and his suit has been replaced with a short sleeve shirt and jeans.

He's opened the blinds to allow the early morning sun to seep into the space as it glistens off the water. Seriously, his views. What did he pay for those?

"Crash Into Me" by Dave Matthews Band plays from a small speaker on the counter.

I silently watch him and swallow down the feeling that I'm glimpsing a rare moment of seeing the *real* him. It's completely at odds with everything I've ever thought about this man up to this point.

Was this what favor number two was for? Some trick for me to have a meal with him? Coming home early on Sunday just to make me breakfast and force me to spend time with him.

He turns to grab something from the fridge and I can't

pry my eyes away, let alone hide back around the corner fast enough.

He catches me, a slow smile warming his face.

"You're up," he says like I live here and this breakfast would be expected.

"I am." My feet feel stuck in cement, I don't dare veer closer.

"Hungry?" he asks. A knock lands on the door. "Hang on." He holds up his finger and answers the door.

My eyes are still transfixed on him, trying to get used to the idea of seeing him in jeans and a V-neck t-shirt.

Roarke's head swivels in my direction. "It's the dog walker."

I nod, still confused by this whole situation.

Ned, the man who's come every time to take Lucy on a walk, steps into the condo, waving at me.

"Good morning, Ms. Crowley." He clicks the leash and the sound of four stomping paws barrelling down the hallway rings out, and then Lucy is skidding to a stop in front of her new favorite guy.

Lucy pays no attention to Roarke who is back in the kitchen now.

"I'll be back in forty or so." Ned heads out shutting the door behind him.

Lucy never gives me a second look. Traitor.

"Hungry?" Roarke's voice pulls my attention away from the front door.

"Um."

Shit, why did I let Ned take Lucy? It was the perfect excuse for me to leave.

"Come and sit. It's going to be at least forty minutes until you can leave." His smile is friendly and kind, but I remind myself he staged this sneak attack.

"You planned this." I break the distance from the hallway to the kitchen.

"What?" he asks the question, but the truth is written all over his face.

"You got me here knowing you'd be home early this morning."

He dishes up pancakes on a plate and sets them to the side. "Not true."

Nickel jumps up on the chair next to me and toddles over to sit on my lap.

"He likes you." He points with his fork to the small ball of fur in my lap.

"Don't change the subject." My gaze stays on him.

He turns and opens the fridge, taking out some soft cat food and heads to the laundry room. Nickel jumps off my lap to the floor, scurrying to his bowl.

"Is this Lucy's food?" he asks me.

"The one in the Ziploc? Yes."

A second later I hear her food hit her bowl and the sound of water running.

He returns to the kitchen. "There, they're all set." He washes his hands and opens the oven pulling out some sort of quiche.

"Just so you know, I'm not a breakfast person."

He takes the dishes out and heads around the corner to his long table.

"Everyone's a breakfast person."

I follow him. "Not me. I'm going to get dressed and be ready when Lucy returns."

He leans his shoulder on the corner wall of the room between the dining room and kitchen.

"Please don't make me use a favor."

His low voice and the undercurrent of pleading softens

me when it shouldn't. My mind must be cloudy from being around him all weekend. Sure, he wasn't here, but his scent was. He let me glimpse into his personal life. The way everything's so organized except for one drawer in the laundry room that has a million different batteries, screws and odds and ends. His sheets might have been washed but either his smell is permanently embedded into them or he has some sort of special spray. I betrayed myself by smelling his shampoo and body wash in the shower yesterday.

There's not a ton of personal pictures, but enough to know there's a family who loves him somewhere in the world and a group of friends he vacations with a lot.

"Give me one reason I should stay."

You're asking a lawyer to give you a reason? Just stay, you obviously want to, my subconscious screams.

"Well, I could list a lot, but I had a shit time yesterday and I just want to get my mind off of it. You owe me nothing, but I'm asking you to stay."

That's not what I was thinking would come out of his mouth. I'd thought it would be something with some sexual innuendo. Some promise to have me sprawled out on his counter and his face between my legs. Not that he would want me here to distract him from something that's bothering him emotionally.

"Let me go get presentable," I say.

For the first time since I woke, I look down at my cami and shorts. My outfit's not super skimpy, but there's not nearly enough fabric for a platonic relationship.

"You look perfect if you ask me."

My hands touch my messed up ponytail and I imagine what my makeup must look like since I didn't want to wash my face at two in the morning when I dragged myself from the couch to bed.

"Just when I thought I was safe from your seduction."

He walks around the kitchen island, his hand extended and I don't fight it when he captures my hand, tugging me lightly forward.

"You'll never be safe from my seduction. Sorry to disappoint you."

It should disappoint me. Newsflash: it doesn't.

"Come." He opens his palm and weaves his fingers through mine. An electric current runs up my arm, one fueled by lust, not anger.

I go willingly, and he leads me to the seat that allows me to look out the window.

"How much did you pay for this place?" I ask, daring a personal question.

He laughs from the kitchen and returns a second later with two plates and silverware.

"I suppose you think that's fair?"

"You know every bit regarding my financial status."

He sits down and dishes out the quiche, pancakes, and bacon on a plate for me.

"This is way too much food for just us," I say, looking wide-eyed down at my plate.

"More people should be here any minute."

"What?" I plant my hands on the armrests to rise.

He chuckles. "See now my company doesn't seem so bad." Then he winks.

That wink should be annoying and grate on me, but for some reason it makes me feel more like a teenager than anything.

I shake my head, falling back down to my chair, crossing my legs and leaning back.

After pouring two cups of coffee, he sets one in front of me. "Sugar, right?" He spoons one teaspoon, holding it above my cup.

I nod. "Is there anything you don't know about me?"

The spoon tips the sugar into the cup, and he stirs it into the dark liquid.

He doesn't look up at me when he responds. "I admit, I know a lot. I know your routine, or at least I did. You might have changed it since then. I know where you live, the addresses to your cabin in Wisconsin and your condo in Vail. On the way to work, you grab a coffee with one sugar and every Friday you treat yourself to a pastry. I know that your schedule is usually jam-packed with events that you have to wear a cocktail dress and a fake smile to. You work out but only in your home or your friend Tad's gym. I know you have a membership to Torrio's, I know the amount of your trust fund when you turned twenty-five. I know how much you've inherited, how much your parents are worth. Where your dad golfs and where your mom shops. I know that you don't buy any games for your phone and only have a select few contacts that you regularly call even though you have fifty times that amount of numbers in your phone."

He sets the spoon down on the napkin between us and I just stare at him, unable to figure out whether I'm impressed or put off by his little speech.

"That being said, there's a lot I don't know. I don't know what makes you start a foundation like RISE. I don't know what your late night snack is or your favorite type of sushi. I don't know what makes you laugh or smile or what little things drive you crazy. So, I might know a lot about your *habits*, but I want to know *you*. Hannah Crowley, the gorgeous, intelligent woman in front of me. That's all."

I pop a piece of bacon into my mouth trying to act like he didn't just make the foundation of the wall I've built between us shaky. Nope, he most certainly did not.

"You so practiced that." I sit up straight, letting my

gaze fall from his because I'm about two seconds from launching myself over this table on top of him.

"I'm a lawyer, Hannah, half my cases are won from my ability to string together a series of meaningful sentences."

I shake my fingers in the air, sipping my coffee. "Why do I feel like you have more to add?"

"That was just my opening statement. I have more to add."

I playfully roll my eyes. "I can only imagine what you're going to say now."

He clears his throat. "I'll make it short."

"Short doesn't seem like your style."

He winks and it starts up the slow-burning hum between my legs.

"We're here today to talk about Roarke Baldwin pursuing Hannah Crowley. Yes, he was the divorce attorney for her ex-husband. Yes, he did do what was in the best interest of his client. Yes, he had a private investigator follow Ms. Crowley to see if he could obtain any dirt on her. He wants an opportunity to get to know Hannah on a personal basis. He's offered her a deal because Ms. Crowley would never agree to a date with him otherwise. I'm sure by the end of the five favors, Roarke Baldwin will prove how worthy he is of Hannah Crowley's time. Whether it's one date or a million. Whether he gets a kiss or something more. He thinks that by the end of this period, court will see his side of this case."

"What could that possibly be?" The light humor in my voice surprises me.

"That Roarke Baldwin really is a good guy." He smiles so wide double dimples crease his cheeks.

I practically melt into his expensive dining chair.

"Good luck with the judge," I comment, forking a

helping of quiche into my mouth to stop myself from doing something stupid.

"I think the judge is softening a little bit."

"The judge thinks you're full of shit," I reply.

His only response is another chuckle that tells me I'm going to need to up my game if I want to come out of this one a winner.

Chapter Ten

____

"You had to actually sleep in his bed?" Chelsea asks, her eyes narrowed.

What happened to the girl who was jumping around and cheering for me to get together with Roarke?

"Yeah, he doesn't want the kitten in the guest rooms. Something about allergies and stuff." I sort through the messages Victoria handed me when I walked in.

"That's weird and sneaky."

"It can be considerate, too." Victoria picks up a folder with the name of the venue on it. "So, at three today we'll see the venue?"

"Yeah," I say, setting the messages to the side.

Chelsea sits in my office with her mid-morning snack, a cupcake today.

"The considerate thing would have been to let her sleep in a guest room."

"Technically, the considerate thing would be to give her the venue without the five favors. So, in this case, I think we shouldn't be surprised."

Victoria has a point.

Chelsea nods in agreement.

"How did Lucy and the kitten do?" Victoria asks.

I fall back into my chair. "Oh, they're the best of friends. The cat slept in Lucy's bed with her both nights. I think Lucy might have been depressed after we left yesterday. She wasn't herself."

"I really hope he's not a creep and doesn't wash the sheets you slept in or something. What if he's some weird Dahmer kinda guy and he's masturbating in the pillowcase you slept on?"

Victoria and I stop and look at her.

She dips her finger into the frosting and sucks it off her finger. "What?"

"That's a disturbing image," Victoria says.

"Maybe Dean and I may have been watching too much ID television. But he could still be a wacko." Her eyes widen like she's ready to bet on how crazy he is.

"I don't think so." I shake my head.

"Huh," Chelsea says, unwrapping the cupcake and taking a big bite, frosting ending up on the tip of her nose.

Victoria leans forward and hands her a tissue.

"You're into him," Chelsea accuses once she's done chewing.

"I'm not actually, but I will admit that there might be a side to him that's new to me."

Chelsea laughs and elbows Victoria in the chair next to her.

"I spent the entire weekend without him. He wasn't even there."

"He really is brilliant," Chelsea says. "He gave you a tunnel vision into the man he is without having to even be present or verbally persuade you. He gave you two whole days to do whatever you wanted in his most personal space with zero pressure from him."

"I didn't snoop." I raise my chin, proud of the fact that I didn't go through every drawer in his place. Sure, I may have started looking for a pen in not the most obvious places, say his en suite's drawers, but I was still technically looking for a pen.

Victoria tilts her head and leans back in her chair. "It really is a damn good plan on his part. Shows how smart he is."

"Don't start siding with the enemy," I say.

"I'm not siding, I'm just giving him some props because you didn't spend one minute with him and you're already softening to his advances."

"That's not true," I insist.

Victoria and Chelsea sit up straighter like scolded children in class.

"When I woke up on Sunday he was making breakfast. I guess whatever he was dealing with, ended early."

Once again, I ignore the part of me that wonders who the woman that called his name was.

Both girls side glance one another.

"Like I said—brilliant," Chelsea says.

"No, no. I really don't think it was planned." *Why am I defending this man?*

Chelsea raises her eyebrows, folding the cupcake wrapper inside the Kleenex she used as a napkin.

"If you say so." She shrugs.

It's clear she doesn't believe me. After a few seconds, I let a long sigh loose and decide to lose the tough girl act. "Do you want to know the truth?"

"Yes," they say in unison.

"I've never been treated the way he treated me last weekend."

"That bad?" Victoria asks and cringes a bit.

"That good," I say. "I show up and the doorman knows I'm coming. Tells me the dog walker is already scheduled and paid for and that I'm not to tip any of the doormen because Mr. Baldwin took care of it. He had the entire condo cleaned before I arrived. He had the fridge and cabinets stocked with food so I never had to go out. Then on Sunday, yes, I was going to leave first thing, but regardless, he made me a huge breakfast and then made an opening argument pertaining to the two of us."

"Oh I like it." Chelsea leans forward and rests her elbow on her knee and her chin in her palm. "I love it that he's a lawyer and then did that. So cute."

"He said all this stuff about how much he does know about me, but that I don't really know him and in the end, I'll see that he's a good guy."

"Aw." Chelsea leans back, waving a hand in front of her face as though to dry the tears ready to spill. "I'm verklempt."

Victoria turns and looks at Chelsea with a scrunched up face. "Verklempt? Really?"

"What? It's a word."

"I know it's a word. I just didn't realize you were Yiddish." Victoria shakes her head and returns her attention to me. "That is definitely a pro-star move." Victoria pulls out another tissue and hands it to Chelsea. "So, what's the problem then?" she asks.

"I can't give him a chance." My lips tip down despite myself.

"Just because of the whole Todd thing?" Victoria is the one to ask because Chelsea's pulled out her phone to text someone.

"I don't know." I put my head in my hands and then

plop it all down on my desk. "I just can't trust him," I mumble into my arms.

"Sorry, I had to text Dean and tell him how much I love him. Stories like that, they just make me realize I got a good one."

I raise my head and give her a look of death through my eyelashes.

"I think Chelsea meant Roarke is a good one, too."

My eyes shift to Victoria who puts her hands up in defense.

"I get the trust thing, I do, but can I ask one question?" Victoria says as Chelsea's phone dings again just imprinting a wider smile on her mouth.

"What?" I sit up, grabbing my pen and clicking it and unclicking it repeatedly.

"Do you want to get in another relationship? Like would you want to date him if he wasn't your ex's divorce attorney?"

I hadn't really thought about it. I was so hell bent on how much I hated *him* specifically, that I didn't really think about it. After the divorce, I didn't think I'd be celibate until I was six feet under, but marriage wasn't in the near future for sure.

"I don't really know. My main focus is RISE right now and, don't get me wrong, I miss sex. Especially when you consider Todd and I were not exactly burning up our sheets toward the end. But, a relationship? I'm not so sure. I guess I would say no at this point."

"Then there you go," Victoria says like that's all there is to it.

"That's so sad. I know I was totally anti-anything, but Han, you can't close yourself off forever. I never imagined it'd be like this with Dean, and I want you to have the same thing. Not to mention I think sex between you two would be off the charts. You could put all that chemistry between you guys to good work."

I shift my eyes from Chelsea to Victoria, willing her with my expression to tell Chelsea to shut up. Victoria's hand lands on Chelsea's forearm.

"These divorcee dating meetings have turned into divorcee dicking meetings now that you two are getting laid on the regular," I grumble.

"Let's remember, I tried to tell you the same thing when Dean first came back around," Victoria reminds her of only months ago when Chelsea was swearing off men.

"I'm not saying completely no, I'm just saying for me to take a chance again, a man would have to be pretty damn convincing."

"He is the best divorce attorney in the Midwest." Victoria's eyes widen. "Convincing people is kinda what he does."

"Good thing I won't make it easy on him." I give her a saccharine smile.

Chelsea chuckles. "I can't wait to hear what favor number three is."

Victoria and I just stare at her like she's missed the entire point of our conversation. As long as I didn't, that's fine.

My mission now is to make Roarke Baldwin prove to me that he's worth me dropping my guard, even a little.

Chapter Eleven

hree o'clock rolls around and myself, Chelsea, and Victoria all step out of a taxi onto the Northerly Island of Chicago.

"This is his connection?" Chelsea asks with amazement in her voice. "I called here when we were looking and they said it was a three-year wait for a weekend date."

"I went to a wedding here once," I admit. "They have the most gorgeous white tent with chandeliers inside. The views are amazing. I'm skeptical that I housesat for nothing."

We're no sooner through the doors when a woman in a pale pink pants suit approaches us with a tablet in her hands.

"Hannah Crowley from the RISE Foundation?" Her eyes are poised on me like she already knows the answer to her own question.

"Yes."

Chelsea and Victoria take up the space on either side of me.

The young woman who's probably in her early twenties, fresh off her college graduation puts out her hand. "My name is Sonya Herrington. I'll be showing you the area we have available to see if it's to your liking."

I shake her hand, inspecting her neatly manicured nails.

"This is Chelsea Walsh and Victoria Clarke," I introduce my two counterparts. Sonya smiles and exchanges handshakes with each of them.

"Please follow me." Her heels click on the marble floor as we walk down a long corridor. I fall in line with her while Chelsea and Victoria lag behind us. "I would have preferred you see it at night, but Roar…Mr. Baldwin said he wanted you to see it as soon as possible in case it wouldn't be a good fit."

I glance over my shoulder and the girls and I share a look that says we're not going to be picky at this point.

"I'd be surprised if Mr. Baldwin could find me another venue besides this one."

Sonya smiles at me like I'm babbling and she doesn't understand a word of what I'm saying. Before I can pose another question, we step into the room.

"We had an event here last night. A charity for the zoo, so I asked that they keep the set up until this evening so you could visualize the space."

Chelsea and Victoria walk in under the permanent structure that appears more like a giant tent than a building. They eye the large crystal chandelier in the center with fabric draped around it, their eyes wide.

"I attended a wedding here a few years back, so I know what a terrific space it is," I say.

Sonya conducts what I expect is a well-rehearsed speech about the views, how many people the room can hold, and the built-in speaker system throughout. Then she goes through whether we'd want buffet or sit down, open or paid bar and how many different appetizers we'd prefer.

As she rounds the exit to an outside area that faces the lake, she misspeaks again. "Roar—Mr. Baldwin thought the outside would be nice in September. However, we do have heaters we can bring out if it ends up being a chilly weekend."

"How exactly do you know Mr. Baldwin?" Chelsea asks.

I shoot her a look to say don't ask questions.

"Oh, well," Sonya stammers.

"Please, it's none of our business." I step outside onto the patio where tall bar height tables are set up, covered in black and gold linens.

"Too bad Navy Pier won't be doing the fireworks in September. Then again that might be why we were able to fit you in." Sonya smiles at me, and we both look out to the long entertainment Pier that juts out of Chicago's shoreline.

"If I'd known this was the location I'd be holding it at, I would've planned for it to be earlier."

"Then maybe you should change the date," a deep voice from behind us interrupts our conversation.

I recognize it and I'm wondering immediately why my friends and co-workers didn't warn me before he came up from behind me.

"Sonya," he says, his arm winding behind her back and kissing her cheek.

"I didn't know you'd be joining us." Sonya seems shocked to see him and displays a nervousness she didn't have before.

"Court got out early." He sets his gaze on me. "Lucky day I guess."

"You'd think you'd be exhausted from screwing people over."

He steps away from Sonya and closer to me, leaning in. "Nah, I never get tired of screwing, Hannah." He purposely uses my name almost as a way of punishing me for my outspoken comment.

"How do you two know one another?" Sonya asks, her finger waving between us.

"I represented her ex-husband." Roarke stuffs his hands into his pockets and rocks back on his heels.

"That's interesting. Is pulling strings for the venue an apology for screwing you over?" Sonya asks, humor laced in her voice.

"Oh, Mr. Baldwin wouldn't—"

"Roarke," he corrects me.

I side glance him. "Roarke," I say his name with bitterness in my tone. "Wouldn't do it for nothing. He demanded five favors in exchange."

Her jaw slackens. "You didn't?"

The way she's so willing to question him makes me think they must have a close relationship.

"You know I have a black heart." For some reason, he says this with some humor.

Sonya laughs like that's the most absurd thought.

"Mr. Baldwin, so nice of you to get us this venue," Chelsea says as she and Victoria join us on the patio.

"Chelsea, right?" he asks, extending his hand.

"Yes. Chelsea Walsh."

He shakes her hand and then shifts his attention to Victoria. "Victoria?"

"You're good with names," she smiles, shaking his hand.

"I think I've seen you with your boyfriend. Reed Warner, right?"

A huge smile splits Victoria's face. "Yes, how do you know him?"

"I run into him now and again at the courthouse. I think he lives out of his office." Roarke laughs as does Victoria.

"I try to steal him away as much as I can."

"Must be working because I haven't seen him in a while."

Victoria smiles up at him and I can tell he's won her over. She's too easy.

Chelsea digs around her purse, pulling out a bag of chips. Victoria elbows her.

"What? I'm eating for two here." She opens it, having no shame and chomping down on a chip.

"You're pregnant?" Sonya asks Chelsea. "I never would've never guessed. You look great."

"She's not too far along," Victoria interjects. "Though she'll probably be one of those belly-only women you can't tell are pregnant from behind."

"Oh I hated those women," Sonya says and I whip my head in her direction.

"You're a mother?" I ask.

She seems way too young.

She nods, her gaze veering over to Roarke for a beat. What am I missing here?

"Sweets were my weakness," she says. "I almost killed for a chocolate cake once."

Chelsea ventures over to Sonya, the two of them talking about pregnancy cravings and whether the whole pickle thing is actually true.

Victoria's phone rings and she heads back inside the tent to answer.

"I guess that leaves us," Roarke says stepping up alongside me.

"Unfortunately."

He ignores my comment. "How do you like the place?"

"What's not to like? It's gorgeous. I have no idea how you got it, but I'm worried that young girl has a crush on you."

He shakes his head, stepping up to the edge of the patio. "She's doing me a favor that's all. Before you get all single white female thinking I'm dating her, I'm not."

"You're so forthcoming."

He turns around at the edge. I try to keep my gaze poised on the lake, but his eyes pull me in instead. "I'm many things, but a liar is not one of them, Hannah. I'll always be straight with you."

"Well, forgive me for not believing you. History, as they say, is usually the best teacher."

He laughs, stepping forward, reaching out to push a stray hair behind my ear. I turn my head away from his touch and the loose strand from my sleek ponytail falls back down.

"When will I live that down?" His voice is low and tight. "We've been over this, he was my client. I did what I needed to do. That will never change." He dips his head down to meet my eyes. "I thought we were moving forward after Sunday."

"Because we shared a meal?" I scoff.

I pick my head up and meet his gaze head-on. I will not let this man intimidate me.

"Because you stayed. Because we laughed. Because we shared. Because I made the best opening statement of my entire career."

"So arrogant." I shake my head in disbelief.

"Don't act like you don't love how arrogant I am. I'm arrogant because I can back it up. You find that quality sexy."

He steps even closer, his lips right at my ear. "Your shoulders straightened when I announced my arrival and you sucked in a breath. I guarantee that if I was to slip my fingers between your legs right now, I'd find your panties wet."

My mouth drops open at his crassness. I really wish it didn't turn me on.

"Wrong." I let the one word fall from my lips. "You'd find the complete opposite."

"If we were alone I might challenge you to prove it."

"Well, we're not alone."

Come on Hannah, you can do so much better than this.

"If what you say is true then favor number three shouldn't be a problem."

My eyes lock with his. "Favor three? You're really whizzing through them."

"Are you complaining?"

"Not at all. The faster we're through them, the faster I'm done having to be in your company." I give him a saccharine smile.

He leans in again and chuckles lightly in my ear. Although not even a fingertip touches me, my body anticipates it, is eager for it like Lucy is when I bring home a special bone from the pet store.

Oh my God, did I just compare myself to my dog salivating over a bone? What is happening to me?

"Let's revisit that after all five favors are fulfilled."

"What's the next favor?" I ask, trying to move the conversation forward.

"I'm sorry to steal you for another weekend, but I need you to be my date for a wedding."

"This Saturday?" I ask. I'm supposed to have a girl's night with my college friends, but I'll cancel to get these favors over and done with.

"It's not local. We'll be leaving Thursday night and coming home Sunday evening at some point."

"What?" My voice raises and Roarke steps back, readying himself for a fight I'd guess. "That is a huge imposition." I cock my hip and place my hands on my waist. "Way more than a favor."

He stuffs his hands back into his pockets, a cocky smirk on his lips. "Well, I think favor one was pretty easy. Who's to say favor four won't be just as simple? We never agreed to the extent of the favors."

I cross my arms over my chest. "So, you could ask me to move to Africa and I'm expected to consider that a favor?"

"You're being a tad dramatic. It's three nights. You'll have your own room and we'll be around other people almost the entire time."

"Almost?" I raise my eyebrows at him.

"You can't fault me for stealing away a few private moments with you."

"Actually I could." A smile fights to tip up my lips, but I'm able to control it enough to stop myself.

"I'll pick you up Thursday at seven pm." His arm extends out and wraps lightly around my waist and for some reason, I don't swat it away like I should. His lips press to my cheek and once again I let myself down by not fighting him off.

I tell myself it's because I don't want to make a scene but who am I kidding? I want to know what it feels like to have his hands on me.

His musky cologne acts like a vibrator right between my legs and I have to squeeze my thighs together. His soft lips only deepen the ache. "Think about changing the date. I'd love to stand out here and watch fireworks with you in my arms."

I stiffen. "We're almost half done with the favors and I still don't want to date you."

He chuckles, his body leaving mine. "Don't worry. You will."

Walking past me, I force my gaze to remain glued to the slow rippling waves washing up against the edge of the wall. "Bye, Sonya. Thanks again, ladies." He waves goodbye to them and then he's gone.

A whole weekend away with only him. Me at his mercy.

I spin on my heel and face my pregnant employee. "Chelsea, I need to borrow your pepper spray."

Chapter Twelve

On Wednesday evening, Lucy and I exit the Uber in front of Victoria and Reed's new place beside her mom's house. She must have been waiting for us, because I'm barely out of the car before her daughter Jade is running down the sidewalk jumping up and down in excitement.

"Hi, Hannah." She claps and falls to her knees. "Hi, Lucy girl." She runs her hand through Lucy's thick fur.

"Hey." Victoria jogs down the steps, her hands outstretched. "Let me help you."

"This dog does come with a shit load of stuff."

Jade's hands stop moving and she looks up at me.

"Sorry," I cringe.

Her shoulders shrug and she continues petting Lucy as she falls to her back, signaling that she wants Jade to rub her stomach.

"She's heard worse. Pete," Victoria references her ex-husband. "Come on in. I know you're probably eager to get back to your condo and prepare for this weekend."

"Oh yeah, can't wait. If I wasn't wearing a dress, I

wouldn't shave my legs." I haul Lucy's bed under my arm and her bag of food with her leash over my shoulder. "You sure about this?"

Jade runs up the sidewalk to their front door, Lucy at her side. "REED!" she screams.

He comes to the door, smiling tentatively at Lucy. "Hey, Lucy," he says, patting her head like she might infect him with the rabies virus.

"Are you sure Reed's okay with this?" I ask as we make our way up the path to the house.

"Yeah, why wouldn't he be? It's all Jade's talked about. Since she leaves for California next week, it will be nice for them to spend time together," she says.

I forgot Jade is going to stay with her father in Los Angeles for a month this summer.

"How are you doing with that?" I ask Victoria.

She shrugs. "I'm fine. It will be fine. I met the nanny over Skype and I'll see her face-to-face when we get there. Reed and I are staying the weekend in a hotel just in case. Then, we're taking Henry back with us and staying longer when it's time to bring her home."

Henry is Jade's little friend from school. "You sure have your hands full."

"Welcome to my life." We step up into the house, Reed taking the dog bed from me.

"Hannah," he says, kissing me on the cheek. "Excited?"

My lips dip and I stare at him like someone just said I have to get a root canal.

He chuckles to himself sliding the bag off my arm. "That bad, huh?"

"Do you know Roarke Baldwin?" I ask.

Reed places the bag of food on the dog bed in the corner of the room.

"Only a little bit. Obviously, I know his reputation, but it's not like we work in the same field of law."

"He knew you were dating Victoria," I say.

Victoria picks up the bag of food and heads to the kitchen where I hear her pour the food into a dish.

"Can I take Lucy out back?" Jade asks Reed.

He gives her a fleeting look. "Yeah, but we're going to have to walk her you know. We only have a postage stamp square of grass back there." His gaze shifts to mine. "City life."

"Well, she's used to just going on concrete. Downtown life." I shrug.

He chuckles again and nods into the kitchen. "Come on. I was just preparing my shrimp linguini. Join us."

If it's a choice between dinner with the Warner/Clarke's or me sitting around alone anticipating spending four hours in the car with Roarke tomorrow on top of an entire weekend, shrimp linguini wins.

"Thanks, I'd love to." I follow him into the kitchen.

"You know how he knows that we're dating, right?" He taps Victoria's ass to slide over so he can reach the stove.

"You lawyers have your ways I'm sure," I say.

"We have private investigators and sources." He holds a piece of pasta in front of Victoria.

She chews it and swallows it down before giving him a chaste kiss. "Maybe a minute more."

He nods and she continues on with what she was doing.

I watch in fascination. Truthfully, I never had this. Todd and I never prepared a meal together. We dined out almost every night when we were married. Our kitchen was only for late night snacks and when we had the occasional gathering, the caterers were the ones to take it over.

"I know he's looked in on me before. I mean during the divorce."

Reed places the spoon down next to the stove and turns around drying his hands on a dishtowel.

"Then I think you can expect he knows everything about you now."

Victoria returns from where ever she went. The woman never sits down.

"Where's the spontaneity then?" I ask.

"Are you looking for spontaneity? I thought you hated him?" Victoria asks with her usual half-cocked grin saying she knows the answer, but she's enjoying putting me in the hot seat.

"I do hate him, but if he wants to win me over—his words not mine—then why find out about my friends and all the personal stuff? Half the fun of dating someone new is discovering who they are."

Victoria pulls out a wine bottle from the fridge, holding it up at me with her eyebrows raised.

I nod because, hello, I'm wound tighter than a spool of fishing line and I need something to relax me.

"Roarke Baldwin strikes me as the type who doesn't like surprises," Victoria says.

Without testing the pasta a second time, Reed grabs two hot pads and picks up the pot, taking it over to the sink. A rush of steam erupts like a volcano as he pours the pasta out into a colander.

My eyes focus in on the wine splashing into the two glasses. "But what would be the point of finding out about you guys?"

Reed turns around bringing the colander back to the other pot with the sauce and shrimp inside. Seriously, Victoria should be thanking the heavens above every night for bringing her Reed.

"I think he only knows about us because I'm the Assistant DA. It wouldn't take a whole lot of digging to find out. When a guy stops pulling all-nighters and starts cutting out early on Fridays questions get raised. Assistants talk and rumors circulate. Everyone knows I found my dream girl." He winks over at Victoria.

A lovesick smile overtakes her face. "Here." She slides the wine glass across the table to me.

Tension fills the space and I wonder if I'm keeping these two from fucking on the counter with my presence. Lucy barks from outside and then I don't feel so bad, remembering that Jade is here, too. Not to mention Victoria's mother lives right next door. Reed must be used to having multiple cock blocks around at this point.

"He knows Victoria works at RISE," I say.

Reed's casual demeanor continues. "I know he has this reputation around the divorce court, and Vic told me how he represented your ex, but honestly, I thought he was a pretty cool guy when I met him at your party."

My party. I snap my fingers. "That's where he figured it all out." Irritation sets in as I remember a couple months ago when a woman I'd invited to a gathering at my place brought Roarke as her date.

Reed's eyebrows furrow. "Hannah, you seem to think this guy is still out to get you."

Victoria hands Reed plates and he dishes out the meal on each then places them on the breakfast bar. Wanting to earn my dinner, I slide from my stool and carry the plates to the already set table.

"Can you blame me?" I sigh.

There's no arguing with Reed. But the fact that he knows more about me than he should, puts me on edge because I'm at a disadvantage when it comes to him.

Victoria brings Jade's smaller plate over to the table.

"I'd say just do what you have to this weekend. Retire to your hotel room saying you don't feel well. Try to mingle with whoever you think will talk your ear off so he can't wedge himself into your conversation. Whatever you do, don't be alone with him."

I nod like she's the Dalai Lama giving me advice on life.

Reed's deep chuckle interrupts us. "You guys are horrible. The man is trying to win her over. You act like he's plotting her murder."

We both whip our heads over to him.

"He's not trying to win me over. He's trying to get up my skirt."

Reed's face turns a nice shade of red. "Well, I can't say I wasn't trying to get up Vic's, but I wanted more than just that."

Victoria glances over her shoulder out the patio door to find Jade and Lucy running around the small backyard. Well, Jade's hopping on all fours and Lucy's pouncing back not really understanding the game.

"Roarke Baldwin doesn't exactly scream carpool man."

Reed shrugs, filling a cup full of milk. "No offense, Hannah, but you don't exactly scream carpool woman."

Victoria smacks him on the chest. "Reed!"

I wave her off with my hand. "No, he's right."

"Do you ladies want my opinion?" Reed sets a cup down in front of Jade's plate.

"Not really," Victoria says, patting his cheek as she walks by.

"I don't need to hear bullshit. Marriage is off the table for me. If Roarke is expecting more than to get up my skirt he's going to be disappointed."

It's not until the words fall from my mouth that I realize what I just said.

The two of them are staring at me and my eyes widen.

"Not that he's getting that either." I shoot them a look that dares either of them to say any different.

"Well, then I'd go with Victoria's plan because I'm not sure Roarke Baldwin is used to not getting what he wants." Reed grabs a beer and heads to the patio door. "Jade, it's dinner time."

She looks up and heads back inside.

"Why do we keep referring to him by his full name? Like he's the president or someone important," I grumble.

Victoria sits down at the table, her eyes focusing anywhere but on me.

"What?" I ask.

Jade points to Lucy and dictates for her to sit before she'll give her a treat. With any luck, that dog will be fully trained when I return.

"Nothing," she says and shrugs.

"Vic?"

She looks at Reed and they exchange a look. "I just think he's like a five-year-old with a candy bar."

"Meaning?"

Jade begins to walk toward the table, but Victoria directs her attention over to her daughter. "Wash your hands, sweetie."

Once we hear the hall bathroom faucet start, Victoria sets her eyes on me.

"I'm just suggesting that he doesn't seem to have a lot of willpower when it involves you."

"Is that a bad thing?" Reed asks, bending over her chair and kissing her neck. "I had no self-control when it came to you."

Her hand lands on the side of his head and his lips never move. "I guess it depends if Hannah wants the attention. I did."

He whispers something I can't hear and his lips don't stop devouring her neck.

"Ew!" Jade screams. "Not in front of the kid."

Reed doesn't stop though and Victoria doesn't move away.

"Love is a beautiful thing," Victoria mumbles to her daughter.

Jade meets my gaze and she rolls her eyes. "I don't agree. I love Henry, but neither one of us will ever be doing that." She twirls her finger in a circle near her temple.

Reed sits down in a chair between Victoria and me. "We'll see about that."

Jade rolls her eyes again, something I notice she's gotten very good at.

"Watch it," Victoria warns and I can't believe they're already at that age. Jade having an attitude.

"Don't you think so, Hannah?" Jade picks up a fork and waits for me to respond.

"Totally. I never want anything like that." I smile over my forkful of food, purposely dodging Victoria's look. "One and done is my motto."

I place my hand up in the air and Jade high fives it. Sad that the only person who gets me in this room is the eight-year-old.

Chapter Thirteen

At seven pm on the dot, a grey SUV stops alongside the curb of my condo building downtown. The low hum of energy surrounding my body that seems to be ever present whenever he's near, tells me it's Roarke.

"See you Sunday, Nate," I say to my doorman. "If I don't return by Sunday night, find that man."

I point to Roarke exiting his vehicle and ignoring the honking horns and taxi drivers flipping him off because he's double parked.

Nate steadily walks across the foyer of the building and opens the door for him.

"Good evening," he says to Roarke.

Roarke nods before his gaze falls on me. His teeth lock over his bottom lip and his gaze flies down my body lighting off sparks inside me like flint to steel. Nate lets the door close and moves to retrieve my bags, but Roarke beats him, snatching up the bags at my feet.

"I thought you'd have more," he says, a smile tipping his lips up.

"Are you saying that you expect me to be high maintenance?"

He shrugs one shoulder. "You *are* Hannah Crowley."

"Now who's making assumptions?" I follow him out of the safety of my condo building. "Thank you, Nate. Please take down the license plate number should anything happen to me."

Roarke glances over his shoulder, lightly shaking his head.

"You are sort of kidnapping me."

He places my bags into the back of what I now see is a high-end Range Rover. Like the man would drive a Ford.

"If memory serves, you're getting something for coming with me." His hand moves up in the air, telling Nate to not open my door. Nate slinks back toward the building. He's obviously used to arrogant men like Roarke who like to tell him how they want things to go.

"Have a good trip, Ms. Crowley," he calls out before he re-enters the building.

"Thank you, Nate."

Roarke opens the passenger door for me.

I climb inside and turn to address him. "I suppose you're right, but I still think three nights is pushing the envelope of what can be considered a favor." I place my purse on the floor near my feet, relax into the leather seat and reach for the seatbelt.

"As usual, we can agree to disagree." The door shuts, and he rounds the front of the car, looking especially good in his three-piece suit while he continues to ignore the insulting names screamed at him from passing taxi drivers. He sits down in the driver's seat, inserting the key in the ignition. "You ready?"

I nod, keeping my head buried in my phone. Good a time as any to organize my apps.

"Are you going to make me use a favor to get you to ditch your phone?" I can see from my peripheral vision that he doesn't bother looking at me when he speaks but turns the wheel to enter Chicago traffic.

"When do you think we'll arrive?"

The SUV stops two feet down the road.

"In about four hours. Sorry, I had a late business meeting and that's why we're leaving late. Just think though, it's less time you have to be around me."

For some reason, his words make it clear to me what a bitch I'm being. Yes, I'm here under the pressure of these favors, but he did secure the venue for me and I did agree to the favors in the first place. Clicking my phone screen off, I cross my legs and stare out at the sea of red taillights in front of us.

"It will probably take us an hour to get out of the city," I say.

He looks at the mirrors, his hands on the steering wheel and then swiftly changes lanes. "Yeah, that's why this isn't ideal, but it won't be half as bad as if we left at five."

For the next ten minutes, Roarke weaves through the side streets of Chicago like a veteran cabbie. I won't tell him, but his driving skills are impressive. If I'm truthful, they're sexy and the truck's not even a stick shift.

"Music?" I ask, pointing to the dial.

"Sure. Go ahead."

"Anything in particular you feel like?"

He slams on the brakes, his arm swinging out over to my torso as my body shifts forward on the seat.

Cars whizz by in front of us. "Sorry," he mumbles.

"Impressive mom skills you got there." I wait for my seatbelt to loosen and reach for the dial on the radio.

"How do you know I wasn't just trying to cop a feel?"

He glances over at me and a tingle erupts in the pit of my belly.

"I don't think you're that daring at this point." I scroll through the presets on the radio.

"Assumptions again. Don't forget, I *am* hoping to seduce you, Hannah."

Why is it that every time he says my name, it stirs something inside of me?

"I thought I was just a date to a wedding?"

"Everyone knows women are more willing to give it up at a wedding."

I tilt my head and stare at him for a second. He keeps the act up for a good couple seconds before a laugh bellows out. His lips tip and his smile sends a warm sensation through my body.

"Did you just make a joke?" I ask with mock astonishment.

The car speeds up once we reach the freeway clear of the downtown traffic.

"Some people enjoy my sense of humor," he says before checking the mirror and changing lanes.

"Can't say I've ever seen it."

Roarke shakes his head at me and presses a radio preset button and classical musical streams through the car. Then he puts his hands at ten and two on the steering wheel and focuses on the road. He hums the tune, oblivious to me watching him.

We continue sailing down the freeway since rush hour is over, the only sound besides the tires running over the cement are oboes and violins. Roarke switches lanes to pass a slow driver in the left lane, effortlessly moving back into the fast lane.

So he's one of those drivers, huh? Not that it surprises me. Never stops or slows, just whizzes back and forth. He's the guy you hope to see pulled over a few miles ahead, though I will say his arrogant and cocky Mario Andretti driving style suits him.

"Okay, even I can't pretend that long." His long fingers press a dial on his steering wheel and the volume decreases.

Confused by the whole situation, I glance over and he's got a shit eating grin on his face.

"What?"

"I just put that on because you keep making assumptions about me. I'd never listen to that shit out of choice. You want to know my music? This is what I listen to." He switches from the radio over to Bluetooth, his phone lighting up in the center console signaling that it's streaming.

"Regulate" by Warren G. begins playing.

I turn my head tilts his way and he raises his eyebrows. "Surprised?"

I nod toward his phone. "May I?"

"Please." He picks up his phone and hands it over to me.

I scroll through his music and all that's listed is nineties hip-hop. Snoop Dog, House of Pain, Salt-N-Pepa, LL Cool J. "Vanilla Ice?" I ask.

He shrugs and a pink tint warms his face. "Don't even try to deny that you loved that song at one point in your life."

I roll my eyes. He'll never get me to admit that I knew the choreography of that dance video by heart and that my best friends and I used to perform it for each other.

"Are you going to stop typecasting me anytime soon?" He lowers the volume of the music and shoots over three lanes to head up the north exit ramp.

"I'd like to survive this trip." My knuckles whiten on the handle of the door.

"Sorry, you're distracting."

We follow the signs to Milwaukee. "Wisconsin?"

He nods.

"Huh, never would have thought."

"I figured." He eases back in his seat, his hands resting on the bottom of the steering wheel as he slows our speed down.

I'm reflecting on his musical tastes when something dawns on me. "Why were you listening to the Dave Matthews Band that morning in your house if you're a hip-hop fan?"

He doesn't speak for a beat, but I continue to wait out his answer. Finally he shrugs and says, "I thought something like that would be more your speed."

That's actually kind of sweet.

When I don't respond right away he asks, "Do you ever listen to hip-hop?"

"If it comes on the radio maybe."

"I figured."

"Who's assuming now?" I tease.

He chuckles, nodding in agreement. "Note taken. I did assume you were more of a Backstreet Boys girl."

Damn him for hitting it on the mark.

"Sorry, or was it N'Sync? Ninety-Eight Degrees?"

I fidget in my seat. "You had it right the first time. Your PI guy must be good."

"I only hire the best." He smirks the usual one that makes my mind conflict on whether I want to slap it or kiss it off his face. Lately, it's been the latter as much as I try to deny my attraction to him.

"That's one thing we have in common, I guess."

"Listen, I don't want to fill this weekend with conversation about how we know each other from the past, but I just want to say…if you'd come to me before Todd, I would have happily represented you."

"Yeah, I don't want to talk about Todd or the circumstances that led me here." I cross my legs and lean against the passenger window.

"I'm just saying, you have no idea how hard it was for me when I got the paperwork back from my PI guy. Your beauty and intelligence and strength radiated out of the pictures. I knew the hell he was putting you through. Then when I saw you at the first meeting." He inhales deeply and pauses for a second. "You have no idea how hard it was for me to keep my composure. For the first time in my career, I wanted to fire my client."

My shoulders lose all the tension from the previous mention of Todd's name. "Why are you telling me this?" I almost whisper.

His hand reaches over, grabbing mine. "Because I'm not trying to torture you by making you do these favors. I've always followed my gut intuition and they're leading me to you. Has been since the moment I saw you and especially after you opened your mouth that first time and threw a jab my way. There's something between us worth exploring."

He lets go of my hand and I miss the warmth of his skin immediately.

God, what is wrong with me?

"I don't know what to say," I admit.

"I don't want you to say anything. I just want you to be open to the possibility that the anger you have toward me could dissolve into something else."

A breath falls from my lips. He's already figured out one number to the safe I've locked myself in since my divorce. I'm not sure I can give him the opportunity to figure out the rest.

His phone rings over the Bluetooth through the small space of the interior and I'm thankful for the interruption.

He glances at the dashboard, where I see the word 'Mom' on the screen. With a groan, he clicks a button on the steering wheel.

"Hey, Mom, is this important? I'm busy."

"Roarke, your sister is in a panic and she wants to call off the wedding!"

His gaze shifts to mine. "I'm driving. Let me pull over and call her."

"She's hyperventilating. She swears Wyatt is cheating on her. I don't think that's the case. I think she's making excuses." His mom sounds traumatized and I feel bad for overhearing what is clearly a family matter. "I swear my own problems with men have turned both of you into a mess of adults who can't believe someone would love you for you."

Again, he glances quickly to me at his side. I try to keep my back straight and eyes out the window like his mom didn't just out his vulnerability to me.

"Mom? I have Hannah in the car."

"Oh, shoot. I'm so stupid. How did I not realize that?" She pauses. "Hello, Hannah, I'm Edie, Roarke's mom."

I look to Roarke for permission to talk which pisses me off the minute I realize I did it.

"Hello, Mrs. Baldwin."

"No, don't you proper speak to me. It's Edie."

I laugh. "Okay, Edie it is. Feel free to continue your conversation. Don't mind me."

Roarke's hand moves to the phone, but we pass by a cop sitting in the median and he drops it back down.

A rule follower. Interesting.

"I'm looking forward to meeting you," Edie says.

"Mom, where is Allie now?"

"I'm looking forward to meeting you, too, Edie." I lightly slap his shoulder for interrupting.

An amused smile crosses his lips.

"She's at Daysie's and you know that girl is just plain trouble. She won't help Allie see Wyatt loves her. Probably take her out to that dive bar down off the highway to get half pissed instead. Please, Roarke."

"Okay, we're a little over three hours away. I'll call her now, drop Hannah at the hotel, and then go to Daysie's if I'm not able to reach her on the phone."

"Oh, I'm such an idiot, I forgot to tell you."

"What?" There's an edge that Roarke has with his mom that I recognize from my own relationship with my mother.

"Well, Wyatt's uncle was able to get leave and we gave him one of your rooms. I hope that's okay. I don't understand why you and Hannah wanted different rooms anyway."

My eyes widen and my stomach churns. Could he have concocted this entire plan?

"Then you have a houseguest for the weekend. I'll stay with you," he says, not sounding pleased.

I guess not.

"Really? Okay…well… I'll have to arrange some things." Her voice is shaky and unsure and I'm wondering who she thinks I am to her son. "I'll wash some sheets, I'll run to the store now and get milk and what other health foods do you eat?"

"It's okay Mom. I'll make do." Roarke shifts in his seat and I'm starting to realize he does this when he's feeling uncomfortable. "I'll be there soon. Let me go call, Allie."

"Okay. Bye Hannah."

"Bye Mrs…Edie."

"Can't wait to meet you and see if you're as pretty as

my son says. Now Roarke, drive responsibly especially once you get past the county line. You know Sheriff Wiltaker waits for out-of-towners."

Roarke huffs out a laugh and his face morphs into a genuine smile. "I will, Mom. Bye."

He clicks her off the line before she can finish saying goodbye.

"You don't have to," I say.

He turns to me with a questioning look.

"You don't have to sleep at your mom's," I say, hardly believing the words that are coming out of my mouth myself.

"I promised you a hotel room to yourself and I don't go back on my promises."

His thumb presses the volume button on the steering wheel and the music volume raises. I guess that concludes our conversation. I sit there, staring at the tall trees and green landscape out the window wondering why I don't want Roarke to be inconvenienced.

"Why don't you want to spend the night at your mom's?" I ask.

His jaw clenches. "She has a new boyfriend."

From the dark mask that falls over his face, I decide to not ask anymore probing questions on that topic. Not like it's my business anyway. After these last few favors are done, I'll probably never speak to him again.

Funny thing is, even I don't believe the lies I tell myself about the man beside me anymore.

Chapter Fourteen

It's another hour before Roarke pulls off the highway. Other than me asking him if I could pick a song to mix up the rap and hip-hop we don't talk about anything else. He obviously listens to this music a lot because he mouths the words to every damn song.

We pull up to a gas station and he unbuckles his seat belt. "I'll make it quick." His phone is gripped in his hands. "If you want to go to the bathroom or get a snack or anything, I'll just be a minute."

I nod, pulling my purse out from by my feet and exiting the Range Rover. "Anything you want?"

He shakes his head, his mind a million miles away. "No, thank you."

I leave polite Roarke in the SUV and head inside following the sign to the bathroom.

Ten minutes later, I have a white plastic bag full of drinks, sanitizing wipes in case I have to venture into another gas station bathroom on our travels, and a few snacks for us before it dawns on me that Roarke might not want us to eat in his car.

I push open the door from the small gas station store and am met by a loud voice coming from inside Roarke's SUV, only it's not his. The phone is synced through the speakers of the car and I'm not sure he's aware of how loud it is. I can hear every word his sister is saying and I'm not sure if I should interrupt or not.

"Roarke, you don't understand. I know they were hers," she says.

I can see that his forehead is pressed against the steering wheel like this conversation is taking all his energy to get through.

"Since when do you believe in happily ever afters?"

Another pause.

"Yes, I love him."

"Trust? You and I both know there are few people you can trust in this world."

"Who is this girl you're bringing anyway?"

Only hearing the sister's side of the conversation sucks. I really want to hear what his answer to that question was.

"You're sleeping at Mom's? What, is she a prude?" The disgust in her voice is obvious.

"Gentleman? I'd like to see what Olivia would say to you being a gentleman."

I pretend I don't care who Olivia is, but of course I log the name in the recesses of my mind for further examination later.

"You're not my father."

Roarke picks up his head and our eyes meet before I do anything other than stand there.

"You gotta go? What the hell?" his sister snips.

The line dies and he opens the SUV door and climbs out.

"Did you get what you need?" he asks, the keys twirling around his finger, stuffing his cell phone into his pocket.

"Yeah. Are you a licorice guy?" I hold up the bag nonplussed, pretending like I didn't just overhear everything his sister said.

A smile tugs at his lips and maybe because I know what family shit is like to deal with, it pulls a smile from me.

"You thought of me?" he asks, approaching.

"I'm not rude."

"I like it." He takes my free hand, uncurling my fingers from my palm and places the keys into it. "I'll be right back."

He heads into the shop and I glance around at the few people filling their cars with gas. Since it's nine o'clock at night, it's pure darkness except for the gas station which is lit up like an alien UFO in the middle of the desert.

Bringing my gaze upward to the dark sky, my jaw slackens at the million or so bright, white stars on display. Other than the highway noise, it's the crickets instead of horns honking and hustle and bustle of the city.

I'm not sure how long I stare in awe, taking in the pure serenity this small gas station parking lot has granted me, but when a hand touches mine, I jerk back.

"Relax." Roarke's voice calms my fight or flight response. "First time out of the city?" His tone is teasing and I let my gaze fall to him.

"It's gorgeous. Do you miss it?" I ask.

His Adam's apple bounces down and up. "No."

He takes the keys from my hands and rounds the front of the Range Rover.

Once I'm back in the comfy leather seat next to him, he opens the sunroof screen so the sky is visible above us, puts the key in the ignition, and before I can think to ask a follow-up question we're back on the highway.

I can't help but wonder why he would bring me here, if he doesn't want to be here himself.

TWO HOURS LATER, we pull off the highway, right into a motel parking lot. Twenty white vans with the same landscaping business name are parked in the far side of the lot.

"This is where we're staying?" I ask, eyeing the peeling paint on the doors and the grass growing up between cracks in the concrete.

He parks the SUV under the awning beside the sliding glass doors.

"I know it's not The Drake but trust me when I say this is the best there is around here."

"It's fine." I was brought up better than to make someone feel bad even if the circumstances are less than ideal. "Are the doors to the rooms on the outside?" I look across the parking lot to a line of doors on the first and second floor of the building.

"They are, but Woods Parlor doesn't have a lot of crime unless you count domestic violence and public intoxication."

I tighten my lips at his mention of two very different offenses. "So, I'm safe you mean?"

"I'll get you settled and then go track down my sister. I'll only be about twenty minutes away if you need me."

Twenty minutes? He can't save me if he's twenty minutes away. I'll already be raped, murdered or whatever by then.

"Okay." I straighten my back, reminding myself, I'm a Crowley and I don't need any type of savior. Thank goodness I have pepper spray though.

"I love when you act like you can take on the world." He exits the car before I can reply.

It's not usually an act, but it is right now.

I follow Roarke into the small lobby where he presses a

little bell and we hear someone grumble from the room behind the front desk, and then a loud boom echoes in the small space.

"You okay, Ted?" Roarke leans over the counter.

"Roarke Baldwin?" A short-statured, round-bellied, bald-headed man emerges in the doorway, rubbing his eyes. "I saw your name on the list and thought maybe I missed you. My shift started an hour ago."

Roarke holds his hand out and the man wipes his on his stained wife beater before accepting the offering. "Chicago did you good, huh?"

Ted isn't looking at Roarke's three-piece suit or the Range Rover parked outside. Nope. His eyes are on me. On my breasts to be precise. He licks his lips and my stomach clenches.

Roarke steps in front of me, cutting off Ted's line of vision. "I have. This is Hannah, she'll be staying here."

"Sorry about booting you out of the other room, but Wyatt's granddad and all." The two men speak in a language I'm unfamiliar with.

"Yeah, I get it. I'll be at my mom's."

"All the way in town?" Ted asks. Twenty minutes is all the way? Twenty minutes could be one block for me at the height of rush hour in the city.

"Yeah." Roarke shrugs.

"So, she's not yours?" Ted points to me as though I'm a dog or a piece of property to be owned.

My fists clench at my sides and I bite the inside of my cheek.

Roarke glances back at me, the side of his lips ticked up into a smile. He's probably already guessed that I'm fuming on the inside. "Not yet, but soon."

"Can we please get the keys?" I ask, done with this whole conversation. "For future reference, I'm nobody's."

I spin on my heel and exit the lobby and sit and wait in Roarke's car. The two men carry on their transaction and Roarke returns to the driver's seat five minutes later.

"I'm going to ignore the fact that that man looked at me like he's on death row and I'm his last meal."

Roarke laughs. "Ted's harmless. We don't get a lot of your type around here, that's all."

"Hate to break it to you, but you're the same type as me."

He starts the car and pulls it five hundred feet ahead, parking out front of room one thirty-three. I cry inside that I'm on the first floor.

"You were born with money, I made my own money," Roarke says.

He's got me there.

I know from my bff Gwen, coming from nothing and gaining everything is so very different than always having the security of money to fall back on. Still...

"I get that you grew up here, but you don't fit in here anymore. Just like I don't."

He chuckles as we exit the car, him opening up the back of his SUV and pulling out my bag. With each step closer to the room, my stomach tightens—I really don't want to stay here by myself.

He inserts the key into the lock and opens the door wide. Surprisingly, the room is decent. The linens look clean and the décor could be worse. I half expected a dark wood headboard that was mounted to the wall with orange and brown linens with pictures of deer frolicking in the woods. Instead, a yellow, grey, and white room greets me.

Roarke puts my bag on the luggage holder and shoves his hands into his pockets. "You have my number. I'll be back tomorrow to pick you up. Just text me when you wake up. We don't have anywhere to be until the rehearsal at four."

My mouth drops open and I cross my arms over my chest. "You dragged me up here for me to sit in a hotel room off the highway until four o'clock?"

A smile tugs at his lips again and I realize my error.

Now he thinks I *want* to be around him.

He takes a step closer to me. "I had no intention of leaving you here until four. I was simply letting you sleep in if you choose to."

"Thank you. I have no car and I'd rather not resort to a vending machine for my breakfast and lunch."

I sound bitchy, I know. I'm purposely being difficult because I'm scared. Fear makes me bitchy when I don't have the control I crave. I don't know if it's the unsafe feeling of the hotel, or the fact someone could kidnap me and drag me into the woods never to be seen again. Ted's peeping Tom eyes didn't exactly leave me with the warm and fuzzies.

"Then I'll pick you up at nine am and I'll feed you." He rocks back on his heels. Other than loosening his tie after the call with his sister, he's still neatly put together like a Ken doll—only with salt and pepper hair.

"Perfect."

"Good." He heads toward the door and the knob turns in his hand.

My gut clutches and my heart races. It's do or die. "It's late. I'm not opposed to you sleeping in the other bed."

His back stiffens with his hand on the doorknob. "Are you offering for me to stay here with you tonight?" He swivels around and I can't tell by the look on his face whether it disappoints him or makes him happy.

"As a courtesy, yes. Ted made it sound like it was far

and I'm sure you're tired. I would hate for a deer to run in front of you and ruin that nice SUV of yours." I hoist my chin in the air.

His eyes flare with mischief. "Are you scared, Hannah?"

"No." I open my bag, placing my clothes in the dresser and hanging up my dresses for the weekend, anything not to have to look at him.

"So you're just being nice then?"

"Yes." I keep my tone calm and collected as though I'd sleep here for a month by myself if I had to.

Not a chance in hell.

"You're sure you don't mind?" His hand lands on the doorknob again.

"Yeah, it's no big deal." I shrug while I close the closet door. "Two separate beds."

"Okay, I'll grab my bags." He exits the hotel room.

I breathe again once the door is shut. I'm totally setting myself up for failure but having the safety of him in this room outweighs my Missing picture being posted on every telephone pole from here to Chicago.

There's not time to process my doubt because Roarke returns. He shuts the door, flips the bar over, and secures the deadbolt. Wasn't he the one who said no crime happens in Woods Parlor?

"Can I sweet talk my way into your bed, too?" he asks, hanging up a garment bag in the closet.

"You never know when to stop."

I go easy on him after his comment because I appreciate the way he's letting me off the hook in this scenario. The first time I showed this man any kind of vulnerability and he didn't throw it in my face.

"When it comes to you, no, I don't."

For the first time, it dawns on me that maybe my odds of landing in Roarke's bed are significantly higher than my odds of being murdered tonight. That thought would have been handy about five minutes ago.

Chapter Fifteen

The pressures of perfection are something I'm familiar with. You're not raised under a microscope without being trained on how to stay calm and collected under scrutiny or high-pressure situations.

With perfection comes willpower.

Willpower to cut carbs.

Willpower to work out.

Willpower to bite my tongue when necessary.

A piece of cake can sit in front of me for hours as I continue a conversation with someone who is devouring theirs. That's not to say I don't stop on the way home for a milkshake. That's the thing with being a Crowley. You only have to worry while in front of others. In the comfort of a room all by yourself with triple locks to keep prying eyes out, you can indulge in a whole cake if you want. As long as you don't go up a dress size. What would your personal shopper at Neiman Marcus think if nothing fit you when you arrive?

Regardless, I tend to believe I'm a strong woman who

can look unfazed when her body heat is rising to dangerous temperatures.

When Roarke walks out of the bathroom in pajama pants and no shirt on, I almost lose my cool. He has to be in his early forties, but his pecs and biceps bulge as he rounds the edge of the bed and slides in under the covers. He doesn't say a word as he makes his trip across the room. He doesn't have to. I'm sure his stealthy eyes caught me peeking up at him over my Kindle.

He passes out quickly after a short goodnight in his usual deep timbre which seems to be an aphrodisiac for my lower region. I would've settled for some teenage dry humping. That's how low I was willing to go.

I put my Kindle down and laid on my right side as I usually do when I fall asleep. The problem was Roarke was in my line of sight. His bare, muscled chest rising and falling. One hand positioned under his head, one leg sneaking out from the sheet a bit. He truly was a male Adonis.

He'd volunteered to take the bed closest to the door. Once again proving he knows I'm not feeling completely safe here, but not calling me out on my bullshit excuse for offering him the other bed. The fact he keeps doing that is starting to piss me off and I have no explanation for why it angers me.

Rolling over to my left, I face the wall and will my eyes shut with the hopes that this weekend goes by fast because my willpower crumbles a little more every second I'm around him.

A LIGHT PERMEATES my eyelids and I blink my eyes open.

I'm sprawled in the middle of the bed, literally in an X,

taking up the entire space. I can't remember the last time I slept that soundly. Usually Lucy's taking up half the bed and pushing one of her paws into me.

A tall figure blocks the light and I turn my head to see Roarke place something on the bedside table. "You snore."

I sit up, wiping the guck from my eyes.

Why did I let him sleep here again? I should've set my alarm so I could get up first and do my hair and makeup.

"I do not," I say with a still groggy voice.

He sits at the edge of the bed, untying his running shoes, sweat pouring off his face. "You do. It's probably the fresh air, maybe allergies."

My face heats to the level of an erupting volcano. "You're joking?" I ask, mortified that what he's saying might be true.

"Yeah." He stands, strips off his shirt and tosses it on the bed.

Now I have to stare at his muscled chest while sweat drips down it like dots of rain on a window, only these drops are slipping from one ab to the next.

I was not prepared for this kind of exquisite torture when I agreed to this trip.

Grabbing my coffee from the nightstand, I take a sip with the hopes of stopping more saliva from pooling inside my mouth.

"I told you I had a sense of humor." He picks up his running shoes, placing them beside his suitcase is. "I have a proposition for you."

He sits back down and though I've always prided myself on my willpower, right now it's taking everything in me not to launch myself across this mattress and on top of him.

"Why don't you put your shirt back on and then we can talk?" I really don't care at this point if I'm tipping my cards to him. I cannot sit here and pretend not to be distracted by his body any longer.

I pull the sheet up over my body. I'm dressed in shorts and a cami, nothing too revealing but I'm sure my headlights are on and glaring.

"Why?" he asks with his signature cocky grin. "You like what you see?"

Yes, yes, I do.

"Nope." My tone is curt and borderline mean. "It's common courtesy when we're sharing a space."

"Common courtesy?" He quirks one eyebrow, amusement lighting his tone.

"Yes. You're in the presence of a lady." I sip my coffee, hoping to keep the smile from my face.

"Shit, how old are you?" He leans back on his hands, not attempting to move for his t-shirt.

"Old enough." I scowl.

"I'm older and even if I suggested I should clothe myself in front of a lady, it'd be dated."

"There's only one thing right in your sentence and that's that you're older than me."

He stares at me for an unnerving beat. If I was anyone other than myself, I'd pounce on him and think of the consequences later.

He stands. "Get ready. We're heading into town." He saunters to the bathroom and closes the door, water rattling the pipes in the wall seconds later.

AN HOUR LATER, I'm back in the passenger seat of his Range Rover trying not to peek over at Roarke in admiration again. His usual suit has been replaced with a pair of light blue linen shorts and a V-neck t-shirt that showcases his broad shoulders. His hair isn't gelled into cement, rather showing the soft curls in a messy weekend look. The man can pull off casual and business. How do I even stand a chance?

"You've got great legs." His gaze doesn't venture my way as we pass a small green sign that says Woods Parlor Population 1034.

"Did someone have a baby?" I ignore his comment about my legs. I was unsure if I should bring shorts so I opted on sundresses. Easier to dress up if I had to.

"What?"

"The population sign. The four looked new."

He grants me a fleeting look and shrugs. "I don't keep up with the town gossip."

I bite the inside of my cheek as tall trees on either side fill out the drive. It's beautiful, but I can't help but notice the lack of people. Growing up in the burbs of Chicago my entire life, woods were reserved for forest preserves the city mandated so every square inch of the area wasn't cement. Even while you're in the forest preserve, you can usually see other people.

Since Roarke wasn't too keen on me asking about the four, I remain quiet. My mind spins to why he brought me here. As a punishment of some sort? Did he want to see what it was like to take the rich society woman out of her element just for shits and giggles?

"Are you going to acknowledge my compliment? Isn't that bad manners?"

"It's bad manners to compliment my physical attributes."

He huffs. "That's the lamest thing I've ever heard."

"Lamest?"

"Who's asking one-word questions now?" He spares a quick glance my way.

A zing fires in my belly. Our banter is something I've come to enjoy in the past week and when Roarke was busy sulking or thinking I kind of missed it. Don't ever tell him that because I'd deny it, even if you offered me Chris Hemsworth covered in chocolate.

Okay, that's BS, who could resist that?

"I'm just saying you're a lawyer and you used the word lamest." I cross my legs and catch his gaze drift in that direction. My breathing picks up just slightly.

"Excuse my vocabulary. Must be because I'm back here in Woods Parlor." He says his town name much like people who make fun of small town people.

"I was just suggesting—"

"I know what you were suggesting," he snaps. "I'll pick up a dictionary while we're in town."

My jaw hangs open and I stare at the side of his face. Who the hell does he think he is to go and get all sensitive on me now? This is what we do.

"I get that you don't seem to want to be here which only confuses me more as to why you brought me, but unless you plan on using a favor to treat me like gum stuck on the bottom of your shoe, stop deflecting your bitterness onto me."

The truck jerks to the side of the road, and he slams on the brakes.

Thank goodness for seatbelts.

He swivels in his seat, facing me with an expression that could scare a mountain lion.

"Listen, I have no idea why I brought you here either." His fingers thread through his hair. "It was wrong, but you're here now. You're going to see where I came from. How fucked up my childhood was. So let me just give you the lowdown now. I don't have a father so don't ask about him. My mom raised me when she wasn't waitressing down at a bar where she screwed most of the clientele at one point or another. My sister, Allie, is the product of one of those one-night stands. Life here wasn't squeaky clean or picture perfect, but we made do."

We continue to stare at one another for a moment before I respond. "Do you think I'd judge you?"

He looks away from me and out the windshield. "You're practically Chicago royalty."

For the first time, Roarke is not the mean shark from the courtroom who facilitated the stealing of half my shit. The man who saunters around Chicago like he owns the city is no longer in this car.

"First of all, I'm not judging you. Second, I don't judge people based on how they were raised—period. I understand how lucky I am to grow up with what I did. And if I made a habit of looking down on people, I wouldn't have started my own foundation with my own money. If you don't want me making assumptions about you, don't make them about me." I cross my arms and stare out the window.

Still nothing but trees.

The weight of silence presses down on my shoulders for a minute before his hand lightly covers mine. "I'm sorry. It's just…there's no excuse for me taking the bullshit overloading my brain out on you. In my demented head, I thought you being here would help you understand me more, but there's ugliness in this town that I should've remembered. A past that still haunts me. But I apologize. Write the date and time of this right now because I might never say this again."

I turn to look at him and tilt my head.

"You're right. I can't very well want you to see the true me if I'm assuming you're like every other rich society woman I've met. I know your foundation, I know the work you're doing and if I really thought you were like that, I would never have invited you along. Let's start the day over, all right?"

My smile forms without a fight. "Fine."

His hand squeezes mine and he straightens his back and merges out onto the road.

"Thank you," I say.

"For what?"

"The compliment about my legs." My cheeks heat.

His grin slowly spreads across his entire face. "You're welcome. You wouldn't be thanking me if you knew what I was really thinking."

My face warms again and I bite the inside of my cheek trying to suppress my grin.

"One day I'm going to tell you exactly what that was—in great detail—ungentlemanly or not."

I cross my legs hoping to stifle the hum of desire between my legs.

How am I going to survive two more nights with this man?

Chapter Sixteen

"I have to run an errand. I'll be back before you can finish your breakfast," Roarke says.

"Fine." I sit down in the booth, picking up the menu placed behind the fake jukebox. "This place is cute."

Roarke stands on the outside of the booth, leaning over and positioning both cups up for coffee.

"Who said I wanted another coffee?"

He smirks. "I doubt they have soy milk, but you're on a vacation of sorts so you can live a little."

I lean back in the seat, my arms over my chest. "This is my vacation?" My eyes shift out the window to a Mayberry-type town.

His smirk grows wider, like it usually does the longer we converse, but he doesn't have time to reply because a woman walks up to our table.

"Roarke?" she asks. Her black waist apron is stained with grease suggesting it's already been a busy morning for her and her blonde hair is pulled up into a ponytail, makeup smeared, but she's an attractive woman.

"Liv?" he asks, backing up a step. I note the sound of surprise in his voice.

She awkwardly rocks forward on her worn out sneakers unsure if she should hug him or not, telling me they knew each other well at some point.

"It's good to see you."

"I had no idea you worked here." Roarke's back stiffens, his hands finding his pockets once again. "How long?"

"Two months." Their eyes lock and for a moment, and suddenly I feel like a third wheel.

Roarke breaks eye contact first, shifting his gaze to the stained linoleum floor.

Liv's bright blue eyes shift in my direction as I gawk at the two of them. "I'm sorry, did you want coffee?"

"Sure." My voice croaks as though I just figured out how to talk.

"Be right back." A smile creases her lips and she ignores Roarke, beelining it behind the counter.

"The one who got away?" I ask.

Roarke puts on the sunglasses that were hanging from the front of his shirt. "I'll be right back."

"You're not going to answer me?"

He turns back around, his hand resting on the edge of the booth. "Not the one who got away, but an ex. Yes."

A sprout of jealousy bursts through the soil in my heart. "Oh."

"Be right back." He heads out of the diner without another look at either of us.

Questions bubble in my head like a baffled cartoon character. They remain unanswered as I watch Roarke walk across the street to a big white building in the middle of the town square.

"Do you take cream?" Liv's voice pulls me back to my surroundings.

"Any way you have soy milk?" I ask, feeling a little pretentious for doing so.

Liv smiles and her effortless beauty waters that tiny sprout of jealousy, causing it to grow another inch.

"We do. One of our farmers makes the best soy milk. Let me grab you some."

How can I be sitting here resentful toward this woman who is only being sweet to me? She should be hating me unless…she was happy to get out of the relationship with him. Maybe he cheated on her or ran off and left her behind.

She arrives back at the table with a little carafe of milk.

"I think you'll love it. Do you know what you want for breakfast?" She poises her pen over the pad of paper in her hand. It's then that I see the ring on her left hand. The diamond is small but the gold band worn. It's not a new marriage.

Ah, that's why there's no jealousy on her part.

"Um… I'll just have the American breakfast. Eggs poached and instead of hash browns, can I have fruit please?"

She scribbles my order down. "Sure thing. Do you know what Roarke wants?" She eyes the empty spot on the other side of the booth.

"I don't."

He knew my coffee order, but I have no idea what he prefers in the morning. I mean he made me that huge breakfast, but is he an oatmeal guy or an eggs man?

"I doubt he eats what he did at eighteen. I'll wait until he returns. If you need anything, just holler."

"Thank you."

I remain in the booth, sipping my coffee and staring out the window. It's a cute town. A little rundown but quaint nonetheless. I'm not sure what kind of place I thought Roarke was raised in, but I'm not sure I pictured this.

A group of men in overalls and dirty shirts laugh and carry on at the street corner. An elderly couple enters the diner and sits a couple of booths down from mine. As I'm busy taking in my surroundings, a police officer walks in.

He's much different than the Chicago police officers I'm used to seeing. His swollen gut falls over his pants where the leather belt that holds his gun is worn and strained. He bellies up to the counter, and another waitress smiles, filling a cup of coffee and sliding the sugar over to him without him asking.

They discuss the morning and the weather and when his radio squawks, he quickly silences it, never granting it his attention.

A minute later, a brunette breezes into the diner, her eyes scanning the booths. An inkling tells me who she is even before matching hazel eyes to Roarke's bore into mine and she points in my direction.

She saunters over like she owns the town and slides into the booth on the other side of me. "Hannah?"

"Allie?" I ask.

A smile wraps around her lips. "Yeah." She sticks her hand out. "Nice to meet the woman behind the man."

"Excuse me?" My forehead crinkles.

"I just saw Roarke and he said you were over here. I had to meet you."

She's the complete opposite of Roarke. Where he's like an aged Redwood, she's more like a willow tree.

"Oh, well, I'm not…"

She waves me off. "He's never brought anyone back here before. Ever. Whoever you are, you're someone to him."

My hand falls to my stomach to stifle the purr of excitement induced by her words.

"Congratulations on your upcoming wedding," I say.

Her lips dip for a second. "We'll see if Wyatt is a rat. I'm rarely wrong on my suspicions." She looks over to flag a waitress down but her gaze sticks on the cop at the counter. "Oh, great. The bastard is having me followed."

"Who?" I ask.

"Wiltaker. He probably told his grandson not to marry me because I'm a Baldwin. Jackass."

The bell rings and the energy in the room shifts. My body alerts me to Roarke's presence before I even look away from Allie.

"It's my brother, right?" she asks.

"How did you—"

"Your face changed. You like him."

Roarke comes over before I can answer and signals for Allie to slide over.

"He's here," she whispers, nodding toward the counter.

Roarke glances over, shrugging his shoulders. "You're being paranoid."

"I am not. He thinks I'm not good enough and he's convinced Wyatt to go sleep with fucking Kylie. Well, screw them both. I don't need either of them."

Roarke's head falls back. "I got your marriage license moved forward so you can get married tomorrow. Quit with the assumptions. Wyatt didn't do anything."

Liv returns to fill Roarke's coffee cup. "Do you guys want anything else?"

Roarke's chest heaves with a breath as though the last thing he needed in this moment was to be reminded of something. I just don't know what.

"Coffee's fine," he says.

"Can I have a Coke, Liv?" Allie asks, peeking her head around to watch the counter again.

"Sure thing," Liv tells Allie. "Sugar is on the table, I'll go get you some milk," she says directly to Roarke.

"I take it black now." His words sound bitter and curt, silencing the table and wrapping us in an uncomfortable blanket.

"Oh, okay." She walks away.

"Asshole much?" Allie organizes the sugar packets with great concentration.

Roarke doesn't even flinch. "Fucking Christ. It's my first day here and already all this shit." He brings the coffee to his lips. "You okay with driving my vehicle home by yourself?"

My stomach clenches. He suddenly wants me gone?

"What?" I ask.

"Stop being an asshole." Allie pushes the container of sugar back where it came from but starts in on the jams. "You can't just make people disappear when you think they've seen too much." Allie's gaze meets mine. "He won't tell you, but he's embarrassed. You know the whole men-not-wanting-women-to-see weakness? Well, Roarke is the king of it."

I bite down on my lip to stop my smile from forming. Why do I like the fact he doesn't want me to see him vulnerable?

Instead of getting an easy dig in on him, I sip my coffee and smile.

"Thank you, Allie. Next time I won't do you the favor of using my charm to get your marriage license on the fast track when you should have applied three weeks ago."

"I'm not going to need it anyway." She shrugs.

Roarke rolls his eyes. "Since Allie feels like being so open this morning, let me tell you about her hang-ups. She trusts no one. Thinks everyone is out to get her, including the man she loves. The man she said yes to when he proposed. Now that man is about to walk in here." Roarke points and sure enough there's a young guy in his twenties steadily making headway toward the door. Definitely a man on a mission.

Allie knocks Roarke's hip. "Let me out."

"Nope."

Her back slides down the booth and Roarke's foot appears on the edge of my booth seat. "Nope again."

"Seriously. I'm not having this conversation with him, especially with his grandpa's judging eyes a few feet away." Allie's willow tree statue straightens and she gets back in her seat, her lips in a tight line.

"Relax," Roarke says, sipping his coffee again.

As if we're on a movie set, a strong wind storms in with Wyatt's giant figure. He stops, gaze searching the room before it rests on the back of Allie's head.

"Allie Baldwin!" he yells.

"Go away, Wyatt." She finishes with the grape jelly row and moves on to strawberry.

Liv silently places my breakfast and Allie's Coke down on the table, before sliding away, clearly not wanting to get in the middle of this showdown.

"May I?" The kid eyes my side of the booth.

I slide over, my purse resting on the edge of the seat.

Wyatt pushes the plate my way and picks up my coffee mug, positioning everything the way it was before he asked me to slide over. Nice kid.

"Thank you," his deep voice says and then he extends his hand out across the table. "Hey, Roarke."

Roarke shakes his hand, a smile on his lips. "Wyatt."

They drop hands and my breakfast stays untouched as

I watch the unfolding of a young lover's quarrel in front of me.

"Look at me, Allie." Wyatt's words bite out of his mouth.

She turns the jam container and starts on marmalade.

"Allie, look at the boy." Roarke elbows her, but her eyes focus in on the different flavors of jelly like she's doing a jigsaw puzzle looking for a specific piece.

"Stay out of it," she grumbles.

"You know I love you. I've loved you since the third grade when you kneed me in the nuts."

I press my lips together to keep from smiling and Roarke's eyes find mine, sharing a similar expression.

"You never understood the word no," Wyatt goes on.

Allie shrugs. "I wanted you to play with me."

"I didn't want to play. You pushed the topic and then everyone laughed when I fucked up and lost the game."

"Let's move on to the present," Roarke interjects like the lawyer he is.

"Wyatt?" The police officer at the counter circles his stool around to face us.

"Hey, Grandpa," he says, waving his hand but never looking in his direction. "I'll be there in a second."

"What's going on?" His big feet land on the floor and he slowly steps over.

Roarke's back grows straighter with each stride.

"Nothing. I'm talking to Allie." He points across the table to his fiancé.

"Didn't even see Allie here," he says.

Should this man be a police officer if he can't even take in his surroundings when he walks into a diner? Isn't that like protocol or something?

"You have to listen to me." Wyatt's eyes are lasered in on Allie's. "Do you really believe I want Kylie?"

"Kylie?" his grandpa questions.

Seriously what is it with this town and one-word questions?

"Grandpa, please go back and finish your breakfast," Wyatt says in an exasperated tone.

"Roarke." The sheriff shifts his attention, his thumbs resting on the belt under his straining stomach.

"Sheriff." Roarke nods at the man.

"Back for the wedding. Nice of you to walk Allie down the aisle."

"Well, she is my sister."

"And as everyone in this town is aware, I don't have a dad," Allie bites back and Roarke nudges her with his elbow.

"I would have fought him to walk you myself even if you did."

Allie glances up and she and Roarke share a look. A 'you're my hero' smile lands on her face.

"Suck up." Allie disregards his comment, staring at me. "He's being soft because you're here."

"Who are you?" the Sheriff asks me, finally concerned about the stranger at the table.

I extend my hand, ready to introduce myself.

"Hannah Crowley, Sheriff," Roarke answers for me.

The Sheriff's calloused hand wraps around mine. "Sheriff Wiltaker. I knew you were from out of town. Should have figured you came in with Roarke."

Roarke rolls his eyes.

"I'm Wyatt." The young kid gives me a fleeting glance. "Allie's soon to be husband."

"So you think," Allie spits.

"You two kids. Stop all the fighting. You're getting hitched tomorrow and you're going to make me a great-granddaddy."

Allie's cold stare stays on Wyatt.

"I told you, Grandpa, we're not ready for kids yet." Wyatt holds Allie's gaze, not sparing a glance at his grandpa.

"You're being foolish. Once you raise your kids, you'll have time to yourselves."

"Allie, can I please talk to you in private," Wyatt pleads.

"Go talk to him," Roarke says.

"Give me one reason why," Allie says, finally pushing the jam container away.

"Because you love me." Wyatt stands and holds out his hand.

The start of a smile forms on her lips. Roarke slides out of the booth, secure in the fact that Allie will give in.

She stubbornly stays in her spot on the vinyl for a few seconds. "You have five minutes, Wyatt Wiltaker." She slides out and exits the diner with Wyatt behind her.

"Young love. I remember once upon a time..." The Sheriff glances over his shoulder to Liv cleaning off a table. "Nice to meet you, Ms. Crowley. Roarke, welcome home. I'll see you two tonight at the rehearsal."

"Have a good day, Sheriff," Roarke says, and the Sheriff ventures to the back of the diner to chat with four men in the corner.

"Your breakfast is cold." He raises his hand for Liv's attention.

"It's fine. I'm not that hungry anyway."

"Good." He slides out, pulling out his money clip and dropping well over the cost of the meal on the table. "I have somewhere I want to take you."

He offers his hand and I accept, leaving the diner without a goodbye to Liv.

Once we're on the street by Roarke's Range Rover, I

spot Allie straddled around Wyatt's waist on a park bench in the middle of the square, lips locked, hands exploring.

"That didn't take long to work out," I say.

"She has no shame," Roarke remarks as he opens up the passenger door for me.

"She's young and in love," I say, sliding in.

"She's going to make his life hell." He shuts the door and I say nothing else because coming from someone who was in a lukewarm relationship most of my adult life, a passionate relationship filled with fire and ice, doesn't sound all that bad.

Chapter Seventeen

Roarke parks in front of a long building with a sign that says Woods Parlor High School, Home of the Spartans. An American flag flies off the flagpole and a bench sits underneath that reads, "Donated by Class of 2016."

The parking lot has a sparse few cars in it. I'm guessing it must be the administrative staff that's here for a few hours during summer break.

"I have to stop here really quick." He exits the truck and by the time I open my door he's pulling it the rest of the way open. "Wait for me next time."

"Yeah, okay, whatever."

"Should I reprimand you about your word choices now? You sound like Allie."

I roll my eyes and say nothing as I walk alongside him toward the building. "You went to high school here?"

"I did." There's pride in his tone that I haven't heard since we arrived in Woods Parlor. "Sorry, we don't have ivy-covered walls and valet parking."

"You know how I feel about assumptions, counselor."

"Am I wrong?" he quirks an eyebrow while opening the door for me.

"No." I chuckle and he joins me.

"So my assumption didn't make me an ass." He follows me into the building where we're met with a big mural in red, white and blue, a Spartan helmet the main focus.

Taking my hand in his, he leads me to the left and then down a hall.

"How many people are here right now?" I ask.

"Are you afraid to be alone with me?"

"No. I'm just curious."

"Probably just the athletic coaches and few janitorial staff. Summer school just ended." He talks like he's on the up and up about his school and I'm left wondering how involved he still is in this town.

"I thought you said you don't stay up on the gossip."

"Summer school dates aren't gossip," he quips.

Embarrassment pinkens my cheeks over the fact that he's right.

His hand grips mine tighter. "I shouldn't have said it like that. Let's just have a nice day, okay?"

"Play nice, Mr. Bald..." His head snaps my way. "Roarke."

A smile replaces his clenched jaw. "Better."

"Roarke!" A man's voice booms from down the hall. He's standing at the end of the hallway in grey athletic shorts and a polo shirt. His hair is thinning, but he appears in great shape.

"Hey, Sean. I'm glad you're here," Roarke says with genuine affection.

We walk up to him and the two men shake hands. "This is Hannah Crowley." Roarke's hand lands on the small of my back and a tingle lets loose in my stomach.

"Hannah, this is Sean, the head coach of the Spartan football team."

The man's eyes dip up and down, faster than most and I wonder if it's because he doesn't want Roarke to notice. Am I really that much of an anomaly in this town? "Pleasure." We shake hands and Roarke's hand never leaves my back.

"If you've got the time, the team is practicing right now." Sean turns around and my eye catches a trophy case right before the back doors.

"You played?" I ask, seeing his picture with a team in the glass case next to a trophy.

"Yeah." His words aren't the proud ones I loved in the car. He sounds contrite. "We'll be right out, Sean."

The man nods and heads out the doors.

I inspect the other pictures seeing graduation class of nineteen ninety-four. Mentally, I do the math. So he's forty-one or maybe forty-two depending on when his birthday is. While my head is busy calculating the difference between our ages, I notice a picture that has a much younger Liv in a cheerleading uniform in Roarke's arms. He's sweaty and there's no silver in his dark hair.

"So what happened between you and Liv?" I ask, my nose still pressed to the glass, wanting to learn everything about this man who I thought I hated.

"You know the song 'Jack and Diane' by John Mellencamp?"

"Who doesn't?"

"Well, turns out Diane wanted Jack's best friend, Evan."

I turn my head to look at him. His hands are stuffed in the pockets of his shorts again, his eyes averted from the glass case.

"I'm sorry," I say, a frown on my face.

"Don't be. I wouldn't be who I am without that experience. I'd probably be like Sean and be coaching right now. Not that that's a bad thing, I'm just happier where I am." I picture the strong, capable, powerful man in front of me suffering a heartbreak when he was younger. It's hard to merge those two visions of him into one whole person.

"But you'd have the girl," I say, pressing despite not being sure if I should. If I even really want to.

He shakes his head. "She wasn't the right one. If she was, I wouldn't have lost her." He sounds so certain.

"But don't you think that…"

"If you're trying to compare Liv to what happened with you and Todd, don't. It's very different. Liv and I were young, I didn't know there was a whole other world out there."

I step closer, reaching for his hands and entwining our fingers together. "You have so many layers, Roarke. Peel just one back for me."

Why am I asking for trouble by begging him to show me his heart?

"I am showing you. Bringing you to Woods Parlor is showing you a part of me almost no one knows about. It's putting on full display why I don't do relationships."

My heart cracks for this man. I squeeze his hands.

"And you haven't even met my mother yet."

"So the question is, do you believe in true love? In fate?"

At some point, one of us must have moved in because our chests are pressed against one another's.

His gaze falls down to me. "Truth?"

I nod, swallowing down my expectations. He might surprise me.

"No."

I step back, but his hands grip in mine, not letting me pull away.

"That doesn't mean I don't want to be proven wrong. I'm a lawyer, Hannah." He steps forward, and my breasts pebble at our proximity. "I see logic, facts. My day is spent dealing with the aftermath of relationships that people thought would be until death do they part but have transformed a couple into conniving and manipulative people wanting harm to the person they once swore they loved the most. But I want a woman to come home to. A woman to warm my bed at night. A woman who doesn't *need* me but wants me."

To my utter horror, tears threaten to spill down my cheeks from his declaration. "And you think I'm that woman?"

He releases one hand, raising it to tuck a strand of hair behind my ear. "I want you to be her, but first I'd like you to let me in by forgiving me for representing Todd. I want to put that behind us and start fresh."

I lean into the strength of his palm. "I'm not sure."

He nods, his eyes falling shut. "Well, good thing I have two more favors."

My heart is screaming at me. My vagina is flailing on the floor in a huge tantrum. My lips are begging for just one kiss. In a sick way I want him to use a favor to kiss me, but instead, he pulls back, takes my hand again and leads me out the doors without another word.

My mind is in a daze as I stand on the edge of the grass field watching boys hit each other. Roarke is talking to Sean in the corner, inspecting some helmets.

"Water break!" the assistant next to me screams and I smack at a bug sucking on my neck.

"Being near these woods sucks," one of the boys who raced over to the sidelines says. "I guess that's why they call us Woods Parlor." A young kid squirts a stream of water into his mouth and then over his face.

Big blue eyes, sandy blonde hair. He's a heartbreaker in the making I'm sure.

"I guess so."

His eyes feast on me and I'm afraid I'll be the cougar fantasy in his spank bank later tonight. "You're Mr. Baldwin's girl?"

Two more boys join him, more interested in the cheerleading practice going on behind me than speaking with me.

"I'm not his girl," I say.

His lips quirk up. "Why not? He's got to be a catch what with how rich he is."

I shrug. "Money's not everything."

"It is when you have nothing." The kid squirts more water in his mouth and swishes it around for a second before spitting it out in front of him. His two teammates nearby are practically drooling over the girls behind me.

The kid's words ring out in my head and a new stream of questions to ask Roarke form in my head. Why did he ever choose to become a divorce attorney?

"If it wasn't for Mr. Baldwin, we wouldn't have the new concussion helmets." He nods and I look over to see Roarke placing one on top of a player's head. "We'd be playing with uniforms from when he played fifty years ago."

"Fifty seems a little drastic, no?" I chuckle. Oh to be young again.

The kid's eyebrows crinkle.

"Did he pay you to tell me what a great guy he is?" I ask, half serious.

Again with the crinkled brows. "I never do what I'm asked."

"True story," one of the friends who I thought was paying no attention says.

"Just ask Principal Montgomery," the other friend chimes in.

"He's the most successful person to come out of Woods Parlor and never abandoned us."

"Water break over." The assistant coach smacks their backs and the boys squirt more water into their mouths and drop the bottles to the ground before running back to the field.

My gaze ventures to Roarke and Sean again, they're shaking hands.

As I watch Roarke across the field, my gut churns because if he wanted me here to prove that he wasn't the person I assumed he was, it's working. He's so much more and so much better than I ever thought.

Damn it all to hell…I'm falling for him.

Chapter Eighteen

oarke and I arrive at the church for the rehearsal that evening. For some reason, after meeting her, I didn't picture Allie marrying in a church.

This time it's not Allie barreling toward me, but a woman with dark loose hair hanging down around her face. She's wearing a dress probably one size too small, her feet fighting against the straps of her sandals.

"Roarke, baby," she coos like he's a five-year-old.

Please tell me this isn't Edie.

"Hi, Mom," Roarke says not giving her a full hug, but more of the acquaintance version of one.

Edie pulls back, her hands gripping his like she's looking him over.

Her judgment should end in an A-plus. It was all I could do not to jump him when I stepped out of the bathroom at the motel. Dark charcoal slacks, a simple white button-down with the top two buttons undone, the usual silver watch adorning his wrist. He's a more casual version of his usual self, but still as edible as ever, let me tell you.

"Always too dressed up. You're in Woods Parlor for

heaven's sake." She waves him off with her hand. "You could have worn jeans."

I briefly appraise my own outfit. I'm wearing a wine colored dress that ends above my knee and a pair of sandals with a heel that would usually challenge the height of a man. Not Roarke though, thank goodness.

Edie's gaze shifts to me and my mouth suddenly dries.

"Hannah, right?" she asks.

She doesn't pull me in for a hug or even smile for that matter. Instead, her hand extends regally, like she's meeting the queen. Except it's almost as if I should kiss *her* hand. I'm understanding Roarke's hesitancy with me meeting her.

"Hi, Mrs… Edie."

I awkwardly go to shake her hand, unsure of what to do but then a loud laugh erupts from her, echoing through the tall ceilings and wooden beams of the old church.

"I'm kidding. Come here you!" She wraps herself around my middle, her face literally between my breasts since she's so much shorter than me. She rocks our bodies back and forth in a swaying motion.

"Mom," Roarke bites out.

"You're the first girl I've met since Liv, but who cares about that hussy."

"Mom," Roarke says to his mother once more.

"You're so much more beautiful than her. You're so elegant, look at you." She pulls my arms away from my body much like she did with Roarke, inspecting me. "Damn kid, I'm baffled as to why she's here with you." Her smile says she doesn't really mean it.

"Gee, thanks, Mom." He pulls one of my hands from hers. "Let her go now. She's not a toy."

Edie's eyes take me in one last time. "I just didn't expect her to be so breathtaking."

"Cool it," Roarke says, his jaw clenching harder with each compliment paid to me.

Edie rolls her eyes. "You have to go practice walking your sister down the aisle. Hannah can come hang with me." Her arm slides through mine, pulling me away.

"Yeah, she'll be there in a minute." Roarke pulls me back the other way and I fall into his arms.

"I swear, you need an enema to get out whatever it is that is lodged up that ass of yours, Roarke." I purse my lips before I burst out laughing.

Roarke shakes his head. "So, you've met the whole family. I'll send you back to Chicago now."

I laugh finding comfort in the way his arms are around my waist. How did I get in this position and how come I don't want to move away?

"It's fine. Wait until you meet my parents."

Roarke freezes, his arms stiffening. Shit. I shouldn't have said that.

"You'd want me to meet your family?" The smirk on his face says he'll tease me endlessly, but I can see that under that arrogant persona he's pleased with the words that came out of my mouth.

"What would I tell them? This is the guy I'm spending time with as part of a five-favor deal?"

Roarke's face falls. "Yeah, I'd kick a guy's ass if he did that to my daughter."

"Roarke? What the hell?" Allie walks into the church in a lace champagne-colored dress, her hair down and curly similar to her mother's. "Let's get this show on the road, you know I get itchy in churches."

Roarke laughs and his hand molds to my cheek. "This conversation isn't over."

He loosens his arms and I step out of his embrace, our arms slowly moving apart until we have no choice but to let go. Just when my fingers unhook from his, he pulls me back into his arms.

My hands land on his strong chest and his face nuzzles into my neck. "Also, it's incredibly unfair that my mom's face has been between your tits and mine hasn't. We need to rectify that, and soon."

Fireworks erupt between my legs.

"ROARKE!" Allie's voice booms out through the church, much like her mother's did minutes ago.

His forehead lands on mine. "I really regret bringing you here." He squeezes his eyes shut for a second.

"Don't. I like this side of you."

"What side is that?"

"The caregiver side. You were right. You're not the man I thought."

His lips tick up. "So, my plan is working?"

His large hands mold to my hips and I'd do anything to feel his lips on mine right now. Are they soft or firm? Will he take charge or let me guide the pace?

Moron, the man takes charge of everything, he's definitely going to go alpha when you kiss.

As much as I want my independence and I'm pro-woman everything, I want a man who does just that. I don't want to have to guide him or tell him anything. Someone who takes care of me in a way that's not controlling or demeaning. Not some jealous jerk who pisses around me to stake his claim, but someone who shows me off for the prize he thinks I am and because he's proud of me. Someone there when I get home. Who knows if I had a bad day or whether I'm tired just from looking at me. Could that man be Roarke Baldwin? I wish I knew for sure.

"Go sit. I'll make this snappy." He winks and then he's gone. Him and his smoldering touch venture out of the church and into the hallway where Allie was screaming for him.

My heels click on the wooden planks of the old church until I find a pew to sit in that's not too near the front. Thank goodness Edie is busy talking to who I suspect are relatives in the second pew. My mind is like a tornado with thoughts whipping around, never landing on an answer. There are only two people who know the full situation, so I open up our group text stream.

Me: *Girls, girls, girls. I'm in trouble.*

Three dots appear immediately.

Chelsea: *Already slept with him?*
Victoria: *You mean I won!?*
Me: *What are you talking about? No I haven't slept with him and won what? Are you guys betting on my sex life?*
Chelsea: *For once I predicted later than Vic. She had you giving it up your first night there.*
Victoria: *Thanks, Chels. I just think…alone in a hotel room? You do the math.*
Me: *Well, I was able to keep my panties on, thank you.*
Chelsea: *What about your bra? Any motorboat action?*
Me: *And to think I was texting you guys for advice.*
Victoria: *We have to have a little fun. What's up?*
Chelsea: *You can't blame me, I need some fun in my life. Dean doesn't want me even walking too far.*
Me: *Tell Dean you aren't the first woman to carry a child. And I think I want to sleep with Roarke.*
Victoria: *Duh*
Chelsea: *I second the duh.*
Me: *Girls!?*
Victoria: *Han, you've wanted to sleep with him for months now.*

Have I? No, I've definitely hated him.

Chelsea: *What's that saying? There's a thin line between love and hate?*
Victoria: *Yep, that's it.*
Me: *I don't love the man.*
Chelsea: *No, but you want to sleep with him.*

It's annoying when they have a point.

Victoria: *I'm the rational one, right?*
Chelsea: *I'm ignoring that assumption.*
Me: *What does that have to do with it?*
Victoria: *If you want him, explore it. Sleep with him and see what you feel after. You aren't committing to walking down the aisle or anything.*
Chelsea: *He screwed her over. Hard to get past that.*
Victoria: *It was his JOB. He's going to great lengths to make it up to her and seriously, Hannah, did he leave you destitute?*

I chew on my inner lip. Of course not. But it's the principle of the thing.

Chelsea: *He still took half her shit.*
Victoria: *It's a divorce, Chels. I know you and Dean didn't have anything to split up, but I took half of Pete's shit, too.*
Chelsea: *Pete's a douche.*
Victoria: *Some days, but all Roarke did was his job. If Hannah had been his client, we'd be singing his praises right now.*
Me: *His reputation in Chicago is not exactly upstanding.*
Victoria: *Sure, but since when do you care what people think?*

Match Point, Vic.

Chelsea: *Vic, are you arguing for the defense now?*
Victoria: *Let's say I had a conversation with Reed about the whole thing last night and the bastard made a good defensive argument about Roarke.*
Me: *You told him about me and Roarke?*
Victoria: *It's Reed. He's like a woman.*
Chelsea: *Um…yeah, no he's not.*
Me: *I second Chelsea on that one.*
Me: *What was his argument?*
Victoria: *He said that Roarke seems to like you. That he's going to great lengths to get you to like him, which isn't his usual style. That Roarke walks around like he couldn't give a shit that there's probably ten hitmen after him at any one time. But that when it comes to you, he's different and that usually means something when you're a guy.*

My heart softens thinking of Reed's earlier revelation to me.

Chelsea: *Damn Reed.*
Victoria: *Hannah, there's no harm in letting him in a little.*
Chelsea: *If you're already feeling something, it's too late. You don't have to give him the keys to the kingdom. Just let him sneak in the window one night. Maybe you win big.*
Me: *Or maybe I lose everything.*
Chelsea: *Nah, you can't lose when you're a millionaire. Lol*

I stare down at my phone, my girlfriends' advice ringing so close to what I've told them in the past.

Me: *Thanks, ladies.*
Victoria: *Just jump, Hannah. We'll catch you if he doesn't.*

I smile, even though they can't see me.

Me: *What would I do without you girls?*
Chelsea: *Live a really boring life. You want to talk about my bowel movements now?*
Victoria: *Shit, Jade's calling me.*
Me: *Rehearsal's about to start.*
Chelsea: *I knew that'd get everyone off this text string. ;)*

I chuckle and silence my phone, shoving it inside my clutch.

Sitting there and waiting for things to begin, I contemplate all the girlfriends I've had in the past. None of them very loyal. All of them with agendas of their own. I have no doubt that Victoria speaks the truth. If Roarke breaks me, they'll be there to piece me back together. And with that revelation, I make a conscious decision to give Roarke a real chance.

Chapter Nineteen

*A*fter the text convo with Chelsea and Victoria, Roarke appeared different to me. As he walked with Allie's arm through his own down the aisle, his attractiveness notched up another level. His eyes found mine and I didn't shift my gaze. After he pretends to give Allie away, he sits in the first pew next to his mother, and I yearn to feel his strong body next to mine.

The pastor finishes his pretend ceremony and instead of Allie and Wyatt pretending to kiss, they go at each other like they've been reunited after months apart. The groomsmen whistle and the bridesmaids clap.

I wonder if they fight on purpose for the make-up sex? I probably shouldn't be thinking that in a church.

Roarke rises from his seat and stops at my pew, his hand out for me.

As I rise from my seat, my hand falls into his and he wastes no time in linking our fingers and escorting me out of the building.

"We have to go to dinner and then we're free," he whispers when everyone starts filing out to their cars.

"Where's dinner?" I ask.

"We're going to a restaurant on the outskirts of town." He opens my door as usual and rounds the front of the Range Rover over to his side.

I spot his mom sliding into an older BMW while a man hops into the driver's seat.

All the cars are in a procession line, winding through the streets of downtown Woods Parlor. After a minute or so, Roarke turns on some music to fill the silence in the car.

Chelsea and Victoria's words continue to wreak havoc in my head. Both the devil and the angel are propped on my shoulders, each weighing in with their advice.

"You okay?" Roarke's hand slides to my knee and a million shivers cascade up my thigh hitting the bullseye between my legs.

I stare over at him, seeing him for the man he is, the man I didn't know he was, only weeks ago. "I didn't know you at all."

He tilts his head, briefly glancing at me, then shifting his eyes back to the road.

"You know me."

"No, I thought I did." I shake my head. "I'm woman enough to admit I was wrong."

He parks in a deserted parking lot of a store without business banners in the windows, leaving the line of cars headed to the rehearsal dinner.

"I'm lost." He cuts the engine, turning in his seat to face me.

"Is this whole thing an act? Like you hired these people to act like your family and say nice things about you?"

He chuckles more to himself than me. "They say nice things about me?"

"You know you're like a hero in this town. Is that why you brought me? To brainwash me into thinking that man in Chicago isn't real?" My hand feels for the handle and I pry the door open, needing air and maybe some distance from Roarke.

A second later, his door shuts and he's at my side near the back of the truck.

"I'm not only the callous, unfeeling man you see me as when I'm working in the city. I'm also the son who still strives to make his mom proud even though he's still filled with resentment for her. I'm the brother who wants to make his sister's life easier and let her have the dream of unconditional love neither of us grew up with. I'm the town quarterback who left and made something of himself who wants to give a younger version of himself a leg up. I'm the boy who got his heartbroken at a young age that defined his jagged line of thinking when it comes to trust."

I lean on the back of the SUV, my hands clinging to the bumper. His declaration is so honest and pure.

"Did you practice that?" I ask softly.

He throws his hands up in the air and walks across the parking lot flattening the weeds sprouting up between the cracks. "No," he bites out.

"Are you mad?"

"I'm starting to get mad. Yes. I get mad when I feel defeated." He swivels around, his beauty and strength more visible against the backdrop of what failure looks like.

"I'm sorry. It's just…" This time I give him my back, walking a few steps away.

My head is in a jumble. How on Earth can I want this man? The man I've loathed for the past year. The man I almost made a voodoo doll of. How did I allow him to weasel his way past my armor?

"It's trust. I get it. In your eyes I deceived you. I'm the person you relate to the worst thing that ever happened to you." His voice is near, but he keeps his distance. "I was a fool to think it'd be easy for you. Like I could charm my way in and expect you to forgive me."

Tears well in my eyes and I clench my hands into fists to stop them from falling.

"I don't know what to think. My divorce wasn't a picnic, but I don't blame you. You weren't the one who cheated. You weren't the one who wanted everything of mine. That's on Todd."

As I turn to face him, I notice he's resting on the bumper of his car, his sunglasses off and his eyes on me. "I helped him get it though."

"You did what you were supposed to do, I suppose." It's hard getting those words out of my mouth, even if they are the truth.

"You don't really believe that in your heart though." The corners of his lips tip down.

"I get that it was your job, but you have a reputation in Chicago. One where you go after the other party with a vengeance."

His eyes lock with mine. "I will never apologize for the job I do. I'm one of the best in my field and I take pride in that. I don't deliberately take everything from someone, but I do make sure my client doesn't get screwed over because their spouse is hiding money. There are laws, Hannah, laws that people like to break. When someone makes the conscious decision to walk down the aisle and promise their future to someone else, it should be taken seriously. When they decide to have a child, those responsibilities shouldn't be taken away once they decide they want to move on to someone else. I'm sorry I represented Todd in your divorce, but he got to me first. I'm sorry you see me as a monster who stole from you, but I got him what the law said was his. That's all."

I keep my gaze locked with his.

"How can you make that argument sound so noble?" The corners of my lips tip up a bit.

He smirks. "You're not the first person I've had to defend my actions to."

I roll my eyes. "So, you've gone after a client's ex before?" The thought nearly sends me into a rage.

Standing, he stalks toward me. "When are you going to understand?" he asks, gripping my upper arms.

"What?"

"You're the only one I want. I wanted for you to be over that marriage for an entire year. I've never pursued another client or a client's spouse. I'm no saint, granted, but I've never wanted a woman to wake up in my bed more than I do you." He pins me with an intense stare for a moment and I think that maybe he's going to lean down and kiss me. Then he frowns and his forehead wrinkles. "But I'm starting to think this just isn't going to work. You're never going to forgive me."

He releases his grip on my shoulders and turns to walk back to the SUV. I miss his eyes on me immediately.

"I do." The words rush out of my mouth.

He glances over his shoulder and he must see something on my face because he turns around fully, not touching me but stepping so close we're nearly chest to chest.

Our breaths are labored and fast. "You do what?" His voice is low.

"I...I forgive you."

Whatever space was between us disappears as one of his hands clutch the back of my head and he pulls me flush to his body.

"No takebacks," he says.

Giving me no time to answer, his lips crash against

mine with ferocity. With one hand holding me where he wants me, his other hand slides to my back. He takes control of the kiss and I melt into his hold. All the doubts and indecision evaporate as we devour one another. His hand glides down my body and cups my ass, positioning me flush against the bulge in his slacks.

I ground against him, desperately seeking more friction. All weekend he's had me on edge and I'm done fighting the growing heat between my thighs. I'm starving for a scream-worthy orgasm and there's no doubt that Roarke would deliver multiple times.

At some point, while we're all lips, tongue, and pent-up lust, he circles us around and my back hits the SUV. Stepping into me, he skims his hand from my ass to my thigh and steps into me, the friction growing.

"If our timing was different, I'd take you right here," he murmurs against my lips and then slams them down on my mouth as though he can only handle not kissing me for a few short seconds.

"People." I pull away from his lips and glance around.

Instead of stepping away, he thrusts into me, effectively hitting the center of wetness in my panties. "I don't care about them. If this wasn't going to be our first time, I'd already have you in the truck with ripped panties, but..." He leans in and kisses me slowly then cups my cheek. "Our first time will not be fast." He presses his lips to mine in a chaste kiss.

"I'm good with fast."

He chuckles, tucking another strand of my hair behind my ear. "You won't be after I've had a whole night with you."

I could melt into the concrete right here with that declaration and I can't wait for him to prove himself right.

Roarke's hand glides down my arm and disappears

behind me, opening the vehicle door. He pats my hip with his other hand in a motion to tell me to climb in. "Let's get this over with."

I sit in the passenger seat of the Range Rover in a lust-filled daze waiting for Roarke to make his way to the driver's seat. He climbs into the truck, puts the key in the ignition and then freezes.

"What's the matter?" I ask.

He leans over and his lips land on mine, his body hovering over mine. The spark between us ignites into a fire and I grip the hairs on the back of his head, keeping him against me.

"We shouldn't? Right?" he asks when he pulls away for a second.

I giggle like a lovesick teenage girl and run my hand along the light stubble on his cheeks. My thighs clench with thoughts of how that stubble will feel between them.

Before I have a chance to answer, his forehead falls to mine. "You need to work on your timing. You give me the green light when there's no possible way of me having you."

"Would you prefer a red light?" I ask, narrowing my eyes.

"Relax Firecracker. I'm kidding."

"Good because…"

He shuts me up with another kiss and I sink into the soft leather seats reveling in his taste.

Too quickly he tears his lips from my mouth, pulls the seatbelt over my body, and starts the car.

"You're so damn hard to resist. A chink in my willpower." He shakes his head, more to himself than me I think.

I smile and look out the window. I shouldn't like that I weaken him, but I do anyway. I like it a lot.

Chapter Twenty

It's a bar-b-que buffet for the rehearsal dinner at a restaurant on the river's edge with tables inside and outside. There are gas-lit fire pits with Adirondack chairs circling the flames. Kids run around the green grass while men hang around the tables jabbering on about all the local news. Women sit in clumps sharing the latest gossip and for a second I feel like I entered the movie Steel Magnolias.

I sip my spiked lemonade, appraising the crowd.

Allie and Wyatt sit at a table with their friends, beer cans and Solo cups piled high in front of them.

Edie sits with her boyfriend and two other women, smoking, laughing and carrying on.

"What do you think?" Roarke's hand winds around my waist and he pulls me to him, his head burrowing into my neck. My body hums as his lips land on the sensitive flesh.

"It's nice."

"It's not the Ritz," he murmurs, his teeth latching on to my earlobe.

My hand lands on his chest and I push him away. He's

too strong and stubborn though, his hand never leaves my hip.

"Pushing me away already?" he asks.

"If you keep talking like I'm some stuck up bitch who can't enjoy anything other than the best, then yes. And the teasing isn't appreciated."

"I do love your firecracker side, but you should know it only makes me even hotter for you."

I chuckle. "You'll have to wait until later tonight."

He sips his whiskey neat and then holds the cup down at his side.

"If I was a better man, I'd wait until we got back to Chicago. Lucky for you, I'm not." He winks.

"If you keep latching on to my earlobe then you'll be taking me in the women's restroom."

He chuckles. "You have no idea how hard it's been the past two hours not to bend you over one of these tables and have my wicked way with you." His hand slides off my hip to my ass and his fingers delve into my flesh.

I rise to my tiptoes and he steps in front of me, blocking us from bystanders. His lips millimeters from mine, I impatiently wait for him to claim them as his again.

"Do you want to know my plans or do you prefer surprises?" His voice is low, and the deep timbre he's perfected makes my insides clench.

"Why don't you give me a sample?"

His straight lips tip up as though he can't control them. It's my favorite smile of his. The impromptu one where he's trying to fight his amusement but fails miserably.

He steps forward, raising his hand above my head and pressing it against the red siding of the restaurant. Leaning forward, he runs his nose up and down my jawline.

"Let's just say you'll find out I have three amazing God-given assets. My mouth, my tongue, and my cock all revved and ready to fulfill your every wish." His teeth grip the fleshy part of my earlobe, tugging once again.

My body heats and I close my eyes, pushing back the thought of raising my legs to straddle his waist and grinding against him just to ease the thrum of energy building in my body.

"Oh aren't you guys cute. Don't let him seduce you, Hannah. He's a heartbreaker."

Talk about a douse of cold water.

Roarke steps back, glaring at his mother. "Always my biggest fan," Roarke murmurs.

"I'm stealing her away. People want to meet this new love of yours from Chicago." Edie slides her arm through mine and walks us away.

I look longingly over my shoulder to Roarke to save me. He watches us leave him, tilting the glass up to his lips.

Disregarding Roarke since he's not going to tell his mother not to kidnap me and I turn back around. That's when Edie's description of me finally hits my brain.

"New love?"

She laughs, patting my hand. "I know women can be blind sometimes, but Roarke has always worn his feelings on his sleeve. Besides, I'm his mama—I can tell what that boy's thinking. Always could."

I want to object. I want to tell her she's way off base. That here and now is the first time I've seen an ounce of vulnerability in Roarke. That the boy she raised and the man I know are completely different and until a few hours ago, I couldn't see that they co-existed in the same body.

Instead, I offer her, "I'm starting to see that."

She stops near a table at the river's edge where there are five women seated, all eyes on me.

A boulder lodges in my throat.

"Sit," the woman throwing off a sweet grandmotherly appearance says, patting the chair next to her.

I do as I'm told and Edie takes the one next to me.

"You'll never remember all our names, but…" Edie introduces the women to me.

She's wrong though because I was brought up to never forget a name. My mother taught me at a young age to always associate something with the name to help me remember better. Hence the woman next to me would be Peachy Pam because her hair color resembles a peach. Or the woman two down from her is Mustache Millie because she has a bit of a mustache. It's a simple technique and I still use it today.

"Pleasure ladies." I nod to the women at the table.

"The pleasure is all ours. Now…tell us your story," Mustache Millie says, sitting up in her seat with her wine glass at her lips.

"Story?"

Peachy Pam pats my arm. "How you met Roarke. There are women around here who have been trying to nail him down every time he comes home. Liv didn't know what she lost until he came back to town as a successful lawyer with his fancy car and big billfold."

"Well…" I try to push away thoughts of Roarke and Liv in love so jealousy won't have a way to take a foothold in me.

I've had men in my life before. It's not like Roarke and I are committed to one another. Heck, I haven't even slept with him, but the thought that Liv was the love of his life disturbs me to the point of becoming a psycho woman.

"We met in court."

"You were married before?" Edie asks me, eyes wide.

I nod. "I was."

"Roarke was your divorce lawyer?" Millie asks,

downing the rest of her wine staring at her friends like I'm giving the lowdown on her favorite celebrity.

"No. He was my ex's."

It dawns on me that this is the story I will have to tell people over and over again if we're a couple. That he represented my ex in my divorce.

"Oh." Millie smirks at her friends and I peg her as the mean girl in high school.

"That's interesting," Pam remarks never looking at the other women.

I glance over my shoulder, finding Roarke talking to a few guys. Our eyes meet and he smiles.

"Yeah, unconventional I suppose," I say, turning back around to face the firing squad.

"We've heard a few rumors about him down in Chicago. Doesn't he have a nickname?" Blue Betty asks, her huge blue eyes filled with question marks.

"Not sure about a nickname, but Roarke has made a name for himself in the divorce attorney circuit to be sure." *Look how polite I can be.*

"So how did it all happen?" Edie asks as a man drops another beer can in front of her.

"I tracked her down," Roarke's voice says from behind me. His hands on my shoulders, his thumb running along the length of my neck under my hair. "I knew the minute I saw the PI photos that she had to be mine."

Pam clutches her heart and falls to the back of her seat. "So sweet."

"You see how beautiful she is, but did you know she runs a charitable foundation to empower young girls?"

His kind words make my cheeks heat and goose bumps rush up my arms when he leans forward to set his glass on the table and takes my hand.

"I should have told my client I couldn't represent him. That it was a conflict of interest after I saw Hannah."

I shake my head as the women look on at him in awe.

Well, everyone but Millie. She's giving the stink eye. "That would have been a good choice," she snips.

Roarke chuckles. "The best thing about this woman is that she keeps me on my toes. Keeps me honest." He leans over and his lips connect with my cheek. "If you don't mind ladies, I'm going to steal her away. I'm sure we'll see you tomorrow."

All the woman nod in agreement and he guides me away with his hand on the small of my back.

"Just keep going," he mumbles and I weave my way through more guests.

"We should say goodbye."

He stops and glances at Allie. She's lip-locked with Wyatt again.

"I think we're good." He threads his fingers with mine as he leads me around the side of the restaurant to his car. "I needed you like a year ago."

Chapter Twenty-One

Roarke pushes the hotel room door open and we circle around the entryway, our lips attached. The door slams and I have no idea if it's his doing or not but I don't really care. He tears his lips off mine and I lean forward only to find him stepping away from me.

"What's the problem?" I ask.

"If we don't slow down, I won't remember this and I need to remember the first time I take you."

The small piece of me that was still unsure if this is a good idea or not shatters with his words.

He remains a few feet away, his gaze feasting on me, a flame of heat searing along the path his eyes take over my body.

"You're so gorgeous." He toes out of his shoes, taking one painfully slow step toward me.

My stomach tightens and I let the moment sink in because one thing is for certain—Roarke will be someone I need to remember, too.

The back of his hand runs across my cheek and along my jaw, his fingers threading through the hairs at the back of my neck, thumb running up and down the center of my neck.

"I feel like I'm in the middle of some teenage kid's wet dream right now."

The weight of the moment breaks and I laugh, my head falling forward and landing on his shoulder. His own chest vibrates with amusement and the scent of his cologne sparks the want that's inside of me when he's near.

Without missing a beat, he nudges my head up and his lips take mine. Slow and leisurely our tongues slide against one another's. I sink into his strength, toeing out of my own shoes.

My heels fall to the floor and Roarke's neck cranes farther down. At some point as I'm lost in our kiss, his hands grip my ass, propping me up in his arms. Not missing his unspoken intention, I wrap my legs around his waist and he sits down on the edge of the bed.

His bulging erection rocks me at my core only spurring me to grind against him more as all my pent up lust for this man demands a release. My hands cling to his shoulders as I rock back and forth, my head falling back.

I need him. I need to be closer.

The sound of my zipper echoes in the quiet room. His teeth scrape along my collarbone while his fingers slide the fabric over my shoulders, falling down my arms. Removing my arms from the top of my dress, it pools around my waist, revealing my black lacy bra.

Roarke's eyes feast on my breasts and I love that he appears to struggle to shift his vision away. No man has ever made me feel as beautiful and wanted as Roarke. With one searing look, my body engulfs in flames that only he can dampen. I crave that feeling the more it comes.

"Fuck," he bites out, one hand cradling my breast, his thumb running over my already pebbled nipple.

My back arches, demanding more of his touch and hopefully his mouth.

Roarke is a man who picks up on signals though. He lowers his head, taking my nipple in his mouth, wetting the lace of a bra that did little to cover me. I grind harder into his lap, the need for a release skyrocketing to new heights. He unhooks my bra and the lace fabric pulls away from my chest. My breathing staggers as his lips travel the same path of his fingers down my arms until my bra falls to the floor.

"Hold on to me," he says and I move my hands back to his shoulders, my fingers digging into his muscled flesh.

He raises both of his hands, grabbing hold of my breasts, teasing my nipples. My eyes fall closed, reveling in his touch. Firm but gentle, nothing like I thought he would be. In my mind, he'd have my dress up to my waist and be thrusting inside of me by now.

"Time to lose the dress, Firecracker." The nickname he's taken to calling me makes it feel like cupid shot an arrow at my heart. I've never been given a special term of endearment by a man. I can't explain it, but it feels so right when he says it. Like it's something only the two of us will ever share with one another.

His hands and lips leave my body and he guides me into a standing position with his hands. As it has been, he controls the situation as his thumbs dig into the space between my flesh and my dress. With a little persistence, the fabric falls to the floor and I step out.

Roarke wastes no time before he yanks me forward and his lips press against my now exposed stomach. "You're way too perfect for me." His fingers slip under my panties, grab my ass and leaving no distance between us.

I twirl my fingers through his silver and brown hair, loving the way it falls in soft waves without the usual gel.

He rests his chin on my stomach staring up at me and I draw back to look into his eyes. Something is going on behind those gorgeous hazels. Something I don't quite recognize, because I don't think I've seen it before. A small piece of me hopes I get to see it again, though. That if Roarke and I somehow make it, he'll never stop looking at me like he's the luckiest guy in the world. A reminder of Todd's dull eyes focused on me, prick my heart with doubt, but I push any more thoughts of my ex away from this moment.

This is my moment with a man who has pursued me without apology. Shamelessly used leverage to adhere us together so he could win me over.

I run my hand running along his stubble. "You're over-dressed."

Our gazes stay locked as our hands glide along each other's bodies, none of our movements rushed. A small part of me wants to commit this to memory—worried that it's because we're lost in this small town far from the day-to-day realities in Chicago.

A shiver crests over my heated flesh as his fingers run up and down my naked body. He slides my panties down my legs and I step out of them, then fall to my knees in front of him. His hand cradles my cheek and my eyes close briefly before I strip him of his dress shirt. Pushing the fabric off his shoulders, his thumb runs along my lips and I snake my tongue out to suck on it. He inhales with a sharp hiss.

Satisfied, I take off his socks, then unbutton and unzip his slacks. He stands, and they join my dress on the floor, leaving him in only black boxer briefs.

I bite back a smile because if I were a betting woman, I would have beat the house. This man screams conservative right down to his underwear choices.

"Let me grab a condom." He leaves me for the first time in the past twenty minutes and my body chills.

I climb up the bed, laying on my back watching him dig through his bag, retrieving the foil packet. A giddiness whizzes through me over the fact that he's mine, if only for tonight.

"You make me wish I had a photographic memory." His voice is rough and strained as he stands at the end of the bed, his gaze searing my skin.

He wraps his fingers around my ankles and tugs me down the bed. "Did you think this would go along the lines of an old married couple with the missionary position?"

I laugh and tilt my head. "You have other plans?"

"I always have plans when it comes to you." He drops to his knees and positions my legs over his shoulders. "I need to know what you taste like."

His thumb runs along my folds, my hips rising off the bed. Dipping his thumb into my opening, he watches for my reaction. "I love that you're this wet for me."

Without another word, the scruff of his beard tickles the sensitive flesh of my inner thighs as he leans in. He licks, sucks, and twirls until I'm writhing under him begging for release. My fingers clutch the comforter, my thighs tightening around his head. He never stops. Not until I scream his name and my body lays limp on the bed.

The sound of the foil packet ripping open draws me from my post-orgasmic haze. I'm ready for more with this man and when the tip of his dick pushes into my wet core, I exhale on a sigh. Roarke slows his movements, his hands caging my head when his lips meet mine and he eases all the way inside me.

He's large and in charge and as he pulls me closer to the edge of the bed, I'm happy to let him do his thing.

He circles his hips and I lose any meaningful thinking

as his hands wrap around my waist so I don't inch up the mattress. My fingers grip the comforter underneath me until my knuckles are white. I arch my back as he drives up and into me, hitting a spot inside of me that makes it feel like too much and yet not enough.

This man has a wonder cock. Everything about him leaves me craving more.

At first, I bite down the urge to scream until he winds the string tighter and tighter. He unhooks my legs from around his waist and pulls my legs straight up so my feet are on either side of his head.

"Fuck," he says. Ohmygod he's right.

I'm right there with him. Fuck, it's so good. Fuck, I don't want it to end. Fuck, I'm going to combust. Fuck. Fuck. Fuck!

My entire body tenses and holds until the string snaps and I scream out his name as wave after wave of ecstasy drowns me.

Roarke pumps into me a few more times until he stills inside me.

"Fuck," he groans, and he lets my legs fall to the sides, his head falling to my neck before he casts light kisses across the top of my shoulder. "That was beyond anything I had imagined and I'd imagined a lot, and often."

I chuckle, still trying to catch my breath with the weight of a man I hated only forty-eight hours ago pressed against me.

A small part of me had wondered if after we'd had sex I'd have worked him out of my mind. That I'd be done with him. As he draws out of me, the emptiness inside me says I'm not even close to being done with Roarke Baldwin.

The good thing is that I think he's just getting started with me.

Chapter Twenty-Two

*A*cool sensation runs down my spine, stirring me awake. Roarke's warm naked body shelters me under the covers of the hotel bed. I moan from the mixture of hot and cold washing over my body.

The bed shifts and his strong hands and corded forearms lock on either side of my head.

"I really wanted to let you sleep," he murmurs.

He uses his tongue to help a new ice cube run down my back. Shivers erupt over my body, but by the time he's working his way back up my back, it's only his wet and hot tongue doing the teasing.

"You're going to be a disaster tomorrow morning," I say into the pillow.

"You mean this morning, and I'll be on a high from having you last night." His lips cast short kisses across my shoulders, tucking my hair to the side.

I swivel my head, craving the lips that have satisfied me so much through the night.

"Mmm," I moan into his mouth, his tongue perfecting the rhythm I've come to expect.

His lips draw to a close and he draws back, his fingers still gliding up and down my spine.

"I need to ask you something?" I can tell that whatever it is, we're not joking around anymore.

I turn on my side to face him. "What?" I ask.

"Us? Are you actually going to give this a go?"

I slide closer to him, my hand reaching around his body, wanting the heat he offers. His expression holds a fair amount of doubt. As though he's stayed up all night wondering if when I opened my eyes, I'd say it was a mistake. It will be hard with my words to convince him. He lives in a world where promises are broken and decisions are regretted every day.

I touch my lips to his jaw. His chiseled jaw that pulls that movie star look of his off so well.

"I forgive you, Roarke." I scoot up on the bed so we're face to face. "Not that you needed my forgiving, because you owed me nothing when you represented Todd. I guess what I'm saying is that I'm putting that in the past and I want to give this a try. The only thing I ask is that you always be truthful with me. I know you think I'm tough, but this is a huge step for me."

He smiles and rolls me over on my back, his eyes locked with mine. "You can trust me." He seals that promise with a kiss and for the next hour, I get lost in Roarke and his wonder cock once again.

▭

THE WEDDING WENT off without a fight between Allie or Wyatt. Roarke handed his sister off to what appears to be, a great man. No one stood to object as they said their vows, no one was late, and so far, we're midway through the reception with no hiccups.

My eyes scan the barnyard grass area lit with candles inside mason glass jars and strings of small lights. Huge bouquets of magnolias have been set on every available surface. I spot Roarke in his tuxedo, two glasses of champagne rest in his hands as he talks with Sean from the high school.

I stand to the side admiring the man who's quickly consuming everything I think about.

I don't have to wait long before he strolls across the grass and hands me a champagne glass.

"Thank you," I say, accepting his offer.

"Heartbeat" by Carrie Underwood comes on and he grabs my glass placing it down on the table before I even get a sip.

"Hey, you just gave that to me," I whine, but allow him to lead me to the dance floor.

The makeshift dance floor is beneath the star-filled sky with extra strands of twinkle lights set in the giant surrounding trees, making it feel straight out of a movie set.

Pulling me close to him, he tucks our hands between our bodies and wraps his other hand around my waist. Only a few other couples are on the dance floor and I'm positive everyone's eyes are pinned to us. But you'd never guess that from the way Roarke holds me close, softly singing in my ear. For a man who keeps his cards so close to his chest in Chicago, I'm surprised he's allowing these people to see him falling for the woman in his arms.

Is he falling for me? I think so. I'm trying like hell not to let the doubt of not being enough, make the ground under our new relationship unstable.

In the past twenty-four hours, I've had thoughts like 'we're rushing' and 'why am I picking him when I could easily find someone else?' As much as I denied my attraction to Roarke, it's always present when he enters a room I'm in. He got me faster than I would've predicted, but I honestly want to give us a try. After all, what girl really doesn't want someone to love her for her? Even if she protests that she's not looking for love.

Shelving those thoughts before I get carried away, I scan the outdoor gathering and notice Allie a few feet away poking her finger in Wyatt's chest.

"I hope there's not trouble in paradise already," I say, nodding in the newlyweds' direction.

He follows my line of vision and shakes his head. "That's just them. They're hot and cold."

We dance in silence for another minute before I ask a question that's plagued me since I started to develop feelings for him. "Why did you decide to become a divorce attorney?"

He glances behind me and I'm not sure who or what is there, but I'd bet that it has something to do with his answer.

"A lot of reasons. One being the money. I know it sounds bad, but I was a poor kid from a poor town. I scraped by to earn my degrees, sometimes working three jobs. I knew I couldn't defend criminals and be a defense attorney, and with the divorce rate rising every year I felt it was a safe bet at a successful career."

He waits for my response, but I don't really have one. What can I say? I grew up never having to worry about money. Jobs? Well, I worked for my father—he made me the businesswoman I am, but it's not like he made me punch a clock. My rent was paid, groceries delivered to my door. Once my trust was released, it sat in a bank account for me, reserved in case the stock market plummeted.

"Not so noble now right?" His smile says he's teasing. "I guess I still hold a lot of resentment about my dad leaving my mom and me behind to fend for ourselves. That'd be reason number two if I had to pick one." He draws back studying my eyes. I can't judge him because he's lived a life without everything I took for granted.

"Okay." I rest my head on his shoulder, my face cradled into his neck. His cologne does crazy things to my libido.

"That's it?" He tucks our hands tighter between us, his cheek resting on the top of my head.

"I just wondered." I shrug.

"Do you have an opinion on my answers?"

"Nope."

"So I give you a few orgasms and you don't fight me on anything anymore?" His chest vibrates with a laugh. "What happened to my little firecracker?"

I shake my head and close my eyes. "Don't get used to it."

He stiffens for a moment but relaxes as Carrie Underwood hits a high chord. "Why did you start RISE?"

I blow out a breath. "That's a long answer."

"We have time."

A few more couples join us on the dance floor and another slow song starts up. Straightening my head, I stare up into his eyes. Can I trust him?

The angel on my right says *he's trusted you with seeing where he came from.*

"You're going to think I'm a spoiled brat."

His hand leaves my hip, dragging along my body until he cradles my cheek. "Never. Come on." He nods for us to leave the dance floor.

A few minutes later, we're ducking through trees and shrubs hand in hand. Roarke's got a bottle of champagne in his free hand and we walk until we reach a clearing and end up at a dock. The moon casts a mirror image on the soft ripples in the lake. A few fishing boats are tied up along the dock, nothing compared to the yachts that filled marinas I grew up around.

The wooden planks whine as we sit down and hang our feet over the edge, each of our shoes laying at our sides.

As flawlessly as I'd expect, Roarke opens the champagne bottle, suds exploding out and dropping down into the lake.

"Crap, usually I'm better at that."

I laugh and my head falls to his shoulder. "I kind of like it that you're not as perfect as you appear."

His eyebrows crinkle as he looks over to me. "I'm far from perfect."

If I was an honest woman, I'd tell him that to me he's perfect. Other than the part about him representing my ex, but I'm trying to see past that.

"You seem like you've seduced a lot of women in your day. Always a gentleman in public, but the way you know your way around a woman's body..." Even in the moonlight, I spot the slight flush to his cheeks.

"I'm glad my act is working, but there isn't an enormous list of women in front of you if that's what you're asking."

Am I? I don't know. Probably. I'm always a glutton for punishment.

"I'm not."

A tinge of jealousy hits me again thinking about the women who came before me. Did anyone of them hold his heart?

"Stop changing the subject, I snuck you out here so you'd tell me about RISE." He hands the champagne bottle to me.

I take a sip and hand it back to him.

"You trying to give me liquid courage?" I ask with a chuckle.

"You know I always aim to make you as comfortable as possible."

I knock my shoulder to his and roll my eyes. "Hmm…I always thought those were 'get in my pants' lines."

He hands me back the bottle, then holds his hands up in the air. "I don't mean them to be."

"Uh-huh."

"So, Firecracker, why did you start RISE?"

No matter how much I try to push this conversation in a different direction, he sets us back on the path. Embarrassment makes me flush and I take a deep breath. "I grew up with expectations. My mom had me in etiquette classes and always tried to instill the belief in me that I should stand in the shadow of the man I married. As I grew older, my fellow debutantes married into wealth similar to their parents. They stood behind the men they married and learned how to throw the best cocktail parties and how to please their husbands by making them look good in the eyes of the people that surrounded them."

"You don't seem the type." He entwines his fingers through mine, the familiar flutter in my belly starts to stir.

"That's because you met me after the fairy tale had torn at the seams. I wasn't the first of my friends to be cheated on, but I was the first one who left. You could say it was my dad's doing. After all, I was the only one of my friends who got an education in business. Most of my girlfriends clung to their mom's teachings of how to find the right personal shopper and where the best place for brunch was. My mom always tried to get me to fill that role, but she never really had that much success. I was much closer to my dad, who was a doting father…as I grew up, I started to realize that my mom had very little interest in me."

"I still remember the first time I figured out my mom had a drinking problem," Roarke says. "The telescope from a kid's perspective can be gentle."

I nod because he's right.

"Yeah, it can be like a punch to the gut when you finally realize what's been there all along. Anyway, we don't need to dig into my childhood issues." I take a sip from the champagne bottle and set it beside me on the dock. "The psychologist my mother hired when I was sixteen because I was acting out delved into that enough. After I found out about Todd's cheating, something snapped inside of me. My mom's response was that men will be men. My response was to hire a private investigator to find out if my father had someone on the side. The thought of my father not being the man I thought he was might've torn me apart more than seeing Todd with his mistress."

"And?"

I shake my hand. "Nope. He was clean. He only goes to the golf course, the club, work, and home. My father has always looked at my mom in awe, like he can't believe she's his. If I couldn't believe in that, I'm not sure I'd ever stand a chance to believe in love again. But while my mother was convincing me that it might have somehow been my fault that Todd didn't stay faithful—that maybe I was too moody or the fact that I didn't organize a thirtieth birthday party for him, sent the wrong message…she even suggested I read books on sex."

"Trust me, you have no problems in that area." He kisses my neck. "I still get hard remembering you beneath me. Todd's a bastard who let the perfect woman slip through his fingers."

I smile at his kind gesture to try and reassure me, but

any doubts of what I could've done to save my marriage left the minute I filed for divorce.

"That's sweet." I take back another swig of champagne, the bubbles tickling my throat. "My dad told me to cut off his nuts. Said he'd pay for the lawyer, but that ultimately the decision was mine. If I decided to stay with Todd, he would respect my choice, but he didn't have to be cordial to him. The funny thing is that I almost felt relieved that I could end the marriage and not be seen as an ungrateful brat who didn't know how good she had it. I hated all the dinners at nine at night when he was just getting home, and always being interrupted by his co-workers or his beeper. I hated the way I was expected to not have an opinion on anything of importance. By the end of our marriage, he was already sleeping in another room, using the excuse of his schedule. I didn't want to be married to Todd, but I felt trapped in that life."

"I hate myself for representing that prick," Roarke grinds out then takes the champagne bottle from me and tilts it to his lips.

"That's the reason I had to start a foundation where girls learn to know that they have a voice. They can speak their minds and have their own thoughts and beliefs they can own and no one should be trying to silence them." I shrug. "I see so many of my friends whose happiness lies in the mood of their husband. I might never have a daughter, but I don't want any girl to live a life like that. You'd think the world was over gender bias, but it's not."

"Just when I think I couldn't be more attracted to you." His hand lands on my cheek and he turns me to face him. "I want to promise you something because I know trusting me is hard for you. I told you I don't break promises. *Ever*. I promise to never speak for you. I'll never order for you at a restaurant. Your opinion is always welcome even if we don't see eye-to-eye, which let's be honest, is going to happen. I promise to value you as an equal, always. If we walk in this relationship together, it's going to be side-by-side—not with me leading and you following."

A tear wells in my eye, because he's the first man I opened up to after my divorce and his response couldn't be more perfect.

I give him a soft smile. "I never knew such a soft teddy bear was hidden under the grizzly bear facade."

He leans in closer. "You never wanted to find out. But I'm glad you did." He presses his lips to mine and his tongue slides along the seam of my mouth. I don't just give him access to my mouth, I open the entire vault and let him into my life, consequences be damned.

<h1 style="text-align:center">Chapter Twenty-Three</h1>

"You're glowing again," Victoria mumbles passing me by in the hallway as she runs to answer an early morning phone call.

"Am not."

"Are too." We bicker like two siblings telling our mom the other spilled the Coke all over the carpet. "Good morning, RISE," she answers. "Oh, hi."

"What's new?" I peek my head into Chelsea's office.

She's pale and has a sheen of sweat over her face. "Not a good morning. Ask me at lunch."

I laugh and step away giving her some space. Pregnancy seems downright awful to me and I'm not even privy to how scared her and Dean must be about the health of their baby since she has a rare condition that decreases her odds of a successful pregnancy.

"It's your dad," Victoria whispers to me, covering the receiver. "Uh-huh. A handicap of thirteen? That's great. You must really be in the zone these days."

I smile at her failed attempt to talk golf with my dad.

"Oh yes, 'course, sorry. I'll just pass you over to

Hannah… Anytime, I'm sure he'd love to. Hold on one second," she says.

My line rings on my office phone and I pick up. "Are you that desperate to talk to someone you choose to torment my assistant with your golf handicap and try to lure her boyfriend out?"

He chuckles, that deep in his throat one I'm used to. The one that means too many cigars the night before. Must have been guy's night out.

"You should come and join me or find a real man who plays. Should've known Todd was a loser from the moment I played with him. Didn't know how to angle his approach."

I pick up my pen, teetering it back and forth in my fingers. "Good thing you don't need to worry about that now."

"Yes, thankfully. I need you to organize your mother's birthday party. I'd do it, but she'll figure me out. I'll say I had to loan you some money, deposit it in your bank account."

My parents have had access to my bank accounts so they could deposit since I was old enough to take out money.

"I'm really pressed for time with the gala, Dad, and Mom's birthday is practically right after. Can't we just skip a big do this year?"

"No." He uses the stern voice I've heard only a few times like when he found me and Beau Thornton with weed in our basement when I was sixteen. I'm still impressed that I kept the secret that Beau pissed himself when my dad hauled him up to the wall by his Lacoste polo.

"Can I hire someone?" I ask.

"Clearly, you have your marketing director handling

the gala. You've been organizing that for months. If you're doing what I taught you to do, you're in the final stages which means there's not much more you can do at this point. I'm asking you to plan a small gathering for your mother. We can use one of the private rooms at the club. She needs to know we love and adore her." The strong female I usually am would tell anyone else absolutely not, but it's my father and as many issues as my mother and I have had over the years, I still love her.

"I'll get it handled. Send me a guest list."

"There's the daughter I raised." I can hear the smile in his voice. "Your mother loves you and has done a lot for you. Remember that."

I don't remark on having to go with my friend and her mother to prom dress shop. Or the fact that she sent someone directly to me to fit me for the debutante ball she made me be a part of. Or the fact that the last time I ate a meal with her the sole focus was her wondering what the social fallout would be of my divorce.

"I have to get back to work." I tap the pen from side to side on my desk.

"I haven't seen you at any functions in a while. Is there a man taking up your time?"

I chew on the inside of my cheek. Do I tell him or leave it for a surprise? Shit. I don't even know how my dad will react. I'm not going to hide Roarke, but he's not from our world. Even if his bank account would rival those that are, he wasn't bred into society like I was.

"I may bring someone to Mom's party. It's early and I don't want to say anything too soon." That's an honest answer and I kind of want to pat myself on the back for coming up with it spur of the moment.

"What's his name? Do I know him?" my dad asks.

"Like I said, you'll find out at Mom's party if we're still

going strong." I reach for my cup of coffee with my free hand and take a swig.

I delay the inevitable. My mom for sure will delve into her own dark web search to find out everything she can about Roarke. She always makes sure she has more information than anyone else, so she'll never be surprised if someone else digs something up before her.

"Okay, okay." He chuckles to himself, lightening the mood. "Let me know if you need anything. Make it small and intimate. You know your mom doesn't like to be a burden."

I just about choke on my coffee. Are we talking about the same woman?

"Sure thing. Just send me the list asap so I can get the invitations out."

"Of course, I'll work on it this morning. I can't wait to meet this boy of yours."

He's far from a boy.

"Okay, Dad, gotta go."

"I'm coming to the city later in the week. I have to talk to Cliff, get an update on our hedge fund. Let's do lunch."

I release a breath. "Sure, give me a call."

"Bye, Han. Don't let this new guy walk all over you."

"I won't, Dad. Bye." My fingers press on the button to end the call and my head falls down onto my desk.

"Didn't mean to eavesdrop, but you have to plan a birthday party?" Victoria arrives in the doorway. "That took the glow from your cheeks." She sits down in the chair in front of me looking all cute in a Tiffany-blue dress.

"Yeah, but I'm calling in a favor from my event organizer. No way I'm planning her party just to be ridiculed about choosing the wrong linens and flowers." I grab my phone searching for the number of the woman who does all the events at the club. She'll make sure everything is up to my mom's standards.

"You really don't like your mom, huh?"

I click on the number and my thumb hovers while I continue talking to Victoria. "Neither of us care much for the other. I'm a constant disappointment and she's always advising me on how I could've been a perfect wife if I'd only cut out my tongue."

"She said that?" Victoria's mouth goes slack jaw.

"No, but heavily implied my sharp tongue needs controlling if I'm ever going to keep a man."

"She's so different than my mother." She shakes her head.

"Your mom is nothing like mine, believe me."

"I thought something was up since she's never set foot in the office or called the office line." She stands, seeing my phone lit up, waiting to call the person. Forever the perfect assistant and I'm going to miss her help when I promote her.

"Yeah, there's no scheduled lunch dates and I'd never trust her with my daughter if I ever had one."

Victoria's mouth dips down. I'm sure it's a buzzkill since her, Jade, and her mom are like a three-generation trio of love. "I'll let you make that call then. Can I handle anything for you? Balloons? Entertainment? Just let me know."

"You're the best ever, thanks."

Her lips turn up into her usual optimistic smile and she shuts the door on her way out.

I make the phone call and luckily Tracy is more than happy to organize a Crowley event. She gushes on how much she loves my mom and I'm pretty sure she'll make the event jaw-dropping amazing. I snap my usual enthusiasm into place because we wouldn't want anyone getting the idea that I don't want to plan her party. Let them believe I'm just swamped with this non-profit foundation I'm running. My mother can spin anything the way she wants. Good ol' mother, reputation is key.

Chelsea walks in as I end the call.

"Am I bothering you?" She sits down in the chair in front of me. No papers in her hand, no phone clutched in her grip. Fear that she's turning in her notice wraps around me.

"Not at all. What's up?" I ask.

"We have a situation. The venue usually uses this one caterer, but that caterer has to work another event for some family member or something. So we need to find a great caterer on short notice for the gala." She cringes, and her outward expression matches my inward one.

"Okay," I say, using my computer to pull up a list of caterers.

"I've literally called all the big ones. I'm on a waitlist, but everyone else has bad Yelp ratings and I didn't think this would be the time to try out a newbie." She crosses her legs, her arms clasped in her lap, her face holding a green tint.

"Are you okay?" I side eye her.

"Let's just say all those sweets I've been eating? I'm not going to have to worry about gaining a pound."

"Morning sickness?"

"Yeah, but as long as my body isn't my own, I'm happy. Means the little bean is still there." She tries to smile, but it doesn't reach her eyes. I can't even imagine what she and Dean are going through. Every day waiting for the ball to drop.

"What have the doctors said?" I press print and the hum of my printer fills my office.

She crosses her fingers in the air. "All good things…so far."

"Special delivery!" Victoria comes in holding a box.

Normally I might have assumed it was for me, but since Chelsea is always getting deliveries from Dean, I'm not surprised when Victoria hands the present over to her.

"We're going to have no money to raise this kid." This time her smile does reach her eyes, her cheeks round, and her eyes glisten.

Do I look like that when I'm with Roarke?

"Um…I'm pretty sure that's an exaggeration," Victoria says.

We both wait, eager for Chelsea to open the gift. Dean is definitely an outside the box kind of gift giver.

She pulls another wrapped gift from the cardboard box. It's in Cubs wrapping paper. She reads the note and places it on my desk then giggles to herself and tears off the packaging.

Victoria eyes the note on the edge of my desk. "May I?"

"Sure," she answers, her concentration intent on opening the box.

"Thought tearing the paper would be a good stress reliever. Love, Dean," Victoria reads it and then sets it back on the desk.

"He's right, that felt good to rip the blue and red," she says with a smile.

She opens the clothing box and I'm expecting to see some sexy lingerie, but she pulls out a little onesie. A note that was folded within the fabric slips back into the box and she places the onesie down to read the letter. This time she reads it aloud. "We can be the first people to raise a crosstown lover. No picking sides. Love, Dean."

Victoria awes as Chelsea holds the onesie back up. It

has the Cubs logo on one side, Sox on the other. The back has a number one and the name Bennett. One tear falls down Chelsea's cheek, and then another, and then another until there's a cascade of them.

"Let's not ruin this." Victoria grabs the box and I snatch a tissue to hand over to her.

Chelsea accepts, dotting under her eyes. "I'm seriously losing all control. He's so sweet. I can't believe he's mine," she sobs, her sentences barely making any sense between the hiccups of her labored breathing. I think she said something about their past and how sometimes you just know and why did she try to fight it.

Victoria and I let her get everything out of her system. "Chelsea, go call Dean and thank him. Maybe ask him to lunch," I suggest because at this rate she'll never find a caterer for me.

"No." She swipes the tears but more fall. "I'll get control of myself. I'm a professional." She says the words like I am Superwoman. She is, but not today. Today she's a pregnant woman whose hormones are tormenting her.

"Go. It's fine. I'm sure Dean will love the surprise."

She stands, and Victoria hands her the box with the onesie and notes, sharing a look to me like this isn't the last of her outbursts. I wonder what stage will come next?

"I'll just go have lunch," Chelsea says.

"Please, we know you're going to have an afternoon delight." Victoria laughs, spurring Chelsea to change her tears into a chuckle.

"Now that you mention it." She wiggles her ass on the way out of my office.

Two minutes later she's waving goodbye and heading out the main door.

"You know she's gone for the day, right?" Victoria asks, walking over to the doorway.

"She deserves it."

"I should convince Reed it's time to have a baby," she jokes.

"Something tells me that boy will do it the traditional way." My phone vibrates on my desk.

"You know it. I keep half expecting him to propose to speed things along. He's hardly the type who waits around for the time to be right." She pats the entryway of my door and heads back to her desk.

My phone dances across my desk, reminding me it's ringing.

"Hello?" I answer, not looking at the caller ID. Hopefully it's not Tracy telling me the club is booked. No way do I want to find a restaurant.

"I miss you." Roarke's deep voice sets my body on high alert.

"You saw me this morning." I pick up my pen, teetering it back and forth.

"Exactly. It's been too long. Torrio's at six?"

"You don't plan on feeding me?"

He chuckles. "Do you want the gentleman to answer that question?"

"No."

"I'll feed you something substantial, but you'll still be hungry after."

I press my thighs together. "You call me at noon to torment me?"

His deep chuckle rings through the line. "Am I tormenting you?"

"What do you think?"

"Oh Firecracker, I hope that I am." A phone beeps in the background and I catch his name said by a sweet woman's voice, one that sounds much younger than my own.

"You have to go?" I ask.

"I do. For the first time in my life, I want to play hooky."

"Well, I just sent home my marketing manager."

"Tempting baby, but I've got back to back meetings with clients. Can't people be civilized?"

The beep comes through again but before she can say anything, he must hit a button to reply. "Please tell Mr. Quinton that I'll call him back."

"No, Roarke. It's fine. I have to go find a caterer for the gala anyway."

"What does Sonya say about the one they usually use?"

"I guess they're not available. Hopefully I'm not having taco trucks, not that I personally would oppose."

"Do you like tacos?" he asks and I'm reminded that he never gives up an opportunity to find out something about me.

"I do."

"Then I'll be feeding you tonight after Torrio's. See you tonight, Han."

"Bye."

The line clicks dead and the fact he called me by Han, something more intimate than my full name, makes me giddy inside.

Until the client's name he spoke to his receptionist finally makes its way through the lust induced haze Roarke initiates.

Mr. Quinton?

It couldn't be him, right? No way.

Chapter Twenty-Four

I scan through my contacts and press the green button when I see her name immediately. It rings and rings, but I get her voicemail, "You've reached Scarlet. I'm probably at Saks with hubby's credit card. Leave a message and I'll ring you right after I grab Starbucks." A long beep sounds.

"Scar, it's Han. Just checking in. It's been so long. Give me a call and we'll do lunch."

I click the red button to end the call and swivel my chair to stare out the window. I rotate my phone in my hand, hitting my thigh with each turn, I flip it. It has to be a coincidence, but with that asshole being friends with Todd, I can see the referral happening over scotch at the club. Todd's annoying voice in my head, 'Roarke Baldwin got me everything I didn't deserve. Hannah can spare it, she's still sitting on millions.'

Since Scarlett doesn't call back, I decide to conduct a social media stalking. Surely, if they're divorcing, Facebook or Instagram will reflect that. Going on my own Instagram account, I'm reminded that I suck at social media. The last picture I posted was the day I got Lucy and some lame comments from my friends are there saying they miss me. If they miss me so much why don't they pick up a phone and call me?

I click on Scarlett's profile and a million pictures of her, David, and the kids are the first thing I see. They're on a beach somewhere and she's all smiles. There's another with David's arm swung over her shoulders with a caption explaining that it was date night. They've all been taken within the last month.

I'm drawing the wrong conclusions. I mean we're in a city of millions, surely there's another Quinton around who could afford Roarke's services.

My phone buzzes with a text and I hope it's from Scarlett, but it's Roarke.

Roarke: *Here's a caterer, I've used him and he's good. Maybe try him out.*

Listed is a name and phone number, nothing else. No company name or address to visit.

Since I'm already on my computer, I type in Google and find nothing. What am I missing here?

Roarke: *Counting the hours until six. By the way, you and Lucy are spending the weekend at my place.*
Me: *You don't dictate what I do.*
Roarke: *My bad…will you and your overzealous dog spend the weekend with me and Nickel?*
Me: *You forgot the magic word.*
Roarke: *Orgasm?*

I giggle and Victoria smiles into my office as she passes by.

Me: *Wrong word.*
Roarke: *Cunnilingus?*
Me: *Wrong again. I'm inspecting my nails now.*
Roarke: *Please will my Firecracker agree to spend the weekend at my house, so I can fuck you until your throat is hoarse from screaming and your body is limp. Better?*
Me: *Well, thank you for the please. I could have done without the other stuff.*
Roarke: *I don't believe you. Want me to continue? Shut your office door.*
Me: *I have to call this mysterious caterer who has no reviews.*
Roarke: *If I was there I'd have you bent over your desk and my hand would be slapping your ass while I drove into you.*
Me: *Well you're not.*
Roarke: *I have two minutes before my meeting. I can get you off if you just hike up that skirt.*
Me: *How do you know I'm wearing a skirt?*

I had left his place early this morning and changed at my house.

Roarke: *I always visualize you with a dress or skirt on. Easy access in my fantasies. ;)*
Me: *You are something, all right.*
Roarke: *I'm all yours. So no quickie orgasm? My client is starting to give me the stink eye.*
Me: *You have a client with you right now!?*
Roarke: *I told you, we're waiting for the meeting to start.*
Me: *And you were going to talk dirty to me?*
Roarke: *I think I've proven that I'm a multi-tasker.*
Me: *Bye, Roarke. See you tonight.*
Roarke: *I'll be thinking about how wet you are. See you at six. Give the guy a call, he's good. Promise.*

I have a feeling that man will forever keep me surprised.

Trusting Roarke has been easy in the few short weeks we've been together and I know he'd never give me a reference he wasn't more than one hundred percent sure would deliver, so I pick up my cell phone and dial the number he sent me.

———

AT SIX ON THE DOT, I walk into Torrio's and I'm not surprised to find Roarke there already waiting. His gaze stays on me the entire journey to my usual table and I'm not embarrassed to admit that yes, I do add a little extra flare to my hips, just for viewing pleasure.

"Just so you know, this table is mine," I say.

There aren't assigned tables at Torrio's, but me and the girls always sit at this same one.

"You're not going to share with your boyfriend?" he asks, putting on a lost puppy dog expression.

I slide into the opposite side of the circular booth, but he slides closer to the middle, patting the space right next to him.

"Do I have to beg for a hello kiss?" he asks as though I'd have a choice. Not that I'm about to deny a lip-tingling kiss from him.

"Boyfriend?" I ask once we part and a Vesper is placed in front of me by the waiter. "Thanks, Lincoln."

"I'm not sure how I feel about Linc knowing your drink order and not me." His raised eyebrows pull a giggle from me.

"Jealous much?" I tease.

"When it comes to you, green is my color." He tips his drink to his lips.

Maybe alarms should be setting off in my mind, but I love the fact that he'd be jealous of another man. God knows, Todd never was. Still, the strong independent woman inside of me says I don't want some caveman who pounds his fist to anyone who gets within a mile radius. But the lovesick teenage girl who's still there says a little jealousy is a compliment.

"Nothing to be jealous about, I would never do that to someone." I push back the crippling lack of self-esteem that suffocated me when I found out about Todd's cheating.

"It's not you I'm worried about. I know what happens in a guy's mind. The fact is that I envisioned you naked when you sat across from me for the first time in that discovery meeting." He leans closer not finishing his sentence. "It didn't do the reality justice."

His fingers skim along my thigh and I press into his touch, always craving more.

"I thought you were going to feed me?" I ask, wanting to speed this night along so we can get back to either one of our apartments.

"After we finish our drinks. Tell me about your day. Did you call Jett?" He continues to sip his scotch neat and I bring the Vesper to my lips, the citrus flavor bursting on my taste buds.

I nod but move us to another topic that's peaked my interest. "We could've gone anywhere, why here?" I have a feeling he's a little more caveman than I originally thought.

I've noticed a few men's gazes cast over to our table, spurring hushed whispers between them.

He chuckles, sipping his drink again. "Can I get anything by you?"

"Is this what I think this is?" I ask again wanting a

straight answer. I'm not even sure how I feel about the fact he brought me here as a trophy to parade around.

"You spend a lot of time here, no?" he asks, finishing the last vestiges of scotch in his glass.

"Yes."

"Come here with your girlfriends?"

I nod, sipping my drink.

"Think of it as saving you the uncomfortableness of having to tell an eager male that you're now taken." He slides his now empty glass away from him.

Again that hear-me-roar woman and the teenage girl fight a few rounds in my head.

"I'm seeing this more as you staking your claim," I say.

His lips turn up into his cocky grin. "Is that a bad thing?"

"It means you're using me as a status symbol or a belonging of yours. I am my own person." I push the Vesper away from me and slide out of the booth.

"Hannah?" he asks, sounding confused.

Keeping up appearances so as to not to give this group more gossip than they already have, I set my gaze on him. "I am not your piece on the side. I am not yours to own, Roarke. I am your…girlfriend. I have my own mind. I make my own decisions. I have my own life. I'm not the shiny fire hydrant at the end of the block you piss around to warn others off."

I turn on my heels heading for the door, smiling politely at the fellow patrons who had their attention set on us the entire time.

"Good night, Sam." I nod, and he opens the door for me.

I stroll down the alley until a hand wraps around my wrist and whips me around, pressing my back to the brick wall.

Roarke steps closer and his steady gaze is fixed to mine, his chest is rising and falling in rapid succession. "You have no idea, do you?" he asks, his tone curt and contrite.

"I don't have time for his." I step to the side, but his hand lands on my hip, stopping me.

"Ms. Crowley." Sam's booming voice echoes down the alley.

Roarke's eyes don't move from mine.

"I'm good, Sam. Thank you."

"Are you sure?" he asks.

"Fucking Christ," Roarke mumbles.

"I'm sure." I lift my voice so he knows this might be a lover's quarrel, but Roarke would never hurt me. Something inside of me says that anyway. I know Sam's eyes will be locked on the security cameras in case I'm wrong.

"Okay," he says reluctantly and the door shuts and my attention shifts back to Roarke.

"Do you have any idea how many men in that room want you?" he asks. "How they ogle you? Make remarks about your tight ass or your perky tits? I've already made threats to half of them already. I'm sorry Hannah, I know you are your own woman and I love that quality of yours, but those men in there will know from today on that you are mine. Am I claiming you? Hell yes, I am."

My chest heaves and I know I should push him away. Shove him to the side and run.

"I'm not going to apologize for it." I feel like he's testing me.

"I don't belong to anyone," I bite out.

He lowers his head, his lips millimeters from mine. "I'm an equal opportunity guy. Would it help if you can claim me too?"

I close my eyes and his lips press to mine and then disappear.

"I've been yours for an entire year," he murmurs.

I wind my hands around his neck, pulling him into me, murmuring between kisses. "I never knew you were so soft." I grin.

His hands slide down and grip my ass, thrusting me into his pelvis. "Does this feel soft to you?"

"Take me home," I say.

His lips are hard and firm as they land on mine again. My stomach rumbles and the vibration of his laugh ripples through his chest. "I need to feed you first."

A phone rings and he steps back from me, leaving my body chilled even though the humidity in the ninety-degree heat should make me sweat.

"I have to get this. Hold on." He steps away, lowering his voice when he answers. A horn honks and then a siren goes off. By the time the siren fades into the background, he's tucking his phone back into his jacket.

"Everything okay?" I ask as he approaches me.

His jaw is tight, but he forces a smile onto his face that does nothing to convince me it's sincere.

"Fine. Just something I forgot to handle earlier."

His hand slides into mine and he leads me down the alley. He'll always have a lot of work related issues and with the whole attorney-client privilege I should get used to not knowing everything when it comes to him.

"So we cleared that up, right?" I ask because I think I may have lost my point somewhere between our kiss and his erection.

"Yeah, we own one another." His hand flies in the air to wave down a cab.

"I have a feeling that this won't be our last fight about this topic."

A cab pulls up to the curb and he opens the door, so I

can slide in. His large body presses to mine immediately and he rambles an address to the driver.

"Let's just enjoy tonight."

His hand lands on my thigh, his fingers dipping between my legs and the topic evaporates from my mind, replaced only with lust.

Chapter Twenty-Five

Roarke: *Meet me at 5491 S. Shore Drive. Bring Lucy.*

I read the text one more time as Lucy and I step out of the car. She pulls on her leash and I barely shut the door before I'm halfway through a tunnel.

"Slow down girl." I try to show her the authority the dog trainer told me to, but I'm the worst dog owner ever or she's the most stubborn dog ever.

Once we're out of the tunnel, Lake Michigan and a large lawn of grass fill my vision. There's families, couples, dogs, and kids enjoying a nice Saturday. My eyes scan all the faces, trying to see why Roarke would have sent me to this.

Then I step farther into the lush green carpet of grass and my eyes find Roarke.

Usually my heart flips when I see him. My entire body responds with flutters and excitement boiling inside of me until I think I might burst. It's the best feeling and I hope it never vanishes if we stay together for a long time.

Today none of those things happen because he's

standing at the edge of the lake with a woman. A blonde who's smiling up at him like he's her savior and not in a brotherly type way. She's all teeth, tits and toes out. She's wearing a short mini skirt with a tight tank top, the strings of a bikini peeking out and wrapped around her neck. She's also much younger than me.

I watch them for a moment, and I know why I'm doing it. Back before I'd been burned, I would have stalked up to them, slid my hand through his arm, and claimed him just like he did me at Torrio's the other night.

But this is after and so I keep my distance, investigating and scrutinizing every smile, every shifting of weight and every look they give one another.

Roarke's hands stay tucked in his shorts. He never leans forward toward her, but she steps closer with every word. With his back to me, I can't see his face, but damn I wish I could when she grabs the hem of her shirt, stripping it off her body to reveal a large pair of tits along with a smooth and taut stomach. Tucking her tank top in the back of her shorts she uses the excuse to push out her tits in his direction.

The war inside of me continues. Do I want him to take the bait just to prove my notion that all men cheat?

Lucy pulls and the leash slips from my grasp.

"Shit!"

Lucy barrels through the picnic goers and I quickly make chase.

"Mommy, that lady swore," one little girl tattles as I race by.

I glance at the mom with apologetic eyes as I run by. "I'm sorry!"

I'm sorry seems to be a chorus as I weave around families trying to enjoy a nice summer afternoon without a dog trampling them.

"Lucy!" I scold, but she completely ignores me, her attention set on something, her feet galloping like a damn horse.

Her tail wags and she jumps off a poor boy's back, skidding to a stop right on the edge of the grass and the sidewalk along the lake.

"Lucy!" I step on her leash until my hands can wrap it around my wrist twice. "I'm so sorry." I apologize and glance up, finally seeing what's in front of me.

Roarke.

His face pales, but without missing a beat, he bends at his knees and pets Lucy.

"Lucy girl. Why do you give your mom such a hard time?" He smiles looking over her to me.

I'm sure my face is beet red from the running and the embarrassment of having ruined people's picnics.

"You asked me to bring her why?" My tone is that of an ungrateful thirteen-year-old who was asked to watch her baby brother.

"It's a gorgeous day and she needs to get out of that condo." Roarke leans over my out-of-its-mind dog, placing a chaste kiss on my lips. "This is Aspen." He holds his hand out to the pretty young girl who was flirting with him.

As usual, I plaster on my wonderful to meet you smile and extend my hand. Her small dainty hand slides into mine for the briefest of seconds before her vision shifts back to Roarke. "Nice to meet you," I say.

"Aspen, this is Hannah, my girlfriend."

Roarke might miss the slight fall of her smile, but he's not a woman. A woman who is scrutinizing this entire situation.

"Oh," she says. "I didn't know."

"And you two know each other how?" My finger wavers between the two.

Roarke runs his fingers through his hair. A telltale sign that it's a question he's unsure how to answer and for a second I regret asking. Until the independent woman stands strong inside of me and says it is my business.

"Well…" Aspen looks to Roarke for an answer.

"We're friends. I helped her out once."

Helped her out with an orgasm, I'm sure.

Then it dawns on me. I guess she could be a client and under the client-lawyer confidentiality agreement Roarke might not be able to tell me much more than what he said.

"That's nice. How he always helps everyone out."

Even I realize how stupid my comment is, but this is uncomfortable and I have a dog that won't stop pulling on her leash every damn time a bird flies overhead, which is all the time down by the lake.

"Yeah, he's like a male Mother Teresa," Aspen says, humor lighting her crystal blue eyes.

Roarke smiles tightly.

"Well, have a great day, Aspen. Perfect day for a run."

He looks up at the sky and grabs a backpack leaning against the rock, then swings it over his shoulder and untangles the leash from my hands.

"Great running into you," she says. "You know how to find me if ever…" Her gaze falls to me and her words trail off. "Nice to meet you, Hannah."

She sets off in a light jog down the sidewalk. Roarke starts walking in the opposite direction and I chance a look over my shoulder, finding her running backward staring at us. She quickly spins around when she spots me and disappears between the other runners and bikers on the path.

"She's cute." My tone suggests there's something more than he's already mentioned.

His arm weighs heavy over my shoulders and he pulls me into his side. "You already claimed me, remember?"

When my only response is an evil eye, he waggles his eyebrows. "I like you jealous. I'll show you tonight how much you don't need to be though."

The usual electric bolt hits its intended target between my legs and I decide to try not to let the mystery girl ruin our day.

"So, what are your plans?" I ask.

His arm slides off my shoulders, and he captures my hand. "You want to know what I have planned for tonight or for right now?"

I hip check him. "Now, Casanova."

He chuckles, stopping us mid-path and a few people grumble having to walk around either side of us. His lips capture mine and I forget about all the people upset about being disrupted and lose myself in his masterful tongue that does crazy things to my sanity.

Drawing our kiss to a close, his hands don't leave my hips and his forehead falls to mine. "You are the only woman I'm seeing."

"I never asked."

"The question was implied and I want you to always remember that. I'm not that type of man."

He waits until I nod that I've heard him, and my heart that's already way too invested pleads desperately to believe him. Unfortunately, Roarke will suffer the consequences from the man who fell in line before him. I remember Todd telling me something similar right after I caught him in a lie about working late. He went on and on about how much he loved me and asked me questions like what kind of an idiot would he be if he cheated on me? I'm regretful now that I believed him, but Roarke has given me no reason to think anything is amiss. One weird phone call and a run in at a park where he asked me to meet him aren't reasons to assume I'm not the only woman in his life.

"Come on. The wine is probably losing its chill," he says.

He takes my hand and we fall in line after an eager Lucy toward a patch of grass.

For the rest of the afternoon, Roarke feeds me watermelon with cheese and crackers while I sip an expensive glass of Pinot Grigio. We lay on a plaid blanket that to my surprise doesn't have square indents that would imply he just took it out of the package this morning. Our shoes are off, and we gaze out at the lake.

"What a beautiful day," I say, eyeing Lucy playing with a few kids from the multi-family cookout a few feet away. She's laying on the ground letting them pet her belly.

"It's only beautiful because you're here with me." Roarke's hip meets mine, his arm behind my back and his lips on my bare shoulder.

"You and your lines. You know they usually say that a man who has so many lines is not truthful."

I look at the boats out on the water that are spurring the waves to crash a little higher over the cement ledge.

"Who says that?" He continues to kiss my shoulder, his hand running up to my cheek. Turning me to face him, his lips land on mine for a second. "I only say what I feel. There's no other agenda on my part." He kisses me one more time, but with families nearby he keeps our affection PG.

I dig through the watermelon, searching for a piece without the frail white seeds.

"Besides," he says, "I've already gotten you into bed. What would be the point of sweet talking you now?"

My hands drop, and I tilt my head with a 'you didn't' expression. He chuckles and I pick up a cracker and throw it at his face.

"Maybe I should sleep at my own house tonight." Both my eyebrows raise.

"You're only hurting yourself if you do." He holds a piece of watermelon in front of my lips, one without the white seeds. A perfectly ripe piece from the outside layer, red and juicy just like I love it.

"You think so?" I ask.

He runs the sweet fruit along my lips.

"You're sweeter tasting than this fruit."

Heat warms my core with his words. He lets me nibble on the piece of cold watermelon and brings my wine glass to my lips.

"That's what I'm going to do to you when I get you home. I'm going to put you on my counter, slide your panties down your legs and bury my head under your skirt until my scalp is sore from you tugging on my hair." The wine disappears and the cold watermelon is back at my lips. "Still want to go to your house?"

I open my mouth, snatching the watermelon with my teeth, sliding it off his fingers. The juicy sweetness explodes inside my mouth and I swallow it down, staring at Roarke the entire time.

"That sounds okay, but what else do you have planned?"

It takes a moment for him to realize I'm joking, but when he does, his fingers attack my ribs and I fall back on the blanket in a fit of laughter. I'm in the moment and it isn't until his hard erection thrusts between my open legs that I realize we're in public.

"Roarke!" I smack his shoulders, but he moans, his lips falling down from my collarbone to in between my breasts.

My eyes blink open and no one is staring above me with disapproving grins, but when I turn to find Lucy, all five kids' eyes are poised directly at me.

"Roarke!" I hit him again and he looks up.

"I'm just getting started."

Then he sees what I'm talking about and he sits up, positioning my skirt over my now wet panties.

"Maybe we're not ready to go out in public yet?" I ask, cringing.

Thank goodness the parents are too consumed in their own conversation, and I really hope we didn't ruin the innocence of childhood.

Roarke starts re-packing the basket and Lucy saunters over, plopping down on the blanket. Three of the five kids follow her.

"Can I be next?" one little boy with spiky blond hair and bright green eyes asks, sitting on his knees, his hand still on Lucy.

"Pardon?" I ask.

"He won so it's my turn." He jumps on me, his small hands trying to push me down.

"Hey!" For some reason, I freeze as this kid starts slapping and using any force he can to get me down to the blanket.

Finally, I get what he's trying to do and I lay flat on my back. He holds my hands on the ground and his friend starts slapping the grass.

"1…2…3… You're done." The kid playing referee hops to his feet and points to me.

The blond kid jumps up, stepping on my leg. He and his friend slap high fives and start celebrating.

"Boys!" Roarke grabs my arm and swiftly helps me up to my feet when he finally clues in to what's happening. "What are you doing? You need to apologize."

They stop all movement. The little girl who ventured over with them is still petting Lucy and staring up at the scene unfolding in front of her. She doesn't seem at all alarmed at the fact that the boys are in trouble. Must be a regular occurrence.

"We're playing WWE," one boy says.

I rub my arm where the kid pinned me, seriously what is he like five?

Roarke bends over at the waist, laughing. I'm still confused.

He gets a hold of himself enough to fill me in. "They thought you and I were wrestling. That I pinned you."

My face heats and not from the sun beating down on us.

Roarke grabs the blanket and I help him fold it so it will fit back in the backpack he brought.

"You boys are so stupid, they were about to have sex," the little girl says.

The blanket drops from my hands. "No, we weren't."

"Yeah you were," she continues to pet Lucy while she speaks, like it's really no big deal.

"No, we weren't," I insist, stronger now.

"Okay." Roarke, ever the diplomat puts his hands between me and the little girl. "We're leaving. Go back to your parents now, kids." He points to the circle of adults in folding chairs laughing and tipping back their Solo cups filled with beer they've been sneaking from a cooler.

The boys walk away, one of them complaining that it's not fair because he wasn't able to wrestle me. The girl slowly raises from her seated form, her eyes on me the entire time. "Cute dog."

Roarke unwinds Lucy's leash from the tree. "Time to see Nickel, girl." He pats her head and swings the backpack over his shoulder.

Leaning into my ear, he whispers, "I'm glad for the interruption because I can't wait much longer to have you."

I don't feel any different and if there hadn't been so many people around, who knows what might have happened on that blanket in the park.

When I'm with Roarke, I forget who I am, where I am —everything revolves around him and I'm not sure if that's good or bad.

Chapter Twenty-Six

Lucy runs after Nickel the minute Roarke unleashes her inside his condo.

"You're going to regret having us here," I say, placing my purse on the entry table.

He sets my overnight bag that he insisted we pick up on the way over down by the door along with Lucy's leash.

"I regret nothing when it comes to you." His chest hits my back, his hands sliding up my ribcage. "Remember what I said at the park?"

I nod.

"You know I never say anything without following through."

I nod again, the warmth between my legs intensifying the farther his hands venture.

"I'll let you choose. Breakfast bar, dining room table or bed?"

"Tough choice," I say, tapping my chin in jest. "I'll go with bedroom."

He spins me around, bends down, and lifts me over his shoulder. "Roarke!" As I hang there, he splays his hand possessively on my ass and his fingertips slide under the elastic seam of my panties, finding the wetness between my legs.

I'm familiar with the journey to his bedroom. He's carried me to bed a few times when I fell asleep on the couch. And we've been in this exact position on more than one occasion.

I'll admit—I don't hate the whole caveman thing *all* of the time.

He flops me down on the bed and my body bounces up in the air. "Thanks for being gentle."

He strips off his t-shirt and moves for his belt. "I'm not feeling very gentle today."

I eye him, rising to my knees and crawling toward him.

His shorts fall to the ground and he kicks them out of the way leaving him in a pair of black boxer briefs.

My nail scrapes along the prominent bulge in the front and my lips cast small kisses on his chest. "I think we should get you some red boxer briefs or blue ones at the very least."

He stares down at me with a smirk. "You don't like my underwear selection?"

God, he's so gorgeous. How am I here with him right now?

"I just think black is kind of boring."

His hand molds to my cheek turning my face up to his. I cup his package, my thumb running over the tip.

"Do you think *I'm* boring?"

I lick up his torso, crawling off the bed one leg at a time until I prop up on my tiptoes, grabbing each side of his face. "You? Boring? Not in the slightest."

This time I control the kiss. It's my tongue sliding in his mouth. It's my lips devouring his. He stands there, his hands venturing up under my shirt and unhooking my bra.

The strapless satin falls to the floor and my pebbled nipples brush along the fabric of my tank top, only growing harder.

"Hmm…" he moans.

His fingertips inch up my chest and goose bumps are left in their wake. My breasts ache to feel his strong palms massaging them.

I break the kiss before I let him take control. "I'm not feeling very gentle either."

I fall to my knees, taking each side of his boxers down with me until they pool at his ankles. He steps out of them and I push them to the side coming face-to-face with his engorged length.

Roarke has a lot of things to brag about and wonder cock is one of them. It points up to his navel and his balls are drawn in tight. He's already halfway there and I imagine once I take him in my mouth, he'll become unglued in a matter of minutes.

"I want you to fuck my mouth," I say as my hand wraps around his length and my mouth covers the tip. My tongue slides along the ridges of his shaft and back around to the tip.

"Damn, Firecracker. You're something else." His head falls back and his hands slide into my hair.

I let him stretch my mouth when he pushes in before releasing him slowly, over and over again and he groans a little longer each time. I tease him to the brink, igniting shivers up my back as he thrusts in and out of my mouth.

I've never hated giving blow jobs, but I didn't exactly pull out my pom-poms when it was my turn to siege the beeje. With Roarke though, seeing him hanging on to his control by a thread, waiting to see what I'm going to do next…his moans that turn into growls that turn into grunts that turn into expletives. And then when his hands tighten in my strands telling me he's trying to hold out as long as he can, but I'm making it impossible. The whole experience is a turn on for *me* and something I want to repeat again and again.

Tipping my head, I suck one of his balls into my mouth as my hand runs up and down his shaft, my thumb spreading the pre-cum along the slit of his tip. Covering his dick with my mouth, I deep throat him again and let him slide out of my mouth—over and over as I take control with one hand wrapped around his girth and my other teasing his balls.

"I'm gonna come." His hips rock harder and I take him as deep as possible until the warmth of his release coats my throat. After a final few jerks, I let him slide slowly out past my lips and wipe my mouth with the back of my hand.

"Just when I think I have you all figured out, you blow me like a pro." He holds his hand out for me and I rise to my feet.

"What are you suggesting?" I ask wide eyed.

He chuckles. "Just that I have some repaying to do."

Roarke gently nudges me back and I fall to the mattress. This time he's the one to fall to his knees, and just like he described earlier he slides his hands up my legs, slips off my panties, and he buries his face under my skirt and repays me in full—with interest.

LATER THAT DAY, Roarke and I snuggle on the couch with Lucy pawing at Nickel's cat toys while Nickel stares on with a grumpy look on his face.

"Why do you have a cat?" I ask.

His gaze darts to where Nickel is laying on the top of

the ottoman. "I shouldn't tell you. You already think I'm soft."

I poke him in the side. His hand covers the spot and he captures my hand when I try to do it again.

"He was a stray. The last kitten in a free box outside a liquor store I sometimes stop at on my home from work. I felt bad for the little furball so I took him in on a temporary basis, but…" His voice trails off, his attention once again shifting to Nickel who looks like he might pounce on top of Lucy.

I smile and he shakes his head, grabbing the remote from my free hand.

"I feel the need to put on *Die Hard* or *The Terminator*. Something manly." The screen flickers as he flips through the channels.

"Nothing wrong with *Dirty Dancing*." I try to snatch the remote back.

He drops the remote when it gets on some show about surviving in the desert. I pick it up and click it back to *Dirty Dancing*.

"For the record, I think it's sweet." I lay my head on his bare chest.

"I remember when you didn't think I was sweet."

I lift up and straddle him and right on cue Lucy barks. She does this sometimes when we're touchy-feely with each other, the little twat swatter.

His hands fall to my ass and as usual, his fingers delve under my panties. It's a habit of his I've come to love. As though he doesn't even want even the thinnest silk barrier between us.

"I'm woman enough to admit when I was wrong."

"So you were wrong?" His eyes dip to my chest. Though it's covered in his DePaul law t-shirt, you'd think I was as bare-chested as him with the way his nostrils flare.

Using his strength, he pulls me flush against him, greeting me with his hardness.

"I was wrong. This one time." I hold up one finger to make my point.

He chuckles and rocks his hips.

Letting out an involuntary sigh, my hands fall to his shoulders as I continue to grind against him to get off. My thirst will never be quenched with this man.

His phone vibrates on the coffee table, but his lips continue to sprinkle kisses along my neck.

Lucy barks at the phone now. I can't see her but I can hear her up on all fours.

"Should you get that?" I ask, my eyes falling shut from the inducing pleasure he's creating.

"No." His word comes out as a throaty whisper.

Will we ever get enough of one another? Will there be a time when he'll want to sleep in another bedroom or his hand won't slide along my ass as I pass him by. Will he stop cornering me to sneak a kiss or ask me to sit with him to keep him entertained while he's making a meal? Will all the little intimate moments fade away like they did in my marriage? My heart tells me no, but there's that annoying part of my brain that says I'm living in dreamland.

The phone starts vibrating right after it stops.

Roarke's lips pause on my skin until it stops ringing again. He positions my lips over his giving me the deepest and hungriest kiss I've ever gotten, besides our first night together. I sink into him, my body hyper-aware that it's been granted another ride on the Roarke roller coaster.

One short beep signaling a text sounds from his phone and then the phone begins vibrating again.

I dislodge myself from his lap, but he locks his arms over my legs so they stay strewn across his lap. Reaching forward, he picks up the phone to see who's calling. The smoothness of his palm running up and down my legs stops and his thumb scrolls down the screen.

"I'll be right back." He gently lifts my legs, stands and places them back on the couch.

Lucy jumps into his spot right away followed seconds later by Nickel who takes a seat on the top of the couch cushions.

This is the second time this week he's sheltered himself away for a call. I don't hear anything, not even a mumble until he comes out ten minutes later, after Baby's dad finds out she's been sleeping with the dance instructor. Just as Baby's world crashes down around her, mine does too.

Roarke emerges from the hall in a pair of jeans, a polo shirt, and shoes. He's even run some gel through his hair. Without missing a beat, he walks directly toward me, leaning down. "I have to run out really quick. I shouldn't be long." He places a chaste kiss on my lips.

At first, I'm stunned. What does he mean he has to leave right *now*?

"Where are you going?" I slide out from under Lucy's body to follow him to the door.

"I have something I need to deal with for a client." He waits, wrapping his arms around my body, pulling me into him. The roughness of his jeans pressed against my t-shirt clad body is not nearly as nice as his cotton pajama pants. "It kills me to leave you, especially when you're dressed in almost nothing." He presses his lips to my forehead.

"Then don't." I grip harder around his middle and his lips fall to the tip of my nose.

"If I had a choice…" His words trail off and I lean my cheek on his shirt, smelling the newly sprayed cologne he put on. "Order in some sushi and I'll be back to eat it off you." His lips linger above mine for a too-brief moment.

I release my hold on him reminding myself that if he's

leaving for something other than work I have no control of that. My relationship with Todd taught me that one thing. If Roarke wants to cheat on me, I can't do anything about it.

He presses lips to mine, my cheek cradled in his palm. His tongue slides into my mouth and all the doubts of his rushed leaving tonight vanish as I rise to my tiptoes to keep the kiss going. One of his hands slides around my back, pushing me into his hold and we stay lip-locked for another few minutes. By the time he closes the kiss, I'm heaving for breath with swollen lips.

"That way you won't forget me." He smiles suggesting that's a figure of speech. Just a tease, but his words sear right into my biggest wound.

Without saying more, he grabs his wallet from the front table, shoving it into his pocket and shutting the door behind him.

I don't have long to stay in my own head because my cell phone starts ringing immediately. Running over to grab it, the name flashing only brings another layer of anxiety to my already sinking stomach.

Chapter Twenty-Seven

My phone continues to ring in my hand while Lucy jumps on all fours on the couch tilting her head back and forth at the noise. Silencing the sound, it vibrates on his glass coffee table, Scarlett's name flashing on the screen in glaring letters.

Once the phone stops, I sit on the edge of the plush couch and stare at it, wondering if she'll leave a message. Is that where Roarke ran out to? To meet David to conjure up a plan to take everything from Scarlett?

A beep rings out in the now quiet apartment. Baby and Johnny's mouths move on the screen with no sound.

Picking up my phone, I cross my fingers that Scarlett is going to go on and on about how busy she is with David and the kids.

From the minute I hear her voice I know that's not the case. It's shallow and has lost the light, airy tone it usually holds.

"Hey, Han, it's been forever. I miss you. Definitely need to do lunch. I'll be in the city next week for a meeting with a lawyer. David filed for divorce, but you probably already know that. I'll be damned if he gets Brody and Nell. Call me back. I could use some advice from someone who's been there."

The line dies and my hand grips the phone tighter.

Is Roarke representing David? God, I hope not, but I clearly heard his assistant saying Mr. Quinton. It would be way too much of a coincidence, especially when you add the ties between David and Todd. Please tell me I'm wrong.

As I see Johnny mouth the classic line about Baby in the corner, I dial Scarlett, my curiosity much too piqued not to find out right away who is representing both of them. Maybe I can actually sway her to meet with Roarke.

"HAN!" she screeches.

I don't remember being quite so happy when I was getting divorced.

I lean back into Roarke's overstuffed sofa, Lucy curling up next to me, Nickel leaning his head into mine.

"I just heard your message. I'm sorry, Scar. I didn't know."

I can hear the kids behind her.

"Well, he's just not happy apparently. Wants to return to the bachelor lifestyle." She's wishy washy about it and I want to ask about cheating but it's none of my business. "Hold on, Nell," she tells her daughter.

"It's not easy and I can't imagine with the kids. It has to be even harder."

"I said no. Don't do that. Sorry, Han, my nanny is sick with the flu so I'm in charge. It's bath time. Of course they were silent when I first called you, and I want to do one thing and it's insane in the membrane." She laughs and I wonder if she's been drinking.

"I hate to ask you this, but who is representing David?"

She cackles a laugh. "I know exactly why you're asking."

It's official, I think she's maybe had one too many glasses of wine or she's on some happy drugs. My therapist tried to put me on them, too, but I refused. No time like the present to deal with your shit.

"So who is it?" I ask.

"BRODY!" she screams. "Out of the bath. You cannot squirt your sister in the eye."

I stay on the line knowing I should let her go, but the assistant's voice rings in my head from the other day.

"I'm sorry Hannah. I guess I don't overpay my nanny after all." She laughs again. "As far as David and me, it's hard. After Brody we still went out most nights—dinners, shows, clubs. Then Nell came and with two kids it's harder. David still wanted to go out all the time. I couldn't keep up with his lifestyle. He probably has some slut on the side, but I honestly don't know. He's a guy's guy you know. He still has his condo in the city. You'll probably see him around." Another kid says something but she covers the receiver. "Daddy is here tomorrow." It's muffled but I still catch the words.

"If you need to talk…"

"Thanks. I was going to reach out to you to talk about representation. You know David, he only wants the best and since he filed I was at a disadvantage." My heart lurches in my chest. So Roarke probably is representing David. "But I found myself a pretty damn good lawyer, too, and I'm not going to let him leave me with nothing."

"I'm glad you found someone. Can I ask…"

"NELL!" she screams.

There's a lot of splashing and screaming in the background and then a crash of glass. "NO!" Scarlett's voice sounds farther away now. Before I can finish my question, the line dies.

I hold my phone out in front of me seeing the call ended. My head falls back in defeat. I just wanted one answer. I'm not even sure why it matters. So what if Roarke is representing David? That should mean nothing to me. Except it does. Can I continue to date a man who represents asshole men who want to leave their wives destitute?

That question plagues me for the next few hours as I watch the movie that comes on after *Dirty Dancing*. I have sushi delivered and wrap up the leftovers and put them in the fridge.

A text rings out from my phone four hours after Roarke left.

Roarke: *Sorry, I'm going to be longer than I thought. Get some sleep and I'll be there when you wake up.*
Me: *K*

I place my phone on the counter and move over to his floor to ceiling windows that look out over the city. Leaning my shoulder on the glass, I stare out at the city, wondering where he is and more importantly who he's with.

I could strangle Todd. Couldn't he have left me *before* he cheated? That way I wouldn't be feeling like it's déjà vu with Roarke leaving so unexpectedly. For Todd it was always an emergency at the hospital. That continued to work until he left me at a restaurant and I found him five blocks down on the corner with a woman. He'd assumed I'd take a cab home, but I had decided to walk instead. I ducked behind the corner until he ushered the young redhead into the back of a cab. When I confronted him, he told me that he was sharing a cab with someone. That for some reason he couldn't get one to stop for him because it was a Saturday night. I naively accepted the answer, but my antenna went up then.

Because of him, I'm doubting Roarke's faithfulness.

"You're the only woman." His voice rings through my head. His truthful hazel eyes hadn't reflected an ounce of deceit yet my stomach still churns wondering why he's been gone this long.

I STIR awake and immediately register the feel of Roarke's body pressed to mine. His arm is draped over my body, his chest against my back. Sliding out from under his hold, I glance to the corner to find Lucy and Nickel sound asleep together on her dog bed. They really do get along well.

Closing the bathroom door, I turn on the shower, needing to get ready for brunch at the club with my parents.

Under the stream of warm water, my mind clears in the morning light. I cannot put Roarke in the same category as Todd. That's completely unfair and he's given me no real reason to doubt him.

The shower door opens and since Lucy or Nickel don't have opposable thumbs, I'm not surprised when Roarke's hands wrap around my waist and his face nuzzles into my neck.

"Sorry I was late last night," he whispers, stepping into the waterfall of his shower.

"You should sleep. What time did you get in?"

He groans. "Two."

A plethora of questions run through my mind. I want to know specifically where he was until two. What kind of client needs him to be out that late? My lawyer billed me triple once when I bothered him on a Friday at six.

"Everything is okay?" I ask instead.

I feel his head nod along my neck.

"You can't tell me?" I ask, digging a little more, but not too much.

"I wish I could." His lips travel down to my shoulder, sweeping my wet hair out of the way to kiss the back of my neck.

Does he? the devil on my left shoulder asks.

"I promise to make it up to you." He twists me around to face him and there's nothing in his eyes but pure regret for leaving me so long last night.

I step into his arms and kiss his chest, wanting him to show me that I really am the only woman for him.

His hands slide down and venture to my ass and his hard erection hits my stomach. When his lips land on mine, my mind hazes and for the moment it's only us. He pushes me against the glass and pulls one leg up to rest on the bench seat. After arranging the nozzle so the water doesn't fall right on him, he lowers himself to his knees and proves that not only does he have a wonder cock, but a wonder tongue, too.

My screams echo against the glass and it's not because of the hot water that I'm flushed when I finally step out of the shower.

Roarke stays in after I leave having let me wash myself up first.

"Thanks to you, I only have a half hour to get ready." I joke as I wrap myself in a plush towel and head into the bedroom.

"You'll be beautiful no matter what," his voice echoes out from the bathroom.

"You don't know my mother." I pick up my clothes

from yesterday, shoving them in my overnight bag and pulling out my bra and panties for today.

"I can't wait to meet them."

"You won't think that afterward, I promise." I see his clothes laying on the chair next to his side of the bed. So unlike him. "Getting sloppy now?"

"What?" The water shuts off and I hear the towel being taken off the rack.

"Your clothes from last night." I pick them up along with my towel to put in the hamper in his closet.

"I was in a rush to get into bed with you," he says, his voice still traveling out of the bathroom.

I head to the closet and throw in my towel, but his clothes are still in my hand.

Don't do it.

Do it.

You're looking for excuses.

You need to protect us.

The war in my head wages on and I pull the shirt up to my nose. The familiar scent of Roarke's cologne relieves my worries.

You're being stupid.

Now you feel better, right?

Dropping the jeans in his hamper, I lift his shirt to my nose and inhale, but this time it's not only Roarke's cologne I smell. There's a faint hint of another fragrance. And since this was a freshly washed shirt when he put it on last night, I know it's not mine. Am I smelling things? I sniff again, my nose traveling all over the fabric like the insane woman I am, the foreign scent more pronounced around one collar.

"What do you think about getting you a dresser?" His voice is suddenly close, and I drop the shirt into the hamper.

He steps into his closet, his eyes on the clothes in the hamper. There's no suspicion to his gaze, only amazement that I put them in there. "Thanks, baby." He kisses my cheek and heads to his rows of meticulously arranged clothes.

All the while my insides are shattering like a sledge-hammer to glass.

Roarke is definitely lying to me.

Chapter Twenty-Eight

_I_ decided not to confront Roarke right away.

Stupid?

Maybe.

I know who I'm dealing with and I want to make sure I have everything in order before I nail him, which means hiring a private investigator to follow him. I want to see with my own eyes and have the proof in hand so he can't sweet talk me into believing something isn't going on.

"Are you allowed to tell me who your clients are?" I ask.

He glances over as we ease off the I-90 in the north suburbs. My tone is curt and he's probably wondering what changed from the shower to now. The fact that I confirmed he's a cheating bastard is what, but he doesn't need to know that yet.

"Depends, but I can't see why you'd care."

"Does the name Quinton sound familiar?" I still want to find out if he's going to screw over my friend or not.

"Quinton?"

I blow out an annoyed breath and his eyes shift my way

once more with a 'what the fuck is wrong with you' expression.

"Yes, Quinton," I snap impatiently.

"Yes. I'm representing a Quinton."

Ha. I knew it.

"David Quinton?"

Again his gaze lingers on me as we stop at the light to turn left toward the club. "Did I miss something?"

"What are you talking about?" I cross my legs, then my arms over my chest. My body language is more along the lines of when we left to go to Wisconsin weeks ago. Before I fell in love with this man and well before he disappointed me.

"I thought your sourness was because you're nervous for me to meet your parents or the fact you don't seem very fond of your mother, but this line of questioning as though I'm on the stand has me thinking I must have missed something."

"I'm just making conversation. I figure you might screw over some of my friends and I have to say, I don't know if I'm okay with that."

He glances over at me and his eyes narrow. "We've been over this, I don't screw anyone over. I get my clients what the law states they are entitled to."

"To you maybe. It's convenient for you to see it that way."

He follows the navigation in his Range Rover since I stopped directing him after we got off the highway. Pulling up toward the club, he stops at the gates.

A security guard leans forward to look inside the car.

"Hi, Len." I wave.

A smile wraps around the fifty-year-old man's mouth. "Hannah? We've missed you." He presses a button. "Have a great brunch."

"Thanks, Len. Give Ruth my love."

"Always." He waves and Roarke drives through the open gates.

"Funny that Len doesn't get the cold shoulder," he mumbles but it's clear he intended for me to hear it.

Roarke parks in a spot and my hand yanks the door open as soon as the SUV comes to a stop.

Before I can exit the car, his hand lands on my left one. "Just so you know, David Quinton isn't my client."

I slide out from his grip not sure how to react after my assumptions were wrong. Stepping out of the car, he's rounding the front before I can smooth my skirt and swing my purse over my shoulder.

"It's Scarlett. She's my client. If you have to know in order for us to go in there like the happy couple we've been since we started dating, then I'll tell you. But please remember you are not to repeat this information." I nod in agreement. "David tried to hire me. Offered me double what Scarlett was paying me."

A heavy weight drops in my stomach.

I had it wrong?

"Oh."

His hand slides to my back and I have no time to think about how I keep making assumptions that aren't true about him before his lips are on my neck. The sweet spot he found that stirs butterflies in my stomach.

"I forgive you," he whispers, his hand tapping the small of my back to get moving.

"Oh do you?" I raise both eyebrows, the usual playfulness not on my face.

Roarke scrutinizes my expression, still in the dark as to why I'm being so bitchy this afternoon.

"Hannah!" a male voice yells my name from somewhere in the parking lot.

"It's my dad," I murmur and Roarke's frown instantly tips up, reminding me he's like a chameleon, able to change with a snap of his fingers into someone else.

Looking around, I spot my dad at the valet. I wave and we head that way.

The other valet opens the door for my mom, holding his hand out for her.

"We're so happy you could make it today." My dad smiles and embraces me with a kiss on the cheek. "You look beautiful." As he steps back his attention moves to Roarke. "Ah, I think our daughter failed to mention something to us, Olive." He holds his hand out to Roarke who's steady hand immediately shakes my dad's.

"Roarke Baldwin. Pleasure to meet you, Mr. Crowley." He does this all with one hand wrapped around my waist.

"Please, it's Gregory and this is my wife, Olive."

My mom walks up to us, her eyes looking Roarke up and down. I can tell she thinks he looks familiar but she's having a hard time placing him. This is how little she notices what happens in my life.

"Nice to meet you," Roarke says. "Hannah's the spitting image of you."

Olive smiles because she doesn't know who he is— she'd hate to offend someone important.

My dad slaps Roarke on the back. "I was just telling Hannah the other day how I'd wished we got to you before Todd did."

I roll my eyes. Roarke glances my way for a second before returning his attention to my father with a condescending smirk on his face.

"You're the lawyer." My mother says it as though it was a test and she got the right answer. "Todd's lawyer."

"Yes, ma'am." Roarke nods.

She half smiles which I know means she's mentally

trying to figure out how much money he might be worth. He wasn't born into money but having money is better than not having it in her world.

"Please don't call me ma'am, just Olive." She smiles fully now, probably figuring that Todd would only hire the best and she's probably conjured up some memory of hearing one of her elitist friends mention his name.

She slides her arm through mine. "He's very handsome," she whispers and leads us forward through the double doors.

Roarke and my dad follow behind, their own conversation turning to golf where I hear Roarke admit he started late in life but loves the game. Funny since not once has he told me he was going to play golf and we're in the middle of summer. Another lie?

For the next two hours, Roarke charms my parents along with their friends. We eat brunch where my mom criticizes my selection of fruit and pancakes. "Sugar is bad and then you're adding carbs on top of that. Come on Hannah, you're only getting older and I'd hate for you to lose that figure."

My savior or the one he wants me to believe he is, piles his bunch of grapes onto my plate. Surprisingly my mom quiets down and concentrates on her friend's conversation about the house for sale on Hillside.

When Roarke excuses himself to use the bathroom, my mind gears up into overdrive wondering if he's making a call to his side piece. My dad takes the opportunity of Roarke's absence to share his opinion.

"Keeping secrets little girl." He slides his arm onto the back of my chair, keeping the conversation between the two of us. Not like the other people care, they're all wrapped up in talking about what the markets are doing.

"I didn't think it mattered. I was going to wait until the

next event." I nod in my mom's direction. "This is probably better anyway."

"Definitely better. He seems nice. Like a good man. Is that so?"

I know why my dad's asking. After Todd, my dad insisted I do a background on anyone I planned to get serious with, and I didn't follow through with Roarke. Maybe because everything was going so fast and I felt like I never had time to breathe, let alone check him out.

"I'll find out soon," I assure him.

He raises his eyebrows. "You should have checked that out before your heart was invested." His matching brown eyes to mine hold disappointment.

"Who said I was invested?"

He chuckles to himself, picking up his coffee mug. "You forget that I know you better than you do yourself. You've already fallen."

"No I haven't."

My dad looks at me like, *prove me wrong.*

"We'll see what comes back."

"I wish you'd looked into him earlier." My dad's lips turn down. "He seems like a good guy, but you just never know."

His belief that a check by a private investigator seemed like a good idea when I was knee deep in tissues and my self-worth was spiraling. I meant to make the call and have Roarke followed, but he disguised our dating as favors and before I knew it I didn't want that path for us. I enjoyed discovering things about him and not reading it on a piece of paper. But things have changed and I'm nauseous just thinking about what I'm going to find out later this week.

"I'm sure it will be fine." I plaster on a fake smile, knowing that bringing him to brunch was a bad idea.

Because once it's proven that Roarke isn't the man I thought he was a few short days ago, I'll have to tell my father that once again my gut was wrong. And everyone knows that half of being a good business person is having great intuition.

"He makes a hell of a first impression," my dad says.

He slides over when Roarke approaches the table, a smile on his face that says he's about as smitten as I am over the man sitting next to me. So I'll break both of our hearts. Great.

"Why don't you show Roarke the fountain?" My dad points out the French doors to the courtyard.

Roarke doesn't miss a beat. He must want me to get out of my parents' scrutiny.

The fountain has water shooting from all five points into the one large spout in the middle. It's nothing like Buckingham but it's nice.

"Finally I get you alone." Roarke sits down on a bench and pulls me into his lap.

"This isn't really a crowd who appreciates public displays of affection." My gaze darts around the surroundings but no one is really around.

"I don't much care what this crowd likes because I need your lips on mine now."

With his words, his hand slides to the back of my neck and he pulls me down to his. The slickness of his tongue doesn't wait to break the seam of my lips. He grows hard underneath my legs as our kiss becomes more than PDA. It's almost X-rated the way his hand slides up my skirt, his fingers dangerously close to my center.

All thoughts of the PI, the perfume, and the phone calls disappear from my consciousness because as always, Roarke has the capability to make my mind fuzzy.

"Ha. Seems like we both walked away winners from

my divorce." Todd's voice sounds from behind us and I freeze.

After a second, I break the kiss, standing to my feet. My face is red and my lips are probably swollen. Todd is there with a look of smug satisfaction on his face, his new fiancée standing at his side. My gaze flicks down to their adjoined hands.

She's younger than me by at least ten years. She's cute and I wonder if I've ever met her. She doesn't look familiar.

"Todd," Roarke says his name like he's a child. He swings his arm around me and pulls me to his side. "I guess our secret is out, but then again yours is, too."

Todd looks down at their adjoined hands and drops his fiancée's. Poor girl.

He looks the same. Tall, thinly built with his khaki pants and button-down shirt, his hair full but shaggy.

"You're dating him?" Todd directs his question to me, but points to Roarke with his now free hand.

"I am." I lift my chin and push back the thought of word getting around that Hannah Crowley has been deceived once again, if Roarke is still playing the field behind my back.

"Good luck with that. Not really your type."

The fiancée matches his steps toward us in her too short sundress and cork-soled sandals.

"How do you know my type?" I place my free hand on Roarke's stomach and my face inches from his neck. I hate myself right now.

"I was married to you for years. I figured your mom would have had a line of suitable men lined up for you." His lopsided grin says he's being sarcastic.

"Good thing she doesn't need to do that." Roarke laughs. One I've never heard come out of him before. His lips press to my temple. "I stole her before they had the chance."

I wish there wasn't truth to that statement but there is. I barely blinked and fell for the one man I hated.

"Did you hear we're getting married?" Todd says in lieu of a suitable comeback. He searches behind him for his fiancée's hand.

Raising their adjoined hands in the air, he attempts to show off the rock on her finger. One that was probably financed partially with my money.

"Well good luck with that." I slide out from under Roarke's hold, grabbing his hand and leaving the fountain.

"You too," he says but I'm too busy leading Roarke away to respond.

I don't have it in me to play a game of one up with him.

Chapter Twenty-Nine

"*E*arth to Hannah!" Chelsea waves her hand in front of my face, pulling me away from my thoughts of what the private investigator I hired is finding out right now.

After brunch yesterday, I told Roarke I had a horrible headache and that I just wanted to go home and lay down. He insisted that he'd take care of me. But somehow, I won the battle and got myself away from his intoxicating cologne and sweet gestures so I could clear my mind to make the call to the investigator. I have to know for sure before investing more of myself in this relationship.

Now I sit in a meeting with the caterer, a friend of Roarke's, or so he says, but the guy is like fifteen years younger than him and doesn't fit Roarke's usual type. Jett's almost black hair and piercing blue eyes would make any girl weak in the knees. Add on the fact he can cook and you've got the panty dropper trifecta.

"Shit, you know how I appreciate a bad boy," Chelsea whispers as we're seated in a restaurant that doesn't open until dinner.

His all black apparel with tattoos up both his arms is a recipe for heartbreak which only reminds me again of the fact that the PI might be snapping a picture right now that could break my heart.

"Well, you're already committed to one of those." Victoria takes a sip of her water.

A loving smile creases Chelsea's lips. "I know. He's been so sweet lately. Always laying his head on my stomach, swearing he's hearing the little bean move."

"And?" I ask.

She waves me off. "Way too early. He just likes to talk to he or she, saying that our bean needs to recognize his voice, too."

"Sweet," I say and Victoria smiles at her, too, before cutting into one of the dishes we're taste testing for the gala.

"I hired a private investigator," I blurt out and each of their forks clink against their dishes when they drop them.

"Why?" Victoria's eyes are big as saucers.

"Because I think he's cheating."

"Are you guys exclusive?" Chelsea asks an innocent yet important question.

"He said I was the only woman but in the past week he's taken a number of phone calls away from me.'

"He's a lawyer," Victoria interjects.

"He left me after getting a phone call one night this past weekend."

Vic looks a little less sure of herself now.

"With what reason?" Chelsea asks, before taking a sip of her water.

"Work."

"There is the attorney-client privilege," Victoria reminds me.

"He came home at two in the morning."

She clamps her mouth shut.

"Then when I smelled his shirt the next morning there was a faint smell of perfume. Not mine."

They both clasp their hands in their laps. Speechless like I expected. It's all the telltale signs. Read any Cosmo it would tell you the same. All I need now is to prove it.

"Why don't you just ask him?" Victoria asks.

"Because I want to have my evidence so he can't sweet talk me. I want to catch him in the act actually. I told the PI that if she sees him in a compromising situation she's to call me and I'll meet her wherever she is."

"What are we, on the set of Cheaters?" Chelsea says. "Can I go with you, because I really want to be like that guy with the microphone asking all the questions." She positions her fist in front of her mouth. "Tell me, Roarke, why would you ruin a relationship with the lovely and gorgeous Hannah Crowley? Have you been diagnosed with insanity?" She giggles but Victoria shoots her a look like 'not right now.' Chelsea's hand drops along with her head. "Sorry," she mumbles.

"Don't be," I chuckle. "You made me laugh for the first time this week."

"Any news from her yet?" Victoria asks.

"She said I'll only hear from her if I can meet her. Otherwise she'll follow him for a week and report back." I push the plate of four different types of potatoes away from me.

Victoria's hand stretches out and covers mine. Chelsea follows suit and we sit in the circular booth like we're having a prayer circle. "We'll pick you up if you fall, Han."

I smile at the two women who I know will do just that. Gwen, too, though I purposely kept her out of the loop when we spoke yesterday. She's crazy busy with work and I don't want to burden her.

"I've already prepared myself."

Just as I say that my phone rings from inside my purse. The girls take their hands back to their own laps, their eyes on me.

I nod seeing the PI number and I fight against the bile rising up my throat.

"Hello?"

"Come to 900 Michigan. I'm outside Bloomingdale's," the sweet voice from a woman that no one would think is the PI says and then hangs up.

"It's now or never."

"Can we come?" Chelsea asks.

"Sure," I say, figuring a little back-up wouldn't be a bad thing.

Chelsea and Victoria slide out, Victoria rushing off to the kitchen to tell Jett we have to leave. When she emerges, she surprises me. "I told him whatever. That he's a great chef and we're cool with whatever he thinks is best."

Chelsea laughs and Victoria shrugs. "We don't have time for another taste test and his shit is awesome. I don't think we have to worry."

"True," I say.

The dark tint of the restaurant is a stark contrast to the sunny day of Chicago. My eyes take a moment to adjust, but Chelsea's already flagging down a taxi.

A yellow cab stops at the curb and she climbs into the front, Victoria and I in the back.

"You don't mind, do you? "Chelsea asks the driver. "The thought of sliding across that seat pregnant..."

The taxi driver shrugs and follows her directions to 900 Michigan, the premier shopping area in Chicago.

After what seems like forever between waiting for pedestrians and traffic the taxi stops at the edge of the tall building with a 900 on it.

I stare up and take a deep breath.

"Can I kick him in the nuts?" Chelsea asks as we ride the escalator up to the Bloomingdale's entrance.

The redhead I hired is sitting in one of the massage chairs. "Hey, Hannah," she greets us. "My partner is still tailing them and they're in the women's section of business attire. There's a child with them. A little girl."

My heart drops to the depths of my stomach before sputtering out a few weak beats. Does he have a child he never told me about?

She pulls out her phone to show me a picture and I can barely see over Chelsea's blonde hair trying to get a glimpse.

"He's been with her this entire afternoon. I have to say though, we haven't seen any untoward affection from either party. He hugged the girl and gave her a high five, but that's all. It's just weird that a man would shop with a woman who wasn't his girlfriend so I figured you'd want to know. I mean…"

"I get what you're saying," Victoria says. "The other day Reed acted like I was prying his fingernails off when I went to look for a pair of jeans."

The PI nods. "I just felt that I should call because other than this, he's been clean all week. Courthouse, office, and home. He went to lunch with a client one day." She slides the screen of her phone over to another picture and there's my friend Scarlett Quinton at a small sandwich place with Roarke. "It's up to you whether you think this is worth confronting him over."

I step away from the phone and she presses her hand to an earpiece. "She's here." There's a pause. "Okay." She stands from the massage chair and her hand falls to her side. "My partner says the woman went into the intimates area after she modeled some pantsuits and the subject had the seamstress come to fit her on two of them. He's been playing goldfish with the young girl while they've been waiting."

"Oh, we're going." Chelsea's already wide eyes grow bigger and she nods toward the entrance.

Take the step, Hannah. Just confront him and then it's over.

I hesitate for a second. I don't know why. But then I remember the humiliation of other people knowing about Todd's affair before I did. How stupid they must have thought I was, the poor in-the-dark wife.

"Let's go." I head toward the entrance, the three women following behind me. With every step, my body weakens. My heart pricks like it's slowly draining of blood knowing it will soon be in little pieces anyway. This is going to hurt so much more than Todd.

How is that even possible? A man who entered my life only a few short months ago will tear me to pieces more than my marriage did.

We enter the intimates and I see a blonde woman leaving the area with bras, garters, and silk panties in her hands. She smiles over to us in her jeans and t-shirt clad body. I register the fact that she's about two sizes smaller than me but refuse to examine it right now.

"What's your name?" Chelsea stops as I pass by to reach Roarke.

My issue isn't with the woman, it's with the man who made the promise to me.

"No Chels," I say.

"Hannah," the PI who was tailing Roarke nods when she says my name signaling that the blonde is the woman who is with him this afternoon.

I swallow past the lump in my throat. Roarke's head peers up over the racks of designer clothes. Did he hear my name?

His face pales and his eyes dart over to the woman with me. Seeing the one woman who was shopping, join a woman already with us, I can see that he already understands what just happened. He's way too smart not to know when someone gets caught in the act. Hell, he's probably seen the live version of this go down in discovery more than the host of Cheaters has.

"What are you doing here?" He weaves through the racks of clothes.

When he clears them and stands on the carpeted path, a little blonde girl follows, her head peering out through the clothes like they're curtains.

"Reese," the woman says and the girl goes to her mom's side. The mom who's holding lingerie in her hand.

"Oh sir, I have the receipt for the suits. You can pick them up next Monday. I can ring up those bras and panties next." The sales associate talks while she's headed down the path toward our group but everyone's eyes are on me and Roarke.

"I'd ask for an explanation but I don't need one," I say with deathly calm.

"You had me followed?" he asks with the nerve to make it sound like I did something wrong.

"I told you I knew the best."

A hollow laugh floats out of his mouth. "Why wouldn't you just ask me if you thought something was going on?"

"I don't need to ask you. I have proof now." I cross my arms keeping my distance because I knew this was going to be the outcome regardless of how many times I begged not to be right.

"Proof?"

"Yes." I sneer back at him and point behind me at the blonde woman.

"I don't think you do."

Chelsea grabs the PI's phone away from her, runs up to Roarke and holds the screen millimeters away from his face. "We have it right here. Who buys lingerie for a woman who's not their girlfriend?" She points to the blonde woman who's now staring at Roarke with sympathy in her eyes.

He glances over to me. "Maybe if Hannah would like to have a one on one conversation, we could clear this all up and you'll see there's no proof of anything." He's mad. I hear it in his tone. In the way his jaw is clenching and how he's holding his hands in fists at his sides.

Well screw him.

"I don't need some conversation where you sweet talk me and convince me that I'm imagining things. That my insecurity of being cheated on before is bringing doubts into my subconscious. Would you be okay with another man buying me lingerie?"

"No, I wouldn't." He shifts his stance and I've never seen him so indignant except for when we were in court.

"Then it's done. Thank you, Roarke, for proving to me you are exactly who I thought you were in the first place."

I storm off down the aisle, not caring one iota that other shoppers are starting to take notice.

"You're being ridiculous!" he calls out after me. "Give me five minutes in the cafe and this will all be cleared up."

"I'd knee you in the nuts if I didn't think it would harm my baby," Chelsea spits out, following me.

"I'm really disappointed in you, Roarke. I thought you were one of the good ones," Victoria says and then I hear nothing else and I don't stop until I'm flagging down a taxi back on the street.

Just as they promised, Victoria and Chelsea are at my side, prepared to piece me back together.

I'm just not sure all the broken pieces will fit back together like they did the first time around.

Chapter Thirty

The next day I sit in my office, my eyes so puffy that I feel like a blowfish after a night of going through two boxes of tissues. The girls tried to spend the night, but I told them to go home to their men. That I'd take a sleeping pill and go to bed.

Roarke hasn't tried to reach out to me since I left him standing between the designer dresses and sexy lingerie of Bloomingdale's. I might never look at a nightie the same way again.

My phone dings and I don't want to acknowledge it, but there are too many loose ends with the gala a week away and so I have no choice but to see who it is.

Gwen: *I'm flying in this weekend. Can I crash with you?*
Me: *YES! When do you get in?*

It's as though someone up above is sending me a gift. Gwen is a bit of a wild child and will surely take me clubbing and help me forget all my troubles. She did a good job after Todd and I'm sure she'll be up for the challenge this time, too.

Gwen: *Saturday at six. I'll catch a cab to your place.*
Me: *I can't wait to see you.*
Gwen: *Me either. I'll call you later.*
Me: *:)*

I set my phone down, my mood a bit lighter, but the memory of Roarke not explaining what was going on when I was standing right in front of him still lurks in the background. If the situation was so innocent, why wouldn't he have said that in front of his side piece?

Because he didn't want to hurt her feelings.
Jackass.

My phone dings again and I grab it with a smile already on my face anticipating whatever it is Gwen has texted me.

Roarke: *You owe me two more favors.*

I seethe and see red as I stare down at his text. I'd thought that the favors were over once he got me under him in bed. Just the remembrance of his lips and hands makes my body tingle much to my utter dismay.

Me: *Seriously?*
Roarke: *Would you like to see the contract?*

I inhale a deep breath.

Me: *You'd cancel the venue?*
Roarke: *Do YOU think I would? You seem to think you know me so well…*

Me: *What do you want?*

If he wants a favor, fine. I'll do it.

Roarke: *My condo at noon today.*
Me: *No.*
Roarke: *No you won't meet me?*
Me: *If I have to meet you it has to be in public.*
Roarke: *I can't have people overhearing what I have to tell you.*

I don't reply. This is a non-negotiable for me. I can't risk falling back into his bed.

Roarke: *Fine. I'll arrange for a secluded table at Torrio's. Final offer.*
Me: *Fine.*
Roarke: *Try to come with an open mind.*
Me: *Are you bringing your girlfriend?*

He doesn't respond to my question but I see the three dots appear.

Roarke: *Noon.*

I toss my phone on my desk, my eyes staring at the time on my computer. I have three hours before I have to be there. After this, there will be one more favor. I should tell him to go to hell. But I've seen a lot of different sides of Roarke and one is his persistence to get what he wants. I wouldn't put it past him to cancel the venue in order for me to hear him out, and we have a contract that says he'd be within his rights to do it. Bastard.

⬭

THREE HOURS LATER, I walk in Torrio's to find Roarke sitting at my table.

Some nerve, this guy.

I step down the stairs surprised at how empty it is in here, but then again, I've never come here mid-day before.

He stands up from the table when I approach.

"I thought we needed to be secluded?"

"Since they don't open for four more hours this is what we're using." He nods to the booth.

A waiter I'm not familiar with brings over a Vesper.

"This gentleman doesn't know what I want. Could you get me a gin and tonic instead?"

He nods, taking the Vesper with him.

"You're angry at me, not at him," Roarke says.

"I think I was polite."

"You weren't."

"Thank you, Mr. Etiquette, I'll remember that," I quip. I sit back in the booth, my hands in my lap.

"After he brings you a new drink I'll tell you how what you saw isn't what you think."

We wait in silence.

"Funny how you think I'm the one at fault."

His eyes dig into mine. "You know what, before we start I want you to look back over the last month or so. I want you to remember how I was with you. I never lied. I was upfront about everything. My past. No one in this city knows my past, but you, because you came to Woods Parlor and saw it firsthand."

I cross my hands over my chest. "You probably hired them all."

He huffs and rolls his eyes. "Fine. Yes, Hannah. I hired an entire town to act like my family. I put those pictures in the glass case for you to find. I even made sure it was Liv that waited on us. I get that you have trust issues. I have them myself, but I would at least hear you out."

The waiter comes over and places a gin and tonic with a lime on a small dish in front of me.

"Thank you. So sweet." I'm overly pleasant to him.

Roarke gets an even more pissed off look on his face. I'll admit that I kind of enjoy that look because it makes him appear even sexier. Funny how the tables have turned.

Once the waiter is a good distance away, Roarke pulls out a business card from the inside pocket of his suit and slides it over.

One Million Degrees. I pick up the rectangle cardboard in my hand and read it over. A non-profit.

"I'm on the board."

"Good for you." I place it down. "Do you want a pat on the back?"

He blows out an exhausted breath.

"I'm really trying here, Firecracker, but you're not." The hurt in his voice, as well as his pet name for me, cut me as deep as it did when I saw that woman holding a bra and panty set that she was going to model for him later that night.

"Fine." I sip my gin and tonic. "Carry on."

"The woman is receiving services from One Million Degrees. She left an abusive relationship and she's been working and going to school at night. The program helps people like her get a fresh start, so they can do something positive with their life. I'd taken her to Bloomingdale's to get her a suit for an interview she had coming up. I'm not really supposed to go that above and beyond but I know what it's like to walk into an interview room and not be dressed the part. To feel like you're going to fail before you've even begun."

"And that includes bra and panties?"

He holds his hands up in the air. "I know that looked horrible. I was keeping Reese busy so she could shop."

"You were buying her the intimates, too?"

"I was." No apology in his tone.

"Nice." I narrow my eyes at him.

"How do you feel when you put on a new bra and panty set? Let's say before a date. Does it make you feel sexier, bolder?"

He leans forward and I hate that he's able to somehow make a point with this. The fact is he was buying another woman lingerie.

"I'm going to go out on a limb and say yes. Maybe you don't know what it's like to wear years' old cotton underwear or a bra with one underwire missing. It doesn't exactly help you feel like you're the best there is out there. I'm not going to defend my actions, Hannah. I didn't have her model them for me and I would never cross that line with someone from the charity whether you were or were not in the picture. In fact, I'd already given the sales lady my credit card. If you hadn't stormed in there with your girl squad, I never would have seen the undergarments in the first place."

"You're blaming me?" I point to my chest.

"I'm not blaming you," he says through clenched teeth. "The only thing I'll apologize for is not telling you what I was doing. I left that night because her ex-husband showed up drunk and pounding on her door. She ended up calling the police. Reese was so scared I ended up staying over there until she fell asleep. I should've told you that day, but you were taking me to meet your parents and I didn't want you having any doubts that I'm the right man for you." He takes a healthy sip of his drink.

"Why did your shirt from that night smell like perfume?"

I thought I'd get a look of surprise or pissed off expression since I'm testing him again, but I get neither of those, only a calm facade.

"Reese had been playing in her mom's things, spraying perfume. Although I shouldn't be telling you this, but I am because I desperately want this behind us. Sonya is another woman I've helped. Jett as well. There are many others spread all over this city and if I have to bring each one here to convince you I'm telling the truth, I will."

Tears prick my eyes and I inspect the business card again. I've heard of programs similar to this. How can I honestly be mad at him for helping those less fortunate?

"I have to go." I slide out of the booth, all my emotions of the past few weeks suddenly too overwhelming, too convoluted to decipher.

"What? No." He stands to follow me and I turn around sharply, my hand landing on his suit vest.

I take in his appearance one more time. He's the dressed-for-success Roarke, the one I like the least. Maybe because it reminds me of my failed marriage or the way I despised him when I didn't even know him.

Feeling the softness of the vest with the buttons, I want nothing more than to step into him and let him convince me that I'm not crazy. That I won't always think the worst of any man in my life. That one day I'll trust someone when they say they only want me. That a year isn't long enough for anyone to push away all the fear the dissolution of my marriage brought on.

"I'm sorry I drew the wrong conclusions. I should have asked when I first started to suspect something but I was so sure, and I wanted to burn you at the stake. I wanted to have the upper hand when I confronted you. I see now how demented that sounds. I thought I was ready for a relationship but I see now that I'm not."

"No." His forehead creases. "Hannah," he pleads, his voice cracking.

I shake my head, stepping closer just to feel his lips to mine one last time. "I never intended to fall for you, but I did." I rise on my tiptoes and press my lips to his.

He stands there looking stunned at how this has played out.

"Always remember my feelings for you were real, but you deserve someone who won't be assuming the worst from you at every turn. Someone you don't have to argue your case to over and over again. I hope you find her."

I step back, my hand falling from his vest.

As I walk away this time he doesn't follow me and I'm glad because I don't think I would have the strength to keep walking away if he tried to stop me. But it's what's best for him.

When I open the door to step outside, he calls out behind me, "You still owe me one favor, Firecracker, and I *will* cash it in."

<h1 style="text-align:center">Chapter Thirty-One</h1>

*I*t's been an entire week and no word from Roarke, which I keep telling myself is a good thing. I've spent my time preparing for the gala to keep my mind far away from my broken heart and how I single-handedly ruined everything.

"So, everything is going as planned." Chelsea comes into my office looking like her old self. No one can tell she's pregnant, she's yet to get that baby bump, or if she has it, she's hiding it well. Gone is the sweets addiction and crying jags which confirm that when one of us is down the other two rise up to take the reins. I'd hoped I would be more of a help in these final stages of planning, but without her and Victoria, the gala would have been a write-off.

She sets a manila folder on my desk.

"What's this?" I ask.

"It's everything we need tomorrow, just in case. You have copies and I have copies. All the contacts for everyone involved. Jett, the bakery, the florist. There's a list of the times everyone is set to speak." She sits down in front of me. "Everything except for one thing. A certain silver fox didn't retract his invitation." She raises her eyebrows my way and my gut churns.

"Do you really think he'd come and make a scene?" I ask a stupid question because this is Roarke Baldwin. Of course he would.

"Yeah, I do. That's why I hired two bodyguards to stand guard at the entrance. I've given them Roarke's photograph so they're to stop him from entering."

My jaw hangs. "You didn't?"

"No, but if you want me to, I will. I have connections." She waggles her eyebrows and I have no doubt that she does. "But from the look of fear in your eyes, my guess is you wouldn't mind an embarrassing act by him?"

She knows me so well after the short time that we've been friends.

"I miss him. Lucy misses Nickel. Do you think it will go away? Like one day I'll wake up and feel like he was never a part of my life? How can I become so invested in someone after only months?"

Chelsea laughs. "You're talking to the wrong girl. Are you sure you made the right decision ending things?"

"Yeah, it's the right decision. One day he'll see I'm right."

Her concern means a lot because when I told Chelsea and Victoria that I walked away after they thought I was crazy. They didn't say it out loud, but I can see it in their eyes and body language.

But I was right to leave him free to find someone who could give him what he deserves. He was right—I could have asked. He'd never lied to me. He apologized for not telling me that morning but he had a good reason to why he didn't. I never thought the saying 'if you love something enough set it free' was true. But it is. Because I love Roarke too much to put him through my tests every time he says he has to work late.

I need to sort myself out. Apparently, I don't have it as together as I thought after my divorce.

Chelsea rises from her chair, the same expression on her face from a week ago when I told her and Victoria what I did at Torrio's. "Whatever you say. I'll see you tomorrow night."

"Thanks for everything, Chelsea."

She stops at the door, a smile on her face. "Always, Han. That's what friends are for."

THE NEXT NIGHT I'm getting ready for the gala when Gwen walks into my bathroom.

"You look stunning, Montana," she says.

Whereas I'm dressed in a long elegant gown, she's in a short sequin dress with a large tulle skirt with fishnet stockings. As if the dress itself isn't going to give my mom a coronary, she has a cut off white t-shirt with big black letters that read Girl Power.

"Shocking as usual." I smile at her in the mirror.

"I refuse to conform. Olive should love it don't you think?"

"I think the girls will love it and you, of course."

She sits on the side of the tub, watching me put my makeup on. Her heavy black eyeliner and mascara applied flawlessly looks great with her pink lipstick.

"I was thinking last night after you went to bed."

"You thinking? I'm shocked." I chuckle.

She sticks her tongue out at me through the mirror. "I'm not just a fabulous pair of tits and ass."

I laugh, deserting the thought of applying my lipstick

when she's in this mood.

"I think you're being really hard on yourself."

"No Gwen." I shake my head, turning back to the mirror, plumping my lips to apply my lipstick. I'll take any excuse to avoid this conversation with yet another person.

"Since when did you ever think you could boss me around?" She raises her perfectly arched eyebrows, crossing her legs.

Gwen is right. She's always challenged me and usually made me a better person for it.

"I think that it's over. What's wrong with being single. You are." I shrug.

She laughs. "By choice. You're hurting yourself and I'm not going to sit back and watch you do it. Todd was an asshole. I told you that from day one. He was spineless. I always said you needed a man who would challenge you, and from what I hear of this Roarke guy, that's him."

I set the lipstick on the counter and spin around to face her. "You don't even know him."

"You're forgetting I sat in the courtroom when that divorce was finalized. I'm the one who took you out for drinks in celebration of shedding one hundred and ninety pounds of grade A asshole."

I giggle. *God, have I missed her.*

"True."

"I would've slipped him my phone number had you not already staked your claim."

She comes over and sits on the counter next to me.

"I hated him."

Her shoulders rise up and down. "You sure about that?"

"Yes, I'm sure."

"He was all you could talk about that night."

"Because I was pissed. He helped Todd take my

money." I pick the lipstick back up and slide it across my lips.

"That's not what you said as you were passing out and slurring your words." She's got her 'I've got a secret expression' on her face. The same one she had before she told me she lost her virginity.

I stop and lean my hip on the counter. "Are you really going to make me ask?"

Her laughter echoes in the small room. "You said you wanted to fall to your knees, unzip his slacks, and see if he's the man you think he is. You wanted to blow—"

I hold my hand up. "Got it, Gwen. I'd also drank half a bottle of Patron."

"You know I always say that the truth comes out when you're high or drunk." She hops down from the countertop and lingers in the doorway. "I'm just going to say one more thing and then I'll leave you alone about it. You are an amazing woman and you're stronger than you think. I might be the only person who saw how hard it was for you when you found out Todd was cheating. I know you see yourself as some damaged person, but you're not. You're a beautiful, independent woman who rose up out of the ashes to do something meaningful with her life. And if Roarke is the man I think he is, he'd rather have you and support you while you work through your stuff, than not have you at all."

I turn and open my mouth to respond but she's gone. Always the one to say her thoughts and disappear.

Inspecting myself one last time, I can almost feel Roarke behind me, kissing my shoulder like he always did, telling me how beautiful I am. Reassuring me I'm the only one for him.

I blink and see it's just me and it's the first time in over a week that I debate if I really did make the right decision.

Chapter Thirty-Two

 walk into the gala and a real smile creases my lips for the first time since everything went to shit with Roarke.

The simple vases with clusters of white roses and greenery on each table under the pleated white tent give off a casual elegant vibe. A makeshift dance floor is surrounded by tables of eight covered in white tablecloths and the tent is open along the sides so you can see the city skyline.

"You like?" Sonya approaches me wearing a nice pink dress and heels, her name tag in place.

"I love. It's beautiful."

"May I walk you around?"

The waitstaff are dressed in classic black and white and flit between tables, filling the water glasses while others straighten the flower arrangements and place cards.

"Definitely."

"So we have the champagne toast ready go after the final speech." She points to the back kitchen. "Over here we arranged a black light room for the girls to write inspiring messages in neon colors."

The entire blocked off room has black dry erase boards with pink, yellow, blue and green neon markers ready to be used.

"I love it."

"I was a little unsure because I know you wanted elegant but since some of the girls and families were going to be here, I figured it could work. I ran the idea by Chelsea and she seemed to agree so we went ahead with it." She leads me over to a long table covered in gift baskets. "This is the silent auction. Whoever hustled to get these did an awesome job. You've got Cubs packages, Blackhawks, a weekend getaway at The Drake, someone even donated a five day trip to Napa with the use of a private jet. It's crazy how much money is in this city. We'll be doing the live auction right after dinner while dessert is being served with the other items."

Her enthusiasm is catching and I love that she seems as excited as I am about all this. "Everything is perfect."

She smiles, winding through the tables. "I wasn't sure how you'll feel about this next part...Chelsea and I had discussed it but she mentioned you've been out of the office a lot the last week. I'm so happy you're feeling better."

I nod but say nothing.

"We decided instead of seating all the speakers together, that we'd sprinkle them in with the families. So the six Winter Classics athletes have been split up in groups of two to sit at tables with users of the programs. I hope that's okay, but we thought if they saw the difference the foundation is making, they'd be more likely to either donate their time or money at a later date. And I think it will make everyone feel included and equal. I'm not sure if

Roarke told you, but I used a non-profit company to get help when I was struggling in community college. The interview training helped me land this job. I just didn't want the people who were part of the RISE Foundation's generosity to feel any separation from the people funding the foundation." Her cheeks blush with a slight pink that matches her dress. "Does that sound terrible? I hadn't meant it to be."

Her innocence and insightfulness amazes me. "It sounded beautiful and very well thought out. Thank you so much for thinking of it."

She shrugs and touches my arm. "I'm so grateful to the One Million Degrees program and that's why I had no problem bumping a profit event for yours." She winks. "Between us of course."

I'm floored by her candidness. "Of course. I'm so happy you got the help you needed to succeed."

She smiles and heads to the podium. "The sound and video guy have the ads ready to go. They'll play those right after the speeches and before the dinner."

"Sonya, I'm truly amazed at how wonderful everything has been planned out."

"Oh!" she exclaims but tapers down her reaction checking to make sure no one noticed. "Don't even ask how, but we got fireworks. They'll go off at ten thirty for fifteen minutes before the end of the evening. Called it another favor."

She winks and although I am so appreciative of her efforts, the word firecracker reminds me of Roarke's nickname for me. I push back the memories beating at the door for entry and smile at her.

"Really? Oh it will be beautiful."

She nods and her hand rests on my arm again. "I have to check on some last minute preparations but enjoy. And if there's anything you need, just grab any waitstaff and tell them to find me."

I pull her into a hug. "Thank you, Sonya."

She draws back. "You're welcome. Any friend of Roarke's is a friend of mine." A soft smile creases her lips and I wonder if she knows. What kind of relationship does he still have with her? "I'm sure he'll be quite smitten when he arrives and sees you." She lightly squeezes my arm and I'm guessing she doesn't know that we've broken up.

"I'm speechless," Victoria says when she arrives a short time later, her arm entwined through Reed's. She's stunning in her black dress with a puffy bottom over her toned legs. Jade is wearing a soft pink dress with a beaded belt around the waist while Reed is in a typical black tuxedo. They look like the perfect American family.

I hold my hands out to the room. "Amazing, right?"

Victoria slides out from Reed's hold, her hand over her heart as she approaches me. "It's beautiful and more than I even imagined. What a great start to RISE." She embraces me and the warmth of her arms brings the hopeful feeling that this will not be our only gala. That RISE will succeed and there will be many more to come.

"Looks great," Reed says behind her.

Victoria draws back from me, giving me the look like 'he's a guy, don't blame him for his lack of enthusiasm.'

"Can I write on the board?" Jade asks.

"Definitely. Start it off, girl," I say.

She runs to the room and disappears. "You guys talk, I'll keep an eye on her." Reed leans forward kissing me on the cheek. "Congratulations, Hannah."

"Thank you, Reed."

With one last look at Victoria, he heads to the room Jade disappeared into.

"Anything I need to do?" Victoria inspects every surface.

"Nope. Just enjoy tonight. I'm going to introduce you and Chelsea at the beginning of the evening and other than that, you guys just have fun." I lean in close. "There's going to be fireworks near the end so maybe Jade can stay later?"

"Reed won that round. Said a late bedtime isn't going to kill her." She rolls her eyes and I wonder how much say he gets these days. Victoria usually holds all control when her ex isn't around and I imagine having Reed interject his opinion must be hard to get used to.

"Holy shit, it's awesome!" Chelsea's voice screeches into the nearly empty room. When we turn, we see her mouth hanging open as she looks around. "Sonya is pure magic. I say we hire her to do all of our events."

"I think you're missing someone?" Victoria says, noting that Dean is not with her.

"Hey, if he thinks I need a jacket in case it gets cold then he can wait at coat check." She thumbs behind her.

Dean walks in handsome as ever in his tuxedo, looking a tad on the exhausted side.

"I'm trying to make sure you don't get a cold." His long strides bring him to us in no time at all.

If I'm not mistaken, there is the smallest hint of baby bump. Anyone who didn't know how flat her stomach was before the pregnancy wouldn't even notice. But in her tight gold dress, I can see the beginnings of her baby bump.

"Ladies. Gorgeous as ever." Dean kisses both our cheeks.

"Hey!" She smacks him in the stomach.

"You know where you stand." He kisses her cheek, then his lips travel to her ear and he whispers something.

Once Chelsea stops giggling, he asks, "Where's Reed?"

I'm sure he's anxious to get out of our girl squad.

"In the black room with Jade." I motion with my hand behind him.

He claps his hands rubbing them together. "A black room. I feel like I'm in college again." He ventures off and Chelsea rolls her eyes.

Why do I miss having a man around to roll my eyes at?

"My hands are itching without anything to do," Victoria says.

The two of us laugh. "Let's get a drink then," Chelsea suggests, even though she'll be sipping on water all night.

"Perfect," I say, thinking I could use a little cocktail comedown at the moment.

The three of us head to the bar with about ten minutes to spare before guests will start arriving. I can only pray that Roarke isn't one of them.

Chapter Thirty-Three

*A*ll the guests are seated and I'm at the podium after introducing Chelsea and Victoria. The video advertising the RISE program is about to play when my voice catches in my throat when I spot the tall man winding through the tables.

Roarke slides into the seat next to mine. The one that was reserved for him but was supposed to have been moved to a different table.

"Please enjoy the…video." I step away from the podium, and the spotlight moves off of me. "Chels," I bite out.

"I saw." She cringes.

"Why is he at my table?"

She shakes her head. "I have no idea. I know I put him at another one." She bites her lip. "I know I've been a little out of it, but that is a detail I definitely didn't miss." I believe her. Part of me wonders if Sonya did it. God knows she thinks he walks on fucking water.

The video continues playing and it's time for all of us

to take our seats. Since we're all at different tables, I'm stuck having to go sit next to him.

"You sit with Dean. I'll sit where you're at," Chelsea mumbles, continuing to head to my table.

I grab her arm at the last minute before it would look suspicious. "You can't. I'm there with half the directors of the school districts."

Her eyes widen. "I forgot. Well, I could act like you."

Victoria laughs.

Chelsea whips around. "What? I could."

"It's fine. I can totally handle sharing a meal with him." Leaving them behind, and not really believing my words, I head to my table.

He already has the table laughing over some story he's just finished telling. Always the charmer.

"Here she is." Roarke stands, pulling my chair out for me.

"I thought you weren't able to make it," I whisper through a smile in case the rest of the table is watching.

"Oh, you're forgetting that last favor." He smiles tucking me into the table.

Situating himself next to me, he places his napkin back on his lap.

He looks good. Damn it to hell does he ever look good in a tux. Forcing myself to be altruistic where he's concerned is going to be difficult.

As the rest of the table busies themselves with salad dressings and bread baskets, I lean in his direction. "Do not ruin this night for me, Roarke."

His shoulders lose the strength they always perceive. "I would never do that. If you'd give me five minutes, we could put all this behind us."

"And do what?" I smile at a woman across the table from us.

"Start where we stopped."

I pivot in my seat to look at him fully. "You don't get it—"

"Hannah sweetie, you are stunning tonight." An elderly wife of the director of Chicago Public Schools diverts my attention from Roarke.

I smile so as to not alarm her there's anything amiss between myself and the man on my right. "Thank you. I do love your dress."

She nods, proud as can be. "Thank you. It's rayon, much to my daughter's chagrin. She keeps on getting me to dress different but my philosophy is the outside doesn't matter. It's the inside. What's in here." She pats her heart. "I don't need to spend an absurd amount of money to look sophisticated and cultured. People can find out who I am when they take the time to speak to me."

I admire her, so completely comfortable in her own skin.

"I think that's wonderful. Hard these days to not fall into the trap of looking like everyone else."

Gwen comes to mind as I hear her laugh from three tables over. Talk about another woman who could care less what anyone thinks about her.

"Now? Can you imagine what it was like when I was growing up? They wanted us dying of heatstroke in a kitchen. I told Earl there's no way you're going to shut me up. If you want to try it, then don't show up to that church to marry me. I have a voice and I'm going to tell you when your thinking is jackass stupid."

I purse my lips to keep from laughing.

"Oh, go ahead and laugh. My granddaughter thinks I'm crazy, but guess what?"

I find myself leaning forward, waiting for her to tell me a secret.

"She's the strong one. Left her husband last year with three kids under four. He tried to hide his income so he didn't have to pay so much in child support, but she had all the documentation. She knew how to get into their 401K, how much they had in stocks. I like to think if I didn't raise her mom to have a mind of her own, she might have not known to make sure she was involved in their financial affairs. Love is beautiful." She eyes Roarke and tilts her head to the side. "But it's also blind. Sometimes you get hit over the head with a sledgehammer and you have to be able to retaliate. What's important is how quickly you get up, don't you think?"

I smile at her. "I do."

"And remember you are worth perfection. No one is perfect but whoever wants to win this." She points to my heart. "Should be striving for perfection."

Why do I get the feeling like she's talking more about me now than in general terms?

"Now you have to treat them with the same respect by letting him in. Trusting that you're in it together. There's no Cinderella story, but there's no reason why a prince and a princess can't slay those dragons together now is there?"

"Oh Eloise, stop babbling on about love," her husband says from beside her.

She eyes Roarke one more time, but he's deep in conversation to his right.

"She gets me." Eloise winks and then waves her finger between us. "Hannah meet my husband, Earl. He's all ears on how he can help get young girls to believe they have a voice that needs to be heard."

She speaks so close to what's in my heart that you'd almost think she had a file on me. I have the urge to grab Roarke's hand under the table, but I stop myself. Everything this woman is saying feels like it's lifting the fog that's been heavy in my brain all week. I don't need a prince to save me, but I do need to trust that if things fail between us, I have the strength to pick myself back up.

I push the thought of Roarke to the side as I carry on a conversation with Earl and the other directors at the table about RISE and what we're hoping to accomplish for the next half hour through dinner.

Roarke sits quietly, never interrupting me or trying to interject his own thoughts on the matters up for discussion. He doesn't try to sell RISE to the table. In fact, if it wasn't for the static electricity that stands my hair on end, I'd wonder if he was still there.

Our dinner dishes are cleared and dessert is about to be served.

"Excuse me, I believe the auction is going to start." I hold my napkin in my hand, but Roarke gets up and slides my chair out for me. "Thank you."

"Always."

Our eyes meet for the briefest moment before I look away.

Although Eloise's unsolicited advice is yet another warning that I'm being stupid, this is not the time to have this conversation.

He sits back down as I head to the podium once more to introduce the auctioneer.

For the rest of the night, RISE profits from more donated money than I thought possible. Roarke has stayed in the backdrop, silently supporting me. He doesn't invade my space or make a scene. I make sure to say hello to my parents and take some time to thank all the speakers so they know how much I appreciate them donating their time. I schmooze some of the deep pockets in the room and everything goes off without a hitch.

I've just turned around from saying goodbye to Jasper

and Lennon Banks with regrets they'll miss the fireworks when I hear a tapping on the microphone.

"Excuse me." Roarke's deep timbre voice echoes through the tent.

I freeze in place—fear and excitement run through my veins as I wonder what he could be up to.

Everyone stops their conversations and grants him their undivided attention, but his eyes are solely on me.

"No, no, no," I whisper as my cheeks heat.

"Who is that?" Lennon asks from beside me.

"Come on," Jasper says to his wife, knowing they need to get back to their kids at the hotel, but she shrugs him off.

"Not a chance in hell I'm leaving now," she says.

He steps up to her, and the three of us stand in a line.

"I thought this would be easy," Roarke starts. "Since I'm used to pleading my cases in front of a judge most days. But this is so much more important than vacation timeshares, joint bank accounts, and retirement plans. This is my own future and this moment will decide whether I get the future I so desperately desire." He pauses and swallows. "I love you, Hannah Crowley."

Gasps sound off throughout the room and everyone turns my way. I try to push the thought of all these people away because he just told me he loves me for the first time and there is something that feels so right about that.

"From the first time I saw your picture, I had a gut feeling that you were the woman I'd been waiting a lifetime for."

A few ahhs echo out from the women in the crowd.

"I don't say that to be cliché, it's true. I've always trusted my gut and it's never steered me wrong. You learn from failure so even if it pushed me to something I failed at, I was okay with that. If it's steering me wrong right now as I stand in front of this room with hundreds of eyes on me while I confess my love to a woman and she turns me down…I guess I'll learn not to do it again. Not that I'd have to because there will only ever be you."

Laughs ring out from the crowd.

"But I hope after I'm done with this speech, my little firecracker will let me guide her out onto that balcony and hold her while we watch real fireworks light up the sky. Because my arms are empty without you and my heart is hollow without your love. I miss you, Hannah. I know what we have is complicated and isn't easy. Trust is hard in any relationship. But you took the chance and got to know the real me. That took courage, but I like to think you got something of a reward by taking that leap."

He winks and smiles that charming one with all white teeth and bright eyes that wins everyone over. The room laughs again while I feel my face grow hotter.

"Our road may have started out bent in the wrong direction. We straightened it together and if it bends again at some point, I have faith in us that we'll straighten it back out—together. I made you a promise that if we're in this relationship, we walk side-by-side. I know you doubt that you'll ever trust me because of your past. Well, I'm here with my hand out because we will walk that journey together, one day and one step at a time. Any branch that lays in our path, we'll step over together. Do you get the common theme here?"

The room echoes with laughter again.

Chelsea has made her way over to us with a big smile.

"Isn't he the cutest?" Lennon says to her.

"Who the hell is this guy?" Jagger Kale, an old friend, comes up on the other side of me. "He belong to you?" The disgust in his voice has me wanting to punch him in the gut.

"You get away from her," Victoria tells him in her mom voice.

"Yeah, Jagger, don't ruin the romantic moment," his wife Quinn says. "Let's remember you were the asshole at one point, too."

"That was when I was clueless, and you hadn't cast your spell over me yet."

Quinn and Victoria pull him away and their conversation drifts away while I study Roarke.

He tucks his hands back in his pockets before he continues talking. "I'm making another promise to you, Hannah, and you *know* I don't break my promises."

My heart hammers in my chest as everyone's gazes shift from him to me and back.

"I promise to be one hundred percent invested in our relationship. I promise to love you unconditionally. I promise to be patient with you when your past experiences creep up on you and make you think crazy things." That one pulls a small smile out of me. "I promise to be the support you need by your side, but never cast a shadow over you. I promise that we will stand united, always."

The room is silent except for the blood rushing to my head and the loud thumping of my heart. Roarke steps down from the podium, stalking over in my direction.

My throat dries as all eyes follow him until he stands in front of me.

"What do you say, Hannah? Can we give this thing between us a true shot and leave all the bullshit behind us?"

"Kiss him!" someone in the crowd screams and Roarke smiles back at them before turning to me.

"I'd make a promise that I'll never disappoint you, but I don't break promises. I can say I'd never do it deliberately. I mean if I bring home the wrong kind of milk or—"

I step forward and press my finger to his lips.

"You love me?" I whisper.

He nods.

"Are you going to make me sign a contract?" My lips tip up and so do his.

"I do like the thought of you being bound to me forever by ink, but I only want you with me if you want to be there. So, do you?"

My heart skips a beat. "I do."

His hand cradles my cheek, and he steps into my personal space.

"Never push me away again." He bends his neck to kiss me, but I pull back.

"You don't tell me what to do."

He chuckles and without saying anything, his lips descend on mine.

"Fireworks!" someone announces.

"I've got my own right here," Roarke murmurs against my lips before dipping his tongue into my mouth.

The footsteps and whispers can be heard heading outside until we're the only ones left in the room.

Once our kiss draws to a close, Roarke steps back to lead me outside, too.

"You owe me one more favor," he says, raising one eyebrow.

"What?" I'm almost afraid to ask.

"Will you move in with me?" His thumb rests on my lips before I can respond. "Your name will be added to the title. We'll own it together. It won't be mine any longer, it'll be ours. If you'd rather me move in with you, I'm good with that, too. The decision is yours. I just can't stand the thought of not being with you night and day."

A big boom sounds off outside from the fireworks.

"I'm a woman who learns from her mistakes. Yes, I'll move in with you."

His reaction is to give me the kiss I've been waiting on all evening. The one where everything else fades away and the only thing left is him.

Always him.

Epilogue

"A new bed?" Roarke asks, walking down the hall to the kitchen.

"A new bed for a new start." I clasp my earring on in front of the dresser mirror, watching him head for a drink.

It's a habit I never realized he had until we moved in together. He always has one drink before we leave to go to a function.

"I like the memories I have of you in that bed. How I tricked you into sleeping in it while you hated me." He turns around, winking.

My hands rest on either side of my ear, so I glare at him rather than give him the finger.

He chuckles, turning back around to head to the kitchen. "You could only be pissed if you didn't fall in love with me," he hollers back from the hallway.

I stare into the reflection of our bedroom from the mirror. The book I'm reading is on the nightstand, along with my charger. On the opposite side, his glasses rest on the book he's reading. Not that there's been a lot of reading going on these days. We're like two horny teenagers since the movers packed up my stuff and hauled it across town. My cousin has moved into my condo now since it's owned by the family.

My eyes water. God do I love him. So much that I'm still surprised myself.

When I've finished getting ready, I grab my heels from the floor and walk down the hallway hearing ice cubes clink in a glass.

"And you promised to give me anything I want, so a new bed it is."

Since he's busy making my drink, I grab the scotch bottle and pour him a glass.

"I don't remember that being part of the speech." He raises his eyebrows and I'd strip him down and have sex with him right here if we had time. Screw the charity event.

"I knew I should have recorded it." I giggle and he kisses me then hands me my drink.

I hand him his in exchange.

"So I have to watch a bunch of bachelors get auctioned off tonight?" he asks.

I nod while sipping my drink. "Are you dodging the bed topic?"

He leans his hip against the counter. "You knew when you brought it up, it was a done deal, right? Like I'd fight you about a bed."

I smile, not because he's going to let me buy us a new bed, but because I knew what his reaction would be and that makes me feel like I truly know him.

"I suppose."

He holds up his drink. "What should we drink to?"

"To all the women who will snag a bachelor tonight?" I joke.

"As long as one of them isn't you."

I slide up to him so we're chest to chest. Without my heels, I only come up to his pecs, but I love the way he can wrap me in a bear hug.

"I found my bachelor." I kiss his chin and then rise to my tiptoes to meet his mouth.

His hands glide down my back until they cup my ass and our kiss deepens.

"I have my own proposition for you," he murmurs.

I fall down off my tiptoes, sipping from my glass. "Your tone scares me."

He chuckles, taking a bigger gulp than usual of his scotch.

My mind runs wild thinking of what his proposition is.

"My tone? It's the same as it always is. You get a new bed and I get…" He reaches into his pocket and my breath seizes in my chest.

"NO!" I scream.

He smiles, pulling out the box that strikes fear into my heart because it will change everything and what we have is good.

Please tell me that box holds earrings or God I'll even take a brooch. Just not a …

"Roarke." My voice wheezes out when he lifts the lid and I see a ring. There's no big center diamond, but it's still a ring—a thick band with more diamonds than my last wedding ring.

"Stop." He holds his hand out in front of him. "I should've prepared you better. This is *not* an engagement ring."

I finally take a full breath.

Thank God.

"Okay then, what is it?" I ask.

"Are you disappointed? It can be an engagement ring if you want it to be, but I thought we, you…"

Just like that night at the Gala, I place my finger over his lips. "I'm not disappointed."

The tension wrapped around his body evaporates. "This isn't a symbol to tell the world I own you either."

"It's not?"

He smirks and takes the ring out of the box. "Well, if it was, you couldn't blame me, Firecracker. I don't want anyone and everyone hitting on you."

"So is that what this is? Like pepper spray for any creeps that come sniffing around?"

He chuckles, reaching for my hand. "Not at all. I know marriage isn't in the cards for us. That a piece of paper isn't what either of us wants or needs to prove our love to each other. But I still want you to look down at your hand and think of me. Think of our home at the end of a long day and the man who loves you completely and faithfully and will be waiting for you when you return to it."

My hand shakes as I bring it to my mouth and drag in a ragged breath.

"I'd get on bended knee, but I know you don't want that. The only thing I want is to seal my promise to you with this ring. That you are mine and I am yours. That's it. Will you accept it?"

"Does this mean I can get *you* a ring?" I quirk one eyebrow up.

He chuckles. "We'll stop on the way to the charity event if you want. I'd love nothing more than to wear a ring that represents what we mean to each other."

I stare down at the ring again and everything Roarke is saying are things we've discussed but usually after post-climax bliss. He's right that I don't feel a need to be married again. What I need is a man who always chooses me and no piece of paper can ever guarantee that.

"I'm asking one more time. Will you wear my ring?"

"That sounds so high schoolish." I giggle and his face grows slightly annoyed. "Yes! I'd be honored to wear your ring."

He slips the silver on my finger and I stare at it with awe and excitement, not with dread and resentment as I eventually did with Todd's ring.

"Platinum?" I ask.

A wicked smile overtakes his face. "Only the best."

I step into him once more and his arm winds around my waist, pulling me flush against him. "I love you."

He kisses me until I'm breathless and then pulls away. "I love you more."

━

"HAVE I mentioned that I'm not really into this bachelor auction thing?" Roarke reminds me yet again as we climb out of the Uber to walk into the hotel ballroom.

"It'll be fun. It's a fundraiser for the First Responders Fallen Heroes. Besides, what was I supposed to say when my parents insisted we take their table after I sent them on that getaway for my mom's birthday? Head over to the silent auction table and bid an absurd amount on a weekend trip and I'll make sure you get a blow job each and every day we're there."

"Done." He kisses my cheek and disappears to the tables of baskets.

"Where's Roarke going?" Victoria and Reed walk up to me.

"I don't know, but I'm following. Nice to see you, Hannah." Reed kisses my cheek. "If I hear one more ohh out of my girlfriend's mouth I might lose my cool." He heads after Roarke to the table and we watch the two men in our lives shake hands and then peruse the baskets together.

"What's up, ladies?" Chelsea approaches, her small belly swelling out of her dress.

"Pregnancy looks good on you," I remark.

Dean swarms her in a hug from behind, his hands rubbing her stomach. "I completely agree." He kisses her neck. "I better not find you with a paddle in your hand." He raises one eyebrow.

"I thought you were into kinky stuff?" Victoria jokes.

"I'm not into sharing." His brooding eyes stay on Chelsea's as he starts to walk off in Reed and Roarke's direction.

"You know you're the only man who can satisfy me!" Chelsea calls out after him.

Someone coughs from behind us and when we look, we see it's a middle-aged lady dressed in tweed.

"We're too far away to have this conversation," Chelsea adds with a giggle.

"Just make sure. No paddle!" He points to her with a smile on his face.

"We'll keep her in check," I promise him.

"Oh, Hannah, you and I both know there's no keeping Chelsea in check." He smirks.

Chelsea blows him a kiss and he too disappears into the crowd.

"I guess it's good the men in our lives like each other, huh?" Victoria's gaze stays on the auction table.

"We all ended up with lawyers. Who would have thought?" Chelsea says, her hands massaging her stomach.

"Should we reprimand them for not getting our drinks?" I ask.

"Nah, we're independent strong women, right?" Chelsea says.

"Totally." Victoria leads the way to the bar on the opposite side of the room.

Once Victoria and I each have a glass of wine and Chelsea has her water with lemon that she's pretending is an actual drink, we sit down at a table near the stage which is all decorated with hearts and arrows. It's corny and cliché but still cute and festive.

"Look at all these men in uniforms." Chelsea's head is turning in each and every direction. "It's not the same, but back in the day Dean could really fill out a pair of baseball pants. His ass is—"

"We got it, Chels," Victoria interrupts her. "How many weeks are you again?"

They laugh because the running joke in the office is that Chelsea's heading into the hormone crazed time of pregnancy and she's going to be mounting Dean every chance she gets, according to Victoria.

"I don't know, she's always been a horn dog." I laugh.

Chelsea throws a piece of confetti off the table at me.

"Not that I'm denying it." She sips her lemon-infused water. "But none of these men hold an ounce of sex appeal compared to Dean."

We all notice a group of three girls walk into the room, laughing and joking with one another and take a seat at the table next to ours.

"Looks like they could be a younger version of us," Victoria says a little wistfully.

"Maybe not younger, but the more single version for sure," Chelsea says.

"Speak for yourselves," I say in a lighthearted way since I'm the senior citizen of our group.

Chelsea eyes the taller of the three, with blonde hair. "I like the blonde, she seems fun."

Now it's me throwing confetti at her.

"Whoa!" Victoria points, wine sputtering out of her mouth to the black tablecloths.

"Holy shit!" Chelsea grabs my hand. "You got engaged?" The disbelief in her tone is similar to the rumbling in my stomach when Roarke first opened the box.

"No." I hold my hand out as the two of them take turns yanking it closer to inspect the ring. "You know I'll never get married again."

"And Roarke thinks what of this?" Victoria asks.

"We're in agreement. Neither of us believes a piece of paper will make us any happier. Don't get me wrong, I get it, I did it once. But I love Roarke and he loves me and neither of us needs the State of Illinois to say we're bound to one another."

"Sweet," Chelsea says. "But I want the paper."

Victoria says nothing and I assume she does, too, but she's too polite to say anything. Afraid it would come off the wrong way.

"To each their own, but for us, this works." I smile, content that Roarke and I understand what it means, even if no one else does.

"So, it's like a promise ring?" Chelsea asks, letting my hand go.

I glance at the diamonds sparkling under the chandelier's light. "I'm not fifteen, but according to Roarke it's a reminder that I have someone who's always thinking of me, who will always have my back."

Victoria sips her wine, her grin growing more and more.

"So that's it. We all have our happily ever afters. Our love stories are over." Chelsea looks like her hormones are about to kick in.

I reach over and place my hand on her stomach.

"They're just beginning."

She grins as a tear slips down her cheek.

"Oh. My. God. Why didn't I think he might be here? Of course he is." The girl at the next table flops her forehead to the table.

"What? Who?" The blonde looks around the room, her eyes scouring over the gorgeous bachelors.

The girl with her head on the table mumbles something.

"I'll take that one." The auburn haired woman says pointing at a cop who walks by. "And here I thought we'd all be watching a bunch of first responders who have their bellies straining their shirts. These guys look like they belong on the runway. They can cuff me anytime." She leans back, sipping her fruity drink and winks at one of the guys.

I'm enthralled in the conversation, so much so that I lose track of the fact that Chelsea's actually picked up her drink and sat at the table with them.

"Focus, Lauren. Maddie needs us."

"Cool your jets, Vanessa. She's not going to pull the trigger. She's just going to obsess over him. She's loved him since forever. Isn't that right, Maddie?" Lauren sits up in her seat and gives her friend a knowing look.

Maddie doesn't pick her head up off the table when she nods. I wonder how long they've all known each other?

"Sorry for interrupting..." Chelsea says.

Victoria's wide eyes focus on mine. "OMG, she didn't."

"She did." I nod.

"You girls are all single?" Chelsea asks.

"Yeah," Vanessa answers warily.

"And friends?"

"No we're strangers," Lauren says and rolls her eyes at her friends.

"This is them!" Chelsea points to the table. "This was totally us six months ago!"

"Oh." Victoria's interest is piqued and she gets up and takes a seat at their table, too.

"What's your story?" Chelsea asks.

All three of the girls seem to look at one another confused about why Chelsea is all up in their business. I don't blame them.

"We should leave these ladies to themselves," I say.

"Nonsense," Chelsea shuts me down. "You don't mind, do you? Are you guys planning on bidding?"

"Hey babe, what's going on?" Dean approaches with a similar looking drink to Chelsea's.

"She's bothering these three nice women." I point to the beautiful girls across from me.

He glances down to her and she shrugs like 'come on this is going to be fun.'

"Yeah, I'll be over here. Don't let her bid for you girls, okay?"

Two of them blush at Dean. Not that I blame them, there's no question that he's a hottie—the boy next door with a sexy smirk.

Roarke pauses briefly at our table, leaning down to speak into my ear. "You okay?"

"Yeah."

"I'm going to join Dean." He nods to the table the three of us were sitting at and heads over.

Seconds later, Reed is sitting with the other two guys at the table beside us.

"Let's get back to you," Chelsea says to the brunette who now has her eyes poised on a man across the room dressed in firefighter gear. They must make him wear that in the hopes that it makes a woman want to throw her cash down to win a date with him.

"Excuse me?" she asks in a tone like someone just offended her. "I'm not sure that's any of your business."

"Maddie loves the hottie in the corner," Lauren says. "The one with the cop and paramedic."

Chelsea's mouth hangs open. "You know Mauro?

The brunette's eyes widen and her face grows beet red in the space of a second before she grabs her drink and sips from the straw.

"Since she was like what? Fourteen?" Lauren says.

"Shut up, Lauren," the Maddie girl says, spearing her friend with an evil eye. "We went to the same school. Sure, he's hot. I just…"

"Admire him from afar," Lauren says, finishing her sentence. "She's loved him since the day she set foot at St. George."

"St. George? You guys went there?" Chelsea asks, practically vibrating in her seat.

At this point Victoria and I are silent, heads bobbing from one person to the other.

"Yeah," Lauren says.

"I went to the public school in the area, Lane Tech." Chelsea beams. "I bet we grew up near each other. It's how I know the Bianco brothers. So you know them, too? Let me call them over." She points to the group.

"NO!" Madison screeches and smacks Chelsea's hand down.

"That would entail Mauro knowing who Madison is," Lauren deadpans.

"Why would he not know you? St. George isn't that big."

Madison and Lauren exchange a look and I see that the tall blonde, Vanessa, seems to be as lost as Vic and me.

"Let's just say they ran in different circles," Lauren

says. "She was too good for him then and she's too good for him now."

"So you think you know better than her?" Chelsea asks Lauren.

"Yep." She crosses her hands in front of her.

Chelsea grabs the paddle in front of Madison and slaps it down in front of Lauren. "You select who she bids on then."

"No way!" Maddie says. "She'll have me with some meathead guy with monster muscles who can't hold a conversation."

Lauren points to Madison. "I resent that comment. Tad was an engineering major."

"And he's still in college trying to make the dream happen," Vanessa says with a laugh.

"Well, he was gifted in other areas," Lauren insists.

"Aren't they all?" Vanessa rolls her eyes.

"It's not my fault you pick the three and a half inch floppy dicks." Lauren nudges Vanessa.

"Then it's settled." Chelsea picks up Lauren's paddle and hands it to Vanessa and then hands Vanessa's paddle to Madison. "You each pick a guy for the other one."

"No way," Madison hands Vanessa's paddle back. "She can't pick for me."

Chelsea relaxes back in her chair and sips her water.

"You've had way too many trips to the bar. Our tastes are completely opposite," Vanessa objects, which kind of surprises me because of the three of them she seemed like the up-for-anything kinda girl.

"It's one date. It'll be fun!" Chelsea insists.

"Then you do it." Madison tosses her friend's paddle into the middle of the table.

"Yeah, that's not going to happen." Dean leans back on two legs of his chair telling us he's been listening the whole time. "She's taken." He rubs her stomach again and Chelsea beams.

"You don't have to do it, but I think it would be fun." She stands and pats Madison's arm. "Don't worry, your secret is safe with me, but Mauro really is a great guy."

Madison's cheeks flush pink and I don't miss the way Lauren's tamped down her dislike for him. Her eyes ping-pong between Madison and Mauro and I hope the gears are shifting. Maybe giving her friend a date with the one guy she's been pining over might be the best gift she could give her.

"Where are all my single ladies?" the MC booms over the microphone and I slide out of my seat and back over to the table with Roarke. His arm instantly comes around to rest on the back of my chair. "Let's meet the first responder bachelors up for auction tonight."

I hope they take Chelsea up on her idea. It seems like a fun thing to do with your single friends. After all, what could possibly go wrong?

The End

Cockamamie Unicorn Ramblings

The last book in a series is always sad for us, but as you know, one day you'll see these couples again. Maybe when you least expect it!

As we mentioned in the Manic Monday CUR, this book idea was born from Piper. She already had the idea for an enemies-to-lovers book about a woman falling for her ex-husband's divorce lawyer who she despised. We were able to work with this idea and bring in the other two books to develop an entire series.

We've loved writing this series! We've loved giving you three very different heroes and heroines with three very different versions of what happily ever after means to them. Each one is a little different, but no less valid in our eyes. To some couples HEA means a white picket fence, two point five kids and a dog. To others, it means just the two of you navigating life's ups and downs, but knowing you're doing it together.

Rayne has especially loved being able to write these stories set in her hometown of Chicago. Which brings us to the next topic… The Bianco Brothers.

Lucky for Rayne, we'll be staying in Chicago for another series. Mauro, Cristian and Luca Bianco will be our heroes for the upcoming series, The Blue Collar Brothers. We've given you a glimpse into our heroines. We're going to let you in on a little secret. For Charity Case we went back to single point of view, giving you only the girls side of the story. But we couldn't tease you with the Bianco brothers and not let you be in their head, so you guessed it —DUAL POV!

Now let's put our hands together for our awesome team!

Letitia from RBA Designs for the wonderful covers.

Ellie from Love N Books for line editing. We're still trying not to give you a manuscript one day with an unrealistic deadline (even if you hit it each and every time).

Shawna from Behind the Writer for using those great peepers and catching a lot more than commas and typos.

Sarah Ferguson and Social Butterfly PR for their usual organization and being one step ahead of us throughout the process.

All the bloggers who carve out time to read and review our books. Your enthusiasm for our books and characters only makes us continue this ride.

All our early ARC readers, first for wanting to read our stuff early and for posting their reviews.

And of course, all our unicorns. <3 Your excitement and love for our characters keeps new voices popping in our heads! Thank you isn't even close enough to how we feel about you all!

xo,

Piper & Rayne

About Piper & Rayne

Piper Rayne is a USA Today Bestselling Author duo who write "heartwarming humor with a side of sizzle" about families, whether that be blood or found. They both have e-readers full of one-clickable books, they're married to husbands who drive them to drink, and they're both chauffeurs to their kids. Most of all, they love hot heroes and quirky heroines who make them laugh, and they hope you do, too!

My Almost Ex

My Vegas Groom

The Greene Family Summer Bash

My Sister's Flirty Friend

My Unexpected Surprise

My Famous Frenemy

The Greene Family Vacation

My Scorned Best Friend

My Fake Fiancé

My Brother's Forbidden Friend

Hockey Hotties

My Lucky #13

The Trouble with #9

Faking it with #41

Sneaking around with #34

Second Shot with #76

Offside with #55

Kingsmen Football Stars

You had your chance, Lee Burrows

You can't kiss the Nanny, Brady Banks

Over my Brother's Dead Body, Chase Andrews

The Baileys

Lessons from a One-Night Stand

Advice from a Jilted Bride

Birth of a Baby Daddy

Operation Bailey Wedding (Novella)

Falling for My Brother's Best Friend

Demise of a Self-Centered Playboy

Confessions of a Naughty Nanny

Operation Bailey Babies (Novella)

Secrets of the World's Worst Matchmaker

Winning My Best Friend's Girl

Rules for Dating your Ex

Operation Bailey Birthday (Novella)

The Modern Love World

Charmed by the Bartender

Hooked by the Boxer

Mad about the Banker

The Single Dad's Club

Real Deal

Dirty Talker

Sexy Beast

Hollywood Hearts

Mister Mom

Animal Attraction

Domestic Bliss

Bedroom Games

Cold as Ice

On Thin Ice

Break the Ice

Box Set